A FATAL OBSESSION

Inspector Thanet shrugged. "What puzzles me is that I have this feeling that everyone's holding back about Carrie Birch. And I can't get a clear picture of her. She's like a negative that's too thin for printing." He made up his mind. "Look, I think I'll just nip down to the hospital and have a word with her mother."

Perhaps, he thought, as he drove toward Sturrenden General, Mrs. Birch might be able to enlighten him about Carrie. Or perhaps he was looking for something that simply wasn't there. Perhaps Carrie really was as uncomplicated as people wanted him to think. No—simple, uncomplicated people just don't get themselves murdered.

And then, there was the packet under the mattress...

No, there was something about Carrie they were all covering up. And he was going to find out what it was if it was the last thing he did.

SIX FEET UNDER

D0650168

Bantam Crime Line Books offers the finest in classic and modern British murder mysteries.
Ask your bookseller for the books you have missed.

SIX FEET UNDER

Dorothy Simpson

BANTAM BOOKS

NEW YORK · TORONTO · LONDON · SYDNEY · AUCKLAND

Author's Note

People often ask me where my ideas come from. Often I don't know. But not in this instance.

In December 1975 the newspapers were full of a story which fascinated me. I followed it, filed it and forgot it—or so I thought. Then, last year, while I was thinking about this book, the idea popped up: why not use that story as a basis for a murder mystery? The characters and setting would of course be my own creation. The result was SIX FEET UNDER.

This edition contains the complete text
of the original hardcover edition.
NOT ONE WORD HAS BEEN OMITTED.

SIX FEET UNDER
A Bantam Book / published by arrangement with
Charles Scribner's Sons

PRINTING HISTORY

First published in the United States by Charles Scribner's Sons
September 1982

A Mystery Guild Selection, March 1983

Bantam edition / October 1985
2nd printing / January 1990

ISBN 0-553-18506-3

Published simultaneously in the United States and Canada

PRINTED IN THE UNITED STATES OF AMERICA

O   11 10 9 8 7 6 5 4 3 2

For Mark, Ian and Emma

Cruelty has a Human Heart,
And Jealousy a Human Face;
Terror the Human Form Divine,
And Secrecy the Human Dress.

The Human Dress is forged Iron,
The Human Form a fiery Forge,
The Human Face a Furnace seal'd,
The Human Heart its hungry Gorge.

William Blake

1

Detective Inspector Luke Thanet was a happy man. He had an interesting job, no pressing financial worries, two healthy, lively children and, perhaps best of all, a wife who was all that any man could wish for. And so it was that on this blustery March evening, blissfully unaware of the nasty little shock that Fate was preparing for him, he stretched out his toes to the fire, settled back into his armchair and reflected that he wouldn't change places with any man in the world.

Reaching for his pipe he tapped it out, scraped it, inspected it, blew through it, then filled it with loving care.

"It's nine o'clock," Joan said. "D'you want the news?"

"I don't think so. Do you?"

"Not particularly."

She went back to her book. Thanet lit his pipe and picked up the newspaper. He hadn't been reading for more than a few minutes, however, when he realised that Joan was unusually restless. Normally, when she was reading, she plunged at once into total absorption. On one occasion Thanet had counted up to a hundred from the time he asked her a question to the moment when she looked up, eyes unfocused, and said, "What did you say?"

Now she fidgeted, crossed and re-crossed her legs, fiddled with her hair, chewed the tip of her thumb.

Eventually, "Book no good?" Thanet enquired.

She looked up at once. "Mmm? Oh, it's all right. Very interesting, in fact."

"What's the matter, then?"

She hesitated, gave him a speculative look.

He laid down his newspaper. "Come on, love. Out with it."

To his surprise she still did not respond. "Joan?" He was beginning to feel the first faint stirrings of alarm.

She shook her head then, a fierce little shake. "Oh, it's all right. There's nothing wrong, not really. It's just that I've a nasty feeling you aren't going to like what I'm trying to pluck up the courage to say."

"Oh?" he said, warily.

She looked at him with something approaching desperation. "It's just that . . . oh, dear. . . . Look, you know we've said all along that when Ben starts school I'll go back to work? Well, that's only six months away now. So I really ought to start thinking about what I want to do."

"I see," Thanet said slowly.

"There you are. I knew you wouldn't like it."

"Darling, don't be silly. It's just that, well, the idea will take a bit of getting used to after all this time, that's all."

"Don't pretend," she said. "You're dead against it really, aren't you? I can tell."

And she was right, of course, he was. They had been married for eight years now and for all that time Joan had been the good little wife who stayed at home, ran the house efficiently and without fuss, coped with two children and made sure that everything was geared to Thanet's convenience. Unlike the wives of so many of his colleagues, Joan had never complained or nagged over the demands of his job, the irregular hours. Now, in a flash, he saw everything changed. Uncomfortable adjustments would have to be made, there would be inconvenience, irritation, arguments. Theory and practice, he now realised, were very different matters. All very well, in the past, to contemplate with equanimity the prospect of Joan returning to work one day, but to accept that that day was almost here . . . No, she was right. He didn't like it at all.

"Nonsense," he said. "We've always said you would, when the children were old enough."

"Oh, I know you've always *said* you wouldn't mind. But that's very different from not minding when it actually happens."

"I thought you'd more or less made up your mind to do an art course."

"No. Oh, I did think so, at one time. I'm very interested, as you know. But . . . I don't know, I'd like to feel I was doing something, well, less self-indulgent, more useful. Oh, dear, does that sound horribly priggish?"

He grinned. "To be honest, yes. But I know what you mean."

"Do you?" she said eagerly. "You don't think I'm being stupid?"

"Not in the least. What sort of thing did you have in mind?"

"Well, that's the trouble. I'm just not qualified for anything. That's why I feel I ought to start thinking about it now, so that if I have to do a course, or any special training, I can get myself organised for September."

"Yes. I can see that. You haven't gone into it yet, then?"

"I wanted to speak to you about it first. Oh, darling," and she came to kneel before him, took his hands, "you're sure you don't mind?"

"No," he lied valiantly. "I knew, of course, that the time would come, sooner or later..."

Very much later, he told himself, as he drove to work next morning. And preferably not at all. He had awoken still feeling thoroughly disgruntled and the weather matched his mood: grey, lowering skies and a chilly wind.

In his office he scowled at the pile of reports awaiting his attention, riffled through them impatiently. It wasn't even as though there was anything particularly interesting on at the moment... With a sigh he opened the top folder, began reading.

A moment later he was on the phone.

"Where's Lineham?"

"Gone out to Nettleton, sir."

"What for?"

"Some woman making a fuss, sir. Name of... Pitman, sir. Marion Pitman. Apparently there's this old girl who's an invalid, a neighbour of Miss Pitman, and her daughter's disappeared."

"What d'you mean, disappeared?"

"Didn't come home last night, sir. The old woman...," the sound of papers being rustled came clearly over the phone, "Mrs Birch, didn't find out until this morning."

"Probably out on the tiles," Thanet said. "What the devil did Lineham have to go out there himself for?"

"Miss Pitman was most insistent, sir. Apparently the daughter, Miss Birch, just isn't the type to... er... stay out all night. A middle-aged spinster, sir."

"Well, as soon as Lineham gets back, tell him I want to see him."

But Lineham did not return and half an hour later Carson rang through.

"Sir, DS Lineham's just been on the radio. That woman he was looking for, they've found her. Dead, sir, in an outside toilet..."

"Lavatory," growled Thanet, who didn't like euphemisms. Poor old girl, what a way to go...

"Murder, sir, he thinks," Carson finished eagerly.

In a matter of minutes Thanet was on his way. As he passed the desk he paused to say, "Manage to get hold of Doc Mallard yet?"

"Yes, sir. We're having to send a car for him. His has broken down."

"Don't bother. I'll pick him up. I have to pass his house anyway."

Mallard came hurrying down the path as Thanet drew up in front of the trim little bungalow into which Mallard had moved after his wife's death some years ago. Thanet had known him since childhood and was fond of the older man, patient with his moods, aware that Mallard's testiness was the result of his inability to come to terms with the loss of his wife. "It's as if half of me has been amputated," Mallard had once said to Thanet in a rare moment of intimacy. "And the half that's left never stops aching."

Thanet greeted him warmly, told him the little he knew of the reported murder.

"Lineham's already out there, you said?"

"Yes."

"Think he'll make it to the altar this time?"

Lineham was supposed to be getting married on Saturday.

Thanet grimaced. "Don't know. I hope so, for his sake. He'll go berserk if it has to be put off again."

Detective Sergeant Michael Lineham was an only child. His father had died when Mike was six and Mrs Lineham had never remarried, had lavished all her love, care and attention on her son. Lineham had fought the first great battle of his life over his decision to enter the police force; the second was still in progress. Twice already the wedding had had to be postponed. On both occasions Mrs Lineham had had a mild heart attack the day before.

"Those attacks," Thanet said now. "They are genuine, I suppose?"

"Oh yes. No doubt of that. Brought on, I would guess, partly by distress over losing her son and partly by the subconscious desire to delay the wedding."

"So there might well be another one, this time?"

"Quite likely, I should think."

Thanet sighed. "I do hope not, for Mike's sake. And for Louise's, of course. She's a nice girl, but I can't see her putting up with these delays indefinitely. And who would blame her? Ah, this is where we turn off."

Nettleton was a small Kentish village of around a thousand inhabitants, a couple of miles from the centre of the ever-expanding town of Sturrenden, where Thanet was based. At one time it had been a completely separate community but over the last ten years the advancing tide of houses had crept inexorably over field and orchard until Nettleton had become little more than a suburb on the very edge of Sturrenden.

"At this rate the English village will be a thing of the past by the end of the century," muttered Mallard.

Nettleton, however, had still managed to retain something of its individuality, perhaps because the main Sturrenden to Maidstone road did not run through the centre of it. Mallard and Thanet looked around approvingly at the picturesque scatter of cottages on either side of the road, the black-and-white timbered building which housed the general shop and post office.

"Village school's gone, I see," said Mallard, gesturing out of the window.

It had shared the fate of so many of its kind and had been converted into a private house.

"One of the biggest mistakes they ever made," the doctor went on. "And now, of course, they're howling over the cost of transporting the kids so far to school. Typical."

"Here we are," Thanet said. "Lineham said to park in front of the church."

There were already several police cars in the small parking area. Thanet got out of the car, locked it and then stood frowning at a small crowd of sightseers clustered on the opposite side of the road around the entrance to a footpath which ran along the back of a row of terraced cottages.

"Ghouls," he muttered—aware, however, that the sudden tension in him, the flutter of unease in the pit of his stomach, had nothing to do with the onlookers. The moment he always dreaded was approaching. He had never admitted it to anyone, even to Joan, but he hated his first sight of a corpse, could never dissociate the dead flesh that he would have to handle from the living person it had so recently clothed. Other men, he knew, evolved their own method of dealing with the situation, erecting barriers of callousness, indifference or even, as in the case of Mallard, macabre levity, but he had never been able to do so. Somehow, for him, that moment of suffering was necessary, a vital spur to his efforts to find the killer. Without it his investigation would lack that extra impetus which usually brought him success.

He and Mallard crossed the road together.

"Move these people away," Thanet snapped at the constable on duty at the footpath entrance.

Preoccupied as he was with the coming ordeal, he and Mallard had walked on a few paces before it registered: in the knot of sightseers one face had been familiar. Whose was it? Thanet stopped, turned to look back, but the little crowd was already dispersing, drifting away reluctantly with their backs towards him.

Thanet shrugged, followed Mallard to the spot where a second constable stood guard, at an open doorway in the ramshackle fence on their right. He peered in at a long narrow garden crammed with mounds of sand and ballast, planks, bricks, paving stones and bags of cement, then picked his way through the clutter to the little brick building tucked away in a corner, behind the fence.

Here Lineham was watching the photographers, who were already at work. They all moved back as Mallard and Thanet approached.

Thanet steeled himself, looked.

The bundle of old clothes, crammed into the confined space between the wooden lavatory seat and the door, resolved itself into the body of a woman, head slumped forward on to raised knees, face invisible. There was dried blood in her sparse brown hair.

Thanet took a deep, unobtrusive breath.

"Which shots have you taken?" he asked.

The photographers had been thorough.

"Better get her out, then," Mallard said. "It's impossible to examine her properly in there."

They spread a plastic sheet upon the ground and Lineham

summoned the constable at the gate to help him. Together they stooped to ease the body out of its hiding place. It was not an easy task. Rigor had stiffened her and Lineham had to struggle to lift the upper half of the body sufficiently to enable the other man to manoeuvre the feet through the narrow doorway. Gently, they lowered her on to the plastic.

"Turn her on her side, for God's sake," said Mallard. "Looks like a bloody oven-ready chicken."

The bent head, knees tucked up to the chest and splayed feet did indeed look grotesque and the two men stooped hurriedly to obey the police surgeon's command.

Perhaps Mallard, too, resented the fact that the woman had been denied any dignity in death, Thanet thought, moving closer as the doctor squatted down beside the body.

The woman was, as he had been told, middle-aged—in her early fifties, perhaps? She was small, slight, and her clothes were drab: brown woollen skirt, fawn hand-knitted jumper, brown cardigan, sensible black lace-up shoes, worn and scuffed. Thanet's limited view of the side of her face gave him a glimpse of sparse eyebrows, muddy skin. There was a large mole sprouting hairs just above the jaw-line.

An unobtrusive little woman, Thanet decided. Unassuming and probably undemanding. And, above all, a most unlikely corpse. Women like this were not usually the victims of deliberate violence. Of a casual attack, a mugging perhaps, yes: that might, of course, be the answer here. If so, it would be the first crime of its kind in a village community in this area. There had been several cases in Sturrenden itself of late, but so far the villages had remained immune.

Thanet grimaced at the thought. Brutality against the old was a particularly repellent manifestation of violence. But in any case this explanation somehow didn't feel right. The victims of muggings were usually struck down and left to lie. Here, trouble had been taken to hide the body.

"This lavatory in use?" Thanet said to Lineham.

"No, sir. The house is empty. It's being done up by a builder, but in any case it has an indoor loo, has had for years."

"Any sign of the weapon?"

"Not yet, sir, no."

"What was her name? Birch?"

"Yes, sir. Carrie Birch."

"Carrie Birch," murmured Thanet. Insignificant though

she may have been, Carrie Birch had been a person with her own hopes, fears and daydreams and she had had as much right as anyone to live to enjoy them.

I'll get him if I can, Thanet promised her silently.

2

Thanet shifted his buttocks into a marginally more comfortable position and resumed his contemplation of Nettleton. From his perch on the five-barred gate he had a clear view of the area which interested him, the area around the church.

At the beginning of a case he always liked to establish in his mind the geography of the place in which the crime had been committed. After that came the people and then . . . ah, then the part which really interested him, the relationships between them. Always, somewhere in that intricate web of attitude, emotion and interaction, would lie the truth of the murder. Who and where and how and why would slowly become evident as his understanding grew, as would the unique position of the victim in that web, murder the inevitable outcome of its weaving.

The row of terraced cottages in which Carrie Birch had lived lay at right angles to the road and almost opposite the church. They looked out upon open fields and in front of them a narrow lane wound its way to a cluster of farm buildings. The gate upon which Thanet was sitting was a hundred yards or so further on along that lane.

Behind the cottages ran a footpath which, according to Lineham, provided a short cut to the church from the far side of Nettleton. On the other side of that footpath and immediately opposite the church was the vicarage, an attractive modern house, brick and tile-hung in traditional Kentish style. The Old Vicarage on the other side of the road was a much larger and presumably therefore uneconomic building, and was the last house in the village. Between it and the church, in what must once have been its extensive grounds, had been built two relatively new modern houses, one a wooden Colt bungalow, the other a much larger and more opulent construction of brick, plastic "weatherboard" and generous expanses of glass.

Thanet already knew that Carrie Birch had lived in number four, Church Cottages, with her mother. Number one, next to the road, was occupied by a young couple and their baby; number two was being renovated, number three housed a family of four and number five an elderly woman. Not, Thanet thought, a particularly promising bunch of suspects. Perhaps someone more interesting might turn up. . . .

Suddenly aware that his buttocks had gone numb, Thanet slid down off the gate and began to rub them, grimacing at the discomfort. He began to walk back down the lane towards the cottages.

According to Doc Mallard, Carrie Birch had been killed between 9 pm and 11 pm the previous evening. She had been struck on the head with the traditional blunt instrument, but in his opinion it might not have been this blow which had caused her death. He was unwilling to commit himself before the post mortem, of course, but there seemed to be indications that she might have been suffocated. After the twelve or thirteen hours which had elapsed since her death the blueness of the features normally associated with suffocation had worn off, but some unpronounceable condition of the tiny blood vessels under the skin of her cheeks was apparently sufficiently marked to give him cause for suspicion.

It seemed possible then that the murder, even if not premeditated, had been deliberate; a blow on the head could be struck in anger, but subsequent suffocation was a very different matter.

An increasingly deafening roar from behind him made Thanet press himself back against the fence as a red tractor came trundling around the bend. Its driver grinned and raised a hand in salute as he rattled by. Thanet waved back.

The tractor turned left on to the main road and almost at once an ambulance entered the lane, pulled up in front of number four. Behind it came Lineham, walking swiftly. Thanet moved forward to meet him.

"That'll be for Mrs Birch, sir," Lineham said, gesturing at the ambulance. "There's no one to look after her now, so the social services have arranged for her to go into hospital. Do you want a word with her, before she goes?"

"Not at the moment, I don't think."

"Don't blame you."

Thanet looked at Lineham sharply. "What do you mean?"

Lineham shrugged. "I had a word with her earlier. Couldn't stand her, myself."

"Why not?"

"Oh, I don't know. I'd guess she ran that poor little woman off her feet and never once said thank you for it. All she can think of now is herself—what's going to happen to her. Why did Carrie have to go and get herself murdered, that's her attitude. Makes me sick."

It was unlike Lineham to be so vehement. Thanet made no comment, however, and the two men strolled on past number four as the ambulance men went up to the door and knocked.

"She last saw her daughter at just before nine o'clock last night, you said?"

"That's right," said Lineham. "Apparently Miss Birch had arranged with a neighbour, the Miss Pitman who rang the station this morning, to go and look in on Miss Pitman's father, who is also an invalid, while Miss Pitman was at the Parochial Church Council meeting. Apparently this was a regular arrangement whenever Miss Pitman was out in the evening. Miss Birch worked for the Pitmans in the mornings, too, cleaning and generally looking after the old man's needs. Anyway, Miss Birch settled her mother for the night before leaving and that was the last Mrs Birch saw of her. She went to sleep and when her daughter still hadn't brought her morning tea at half past eight this morning—she used to bring it at eight, regular as clockwork—Mrs Birch panicked. She tried shouting, ringing the little handbell she has in case she needed her daughter in the night, but there was no answer and in the end she managed to get help by banging on the wall between her bedroom, which is on the ground floor, and number three."

"Who lives there? A family of four, you said?"

"That's right. Name of Gamble. He's a fitter at Brachey's, on night shift at the moment. He was in bed and sound asleep by then and his wife and son had already left for work. His daughter Jenny was still at home, though, and she heard Mrs Birch banging on the wall."

"How did she get in?"

"The Gambles have a key to number four, in case of emergency."

"Is the daughter usually at home in the daytime?"

"No, she works in Boots in Sturrenden."

"Funny, leaving the spare key there, then, if there's usually no one except the father home during the daytime, and he's in bed. Why not leave the key with the other neighbour, the woman in number five?"

Lineham shrugged. "She's a bit of a recluse, I gather. Not the sort of person you leave keys with."

"What's her name?"

"Cox."

"Miss?"

"So far as I know."

They had reached the end of the lane now and turned to watch as a small procession wound its way out of number four: the two ambulance men, a bulky woman in a wheelchair and a second woman carrying suitcase and carrier bag.

"Who's that?" asked Thanet.

"Miss Pitman. She's been sitting with Mrs Birch until the ambulance came. When Jenny Gamble found that there was no sign of Miss Birch and that her bed hadn't even been slept in, she ran across to the Pitmans'. The Gambles haven't got a phone."

The two men stepped back against the fence as the ambulance edged its way past them and drove off in the direction of Sturrenden. Thanet looked with interest at the woman who was hurrying along the lane towards them.

"Miss Pitman?"

"Yes?"

Thanet introduced himself. "I'd like a word with you, if I may."

She was in her early forties, he guessed, a tall woman with untidy brown hair and a harassed expression.

She put a hand up to her forehead. "Yes, of course, Inspector. It's just that . . . oh, dear, everything is haywire this morning. Poor Carrie, and then Mrs Birch. . . . And I really must see to my father, he's an invalid. Do you think you could possibly come over to the house with me? I must check that he's all right."

Her eyes, Thanet noted, were beautiful, large, velvet-brown and expressive. He took pity on her.

"Of course, Miss Pitman. But there's no desperate urgency. There are one or two things I must see to here. Why don't you go on and attend to your father and I'll be across later? The bungalow, isn't it?"

"That's right. Oh, thank you, Inspector. That's very kind. Do you want this? It's the key to the Birches' cottage."

Thanet took the key with a murmur of thanks and watched her go. He firmly believed in the value of courtesy to the public. There were, of course, occasions when it was a complete waste of time, but on the whole he had always found that polite consideration elicited the highest degree of cooperation from witnesses.

"Come on," he said to Lineham. "I want to have a look around number four."

As they passed number two, however, a man erupted from the open doorway, hammer in hand. For a split second Thanet wondered wildly if Fate had decided to hurl the murderer into his arms, blunt instrument and all.

"'Ere," said the newcomer. "You in charge of this lot?" Tall and muscular, wearing tee-shirt and jeans, he was an impressive figure. Bright blue eyes glowered at Thanet from a face barely visible behind its luxuriant growth of hair.

"I'm in charge of the murder enquiry, yes," said Thanet calmly.

"Well, when am I going to be able to get at my stuff?"

"Stuff?"

"Been held up all morning, haven't I? While your lot's been poking around in the back garden. Bill and me wanted to get on with them new partitions on the first floor this morning, and so far we haven't been able to do a bleeding thing."

"I'm sorry that you've been inconvenienced," said Thanet, keeping his anger at the man's manner well under control, "but a woman has been killed, you know, Mr . . . ?"

"Arnold," said the man, Thanet's mild tone having its desired effect. He looked suitably abashed. "Jack Arnold. Yeah, well, I know you've got to do your job, but I got to do mine, haven't I? I mean, time's money, isn't it? And there's little enough profit in these sort of jobs nowadays as it is."

"I'm sure we can come to some arrangement," Thanet said.

He turned to Lineham. "How are the men getting on in the garden of number two?"

"They should be almost finished by now. I'd have to check." Lineham's face was wooden and Thanet knew by experience that the sergeant was hiding his amusement with difficulty.

"If you tell Sergeant Lineham what you want, I'm sure he'll be able to arrange for you to have it."

"Twelve eight-foots of three by two and two twelve-foots of three by two, and them big sheets of plasterboard," Arnold said promptly. "Thanks, Guv."

"Perhaps you'd better go with the sergeant, Mr Arnold, and make sure you get what you want," Thanet suggested, seeing Lineham's eyes glaze. "When you've finished, Lineham, come along to number four, will you?"

"We can go through the house," Arnold said, turning away with alacrity.

"Just one or two small points," Thanet said quickly. "That outside lavatory. Was it ever used?"

Arnold turned back reluctantly, impatience in every line of his body. "No. There's a toilet in the house, see. The landlord had toilets and bathrooms built on to the back of all these cottages a few years back, before he decided to sell them off as they come vacant."

"Are you working here alone, except for . . . er . . . Bill?"

"Most of the time, yes. But we sub-contract the special jobs like wiring and plumbing."

"What time do you arrive for work in the mornings?"

"Eight o'clock."

"And you get into the house which way, front or back?"

"Front, always."

"Did either of you go into the back garden before the alarm was raised over Miss Birch's disappearance?"

"Naw. No reason to, see. We was finishing off taking out that old partition wall—the one we're wanting to get on with."

Thanet ignored the hint. "Did you know her?"

"The old . . . Miss Birch, you mean? Not really. Passed the time of day, that's all, when she went past in the mornings."

"What was she like?"

Arnold shrugged his massive shoulders. "Dunno. Quiet. Mousy type. Couldn't say, really."

"All right. Thank you." Thanet turned away.

At the gate of number four he hesitated, then walked back

the few paces which took him to the other side of the narrow lane. He stood looking at the row of cottages. It was obvious, from here, which of them were in private ownership and which were still rented out.

They were Victorian, he guessed, built of ugly yellow brick with slated roofs. Except for the two end cottages which, he had noticed earlier, both had attic windows in the gable end, each had one window and a front door at ground level and two windows on the first floor. Number one, where the young couple lived, was spick and span, with gleaming white paintwork and a yellow front door. The downstairs sash window had been replaced by a curved bow window with small square panes, one or two of which were bottle-glass. A similar bow window had already been installed in number two, which Arnold was renovating, and in number three, where the Gambles lived. This house, too, looked well maintained. The other two, numbers four and five, looked dingy and neglected by comparison, the paintwork peeling, the roofs in poor condition.

It was interesting, Thanet thought, just how much could be learned about the occupants of houses just by looking at the curtains. Young Mrs Davies sported frilly net curtains, looped back, the Gambles bright modern prints, the Birches traditional half-net curtains flanked by drab florals and the last house in the row, where old Miss Cox lived, full-length nets. Thanet looked thoughtfully at the latter before crossing the road again to let himself into number four.

The front door, he discovered, led directly into a small living room which was spotlessly clean but depressingly furnished in indeterminate shades of brown and beige. It was dominated by a large colour television set and in the most comfortable corner of the room, away from draughts and next to the gas fire, stood an upright armchair with padded seat and back and wooden arms, flanked by all the impedimenta of an invalid's day: footstool with neatly folded rug, round table cluttered with pill bottles, women's magazines, water jug covered with a folded tissue, jar of boiled sweets.

Behind the living room was old Mrs Birch's bedroom. An ancient iron range and built-in dresser testified to the fact that this had once been the kitchen. Now, the cooker, kitchen sink and cupboards were crammed into what was little more than a narrow passage leading to the new bathroom which had been built on behind.

Thanet did little more than glance at all this. What he was really interested in was Carrie's bedroom. The staircase, he discovered, was hidden away behind a door beside the head of the bed in the former kitchen. The stairs were steep and narrow and led to a minute landing with two doors. Thanet pushed open the one on his left. This bedroom was at the back of the house and had no doubt once belonged to Mrs Birch. A dressing table still stood under the window, its mirror spotted with age and clouded by neglect. The overflow from the cramped scullery appeared to have crept up here; vacuum cleaner, aluminium stepladder, sweeping brush and mop stood against the wall just inside the door.

The front bedroom, then, must have been Carrie's. Thanet opened the door with keen anticipation. What had she been like, that little mouse of a woman? Disappointingly, her room appeared to offer little enlightenment. It was clean and neat, drably furnished with brown linoleum and a threadbare rug beside the bed. The green candlewick bedspread was bald in places, neatly darned in others.

Thanet crossed to the bedside table. The alarm clock had stopped at twelve fifteen, presumably because its owner had not returned to wind it last night. There was also a small round biscuit tin painted blue, a pair of spectacles and a paperback book. Thanet inspected the latter. *Victory For Love*, it was called, and the cover depicted an extravagantly beautiful girl gazing up adoringly into the face of a suitably square-jawed hero. So he had been right. Little Miss Birch had indeed had her daydreams, her escape-hatch from the narrow confines of her life. There was a small cupboard in the bedside table and Thanet opened it, peered in. It was crammed to the top with similar books.

The only incongruous feature of the room was a full-length mirror composed of mirror tiles stuck on to the wall beside the window. Thanet frowned, crossed to run his fingers over the satin-smooth surface. Why should Carrie Birch have taken the trouble to put up such a thing? She certainly hadn't struck him as being the sort of person to spend much time gazing at her own reflection.

Beside the fireplace there was a curtained alcove which presumably served as a wardrobe and Thanet went now to examine it. Yes, here hung Carrie's clothes, a much-mended and indescribably dreary collection. Just looking at them made Thanet feel depressed. What a miserable life the woman must have had, with only her paperback romances to relieve its tedium. What, then, could have singled her out for murder? Pure chance? No, he still couldn't believe that.

So, there must have been something.

He glanced again around the comfortless little room, his gaze lingering on the mirror. If Carrie had had a secret, it was not hidden here, it seemed. Unless . . .

He went back to the bed, lifted the mattress and ran his hand along the springs. His fingers encountered something hard and flat. With a surge of excitement he pulled it out. It was an oblong packet wrapped in brown paper and secured with an elastic band.

Fumbling in his eagerness he removed the band, unfolded the wrapping. Then he stared in disbelief at its contents.

It was a bundle of pound notes. Fifty at least, at a guess.

Carrie's savings, hoarded for a rainy day . . . or for some long-desired treat?

He put the bundle on the floor, grasped the edge of the mattress and heaved it aside.

Neatly arranged in a row right down the centre of the bed were many more similar packets. A swift examination confirmed that their contents were identical to those of the first and a rapid calculation produced an astonishing answer.

Little Carrie Birch had had almost a thousand pounds hidden under her mattress.

3

"Where the hell did she get it from?" Lineham's language, like his face, proclaimed his amazement; his mother did not approve of swearing.

"Your guess is as good as mine. Interesting, though, isn't it?"

"I'll say." Lineham grinned. "I bet her mother didn't know about this little lot." The idea obviously gave him pleasure.

"No. But the point, as you say, is, where did she get it?"

"Saved it?"

"It would have taken her years," said Thanet. "Cleaning isn't exactly the most lucrative occupation in the world. Besides, I should think her mother would have known what she earned down to the last penny, from what you say of her."

"She won it, then."

"How?"

"Football pools, sweepstake, lottery, premium bonds?"

"She'd have had to have some sort of written notification of a win on any of those. I can't see her keeping it from her mother."

"Stole it?" suggested Lineham.

"From whom? It's a sizeable sum not to have been missed. If she did, its loss would surely have been reported. You'd better check, I suppose. The only other possibility, it seems to me, is. . . ."

"Blackmail!" said Lineham, triumphantly.

Thanet nodded. "And in that case, of course, the question is, who was the victim?" Thanet walked across to the window and looked out across the fields. The red tractor was working in the distance and over to the left he could just catch a glimpse of the farm buildings, half hidden behind a clump of tall trees.

"Who owns the farm?"

"Man called Martin."

"Do these cottages belong to him?"

"I don't know. I could find out."

"Do that." Thanet turned away from the window. "Well, we'd better get on with it. You go and see what the neighbours have got to tell you about last night, if you can find any of them at home. And find out all you can about Miss Birch— what she was like, where she went, who she talked to, the usual sort of thing. Not a word about the money at the moment, though. I'll go across and have a word with Miss Pitman. She should have finished seeing to her father by now."

"What shall we do with all this?" Lineham nodded at the packages of pound notes.

"Leave it where we found it for the moment. We don't really want to cart it around with us all day and I should think it's most unlikely that the place'll be burgled, with the area crawling with coppers."

The two men replaced the mattress and left the house, Thanet locking the door behind him and pocketing the key.

"What happened to the key Jenny Gamble let herself in with this morning?" he said.

"That's it, I think. Miss Pitman kept it."

The two men looked at each other. "My God," Thanet said. "I'm slipping. Miss Birch's bag! Where is it? She wasn't wearing a coat, so I didn't think... For that matter, where *is* her coat, if she'd been out?"

"Perhaps she came back?" said Lineham.

"Better check," Thanet said. The two men went back into the house and made a quick but thorough search. Lineham found two empty handbags on the floor of Carrie's makeshift wardrobe, but there was no sign of one in use. A worn brown coat hung on the back of the scullery door.

"Looks as though this was the one she used most," said Thanet. He would have to ask Miss Pitman. "I'd give a lot to know where that bag is now," he said.

Outside again. "I'll start with Mrs Davies," Lineham said. "I'm pretty certain she's in."

As they set off down the lane Thanet experienced a prickle of unease between his shoulder blades. He turned around, expecting to see that there was someone coming along the road behind them, but the lane was deserted. He frowned, scanned the windows of number five. Had he seen one of the net curtains move? He couldn't be sure. The movement, if there had been one, had been very slight, glimpsed only on the very periphery of his vision. It would not, of course, be surprising if old Miss Cox was watching them. She must be aware that they would want to see her, would probably be looking out for their visit. Well, Lineham would be along shortly.

"What's the matter?" said Lineham.

"Nothing," Thanet said, walking on.

He and Lineham parted and Thanet crossed the road to the Pitmans' house which was uncompromisingly called The

Bungalow. Miss Pitman had obviously been looking out for him; the front door opened as he walked up the path.

"Do come in, Inspector. I'm sorry I was in a bit of a state, earlier." She stood back to let him pass. She had tidied her hair, put on a little discreet make-up and looked altogether more composed.

"Not at all. It must have been a very distressing morning for you."

The room into which she led the way overlooked the garden at the back and was light and airy, with large windows on both outside walls. The colours echoed the view outside. There was a grass-green carpet, a settee and armchair with loose covers in an attractive design of sprays of green leaves on an off-white background. The floor-length curtains were made of the same material and there were a couple of Victorian button-back chairs, one covered in cream, the other in a deep, muted blue. The large stone fireplace was flanked by ceiling-high bookshelves and the general effect was comfortable, attractive and unpretentious. Thanet felt immediately at home.

"Your father's all right?" he said politely.

"Oh yes, fine. He's eighty-two, you know, and needs quite a lot of care. He is badly crippled with arthritis and can do very little for himself now. I don't know what I'm going to do without Carrie, I really don't. Oh, I'm sorry, that sounds so selfish. . . ."

"Understandable, though, if you relied on her." Briefly, Thanet verified the information Lineham had given him: Marion Pitman had arranged for Carrie to come in at about nine the previous evening to check that all was well with her father. He also learned that Carrie had never bothered to put on a coat to cross the road unless it was bitterly cold or pouring with rain, and that she had invariably carried an old black handbag. Marion herself had attended the PCC meeting at the vicarage, leaving the house at seven twenty-five and returning at ten fifteen.

"That was when the meeting ended?"

"No. It ended at ten, but I stayed on for a few minutes to discuss something with the vicar. I'm treasurer, you see."

"So most people would have left at ten?"

"That's right."

"And on your way home, did you see or hear anything suspicious?"

"I'm sorry, no. Since . . . since Carrie was found, I've thought and thought about it, just in case there could be anything relevant. But there was nothing."

"A pity. Miss Birch worked here every morning, I believe?"

"That's right. I teach part-time, you see, in a school for handicapped children in Sturrenden. Carrie's coming made that possible. It's not that my father needs constant attention, it's just that she was here if he needed anything. I don't like leaving him alone for long periods."

"Had she worked for you long?"

"Oh yes, for years. She first came when I was teaching full-time, it must be, oh, fifteen years ago now. She cleaned the house for me, two mornings a week. Then, as my father's health deteriorated, she came more often until eventually it was every morning. As I say, I don't know what I shall do without her."

"You got on well with her?"

"Oh yes. Of course."

Thanet detected some slight reservation in her voice. "But . . . ?" he said.

"Nothing." She gave a little, nervous laugh. "Really. I didn't see very much of her, of course. I was always out when she was here."

"Except in the school holidays."

"Well, yes."

Her reluctance intrigued him. "What was she like?"

"Carrie?" Miss Pitman looked away, out of the window, as if trying to catch a distant glimpse of the dead woman. "Quiet. Unobtrusive. Got on with the job. Undemanding. She didn't say very much, really."

"What did you talk about? On the odd occasion when you must have had a cup of coffee together, for example?"

"Nothing much. The weather. Village affairs."

"Nothing personal?"

"Not that I can remember."

"She never, for example, said anything about her relationships with other people?"

Miss Pitman looked startled. "Who, for example?"

"I don't know. I'm hoping you'll tell me."

"I don't think she knew many people, other than very casually. She worked for the Selbys two afternoons a week. They live in the Old Vicarage."

"Had she been with them long?"

"Ever since the Selbys came to live here, about five years ago. Irene Selby asked me if I could recommend a cleaning woman and although... I suggested she approach Carrie."

"Although?"

Miss Pitman shook her head. "Nothing."

"The Selbys are a big family?"

"No, just the three of them. Susan, their daughter, is seventeen and still at school. But it's a big, rambling house to manage alone."

"And Mr Selby?"

"Major. He's managing director of Stavely's."

Stavely's was a thriving timber yard in Sturrenden.

"He's standing for the County Council elections next month," she added.

"And how did Mrs Selby get on with Miss Birch?"

"All right, I believe. I'm afraid I couldn't really say. We've never discussed the matter."

"Can you tell me anything else about what Miss Birch used to do with her time?"

"She used to clean the church. But apart from that, nothing much. Her mother was very demanding."

"Did she ever complain about her mother?"

"No, never. But no one could help noticing how Mrs Birch treated her."

"Didn't she belong to any village organisations? WI for example?"

"No."

"You make her sound a pathetic little creature."

"Well I suppose she was, rather."

"And yet," Thanet said softly, "I have the feeling that you had reservations about her."

"Reservations?"

Thanet said nothing, simply waited. But Miss Pitman merely gave that nervous little laugh again and shook her head.

"I can't imagine what you mean, Inspector."

Thanet could see that it was pointless to pursue the subject at the moment.

"Do you think I could have a word with your father now?"

Her laugh was a little too loud, explosive with relief. But there was genuine amusement in it. "You don't think I'd get away with keeping you from him, do you? He'd be furious.

He may be frail but believe me he has all his wits about him and he's been looking forward to your visit all morning!"

Thanet grinned, stood up. "Then we'd better not keep him waiting any longer, had we?"

Old Mr Pitman was sitting up in bed, looking expectantly towards the door. This, too, was an invalid's room, but very different from Mrs Birch's. There was colour, light and evidence of much activity. The bedspread was scattered with books and newspapers and beside the bed there was a large Victorian mahogany tea-trolley, its three tiers laden with many more books, a radio, tape-recorder and rack of cassettes, boxes of slides, viewer, stamp catalogues and albums, magnifying glass, tweezers, scissors and a jar of felt-tipped pens.

The owner of all this ordered clutter looked alarmingly frail, the skin stretched taut over nose and cheekbones, hanging in loose folds about the neck. He had once, Thanet guessed, been a tall, strong man but now he was merely gaunt, shrunken and twisted sideways against the mound of pillows, as though it was impossible for him to sit upright. His hands, resting one on top of the other on the neatly folded counterpane, were blotched with the brown spots of old age, swollen and misshapen with his disease. The eyes which twinkled out at Thanet beneath the quiff of white hair, however, were piercingly alive and brilliant, clear periwinkle blue. It was as though all the old man's life and energy were now concentrated in his mind, visible only through those penetrating blue orbs.

"Come in, come in," he said. "Sit down." And he nodded at an armchair set beside the bed. "Where I can see you properly."

"This is Inspector Thanet, father." Marion Pitman approached the bed and, in a ritual that was clearly so familiar as to be second nature to them, she put her arm around his shoulders and helped him to lean forward, plumped up his pillows and eased him back against them.

"Thank you, my dear," he said. "Now, off you go. The Inspector and I will do very well without you." But there was no sting to the words and he watched her fondly as she left the room. "She's a good girl, Marion," he said, when the door had closed behind her. "I don't know where I'd be without her. Well, I do, of course, in hospital. Though I sometimes think it would be much better for her if I could persuade her to let me go. It's not much of a life for her, you know, looking after an old wreck like me. However," he said briskly, "you haven't come here to talk about us. How can I help you?"

"I believe Miss Birch came here last night?" Thanet said. "Do you by any chance remember exactly what time she arrived and left?"

"Certainly: I've had plenty of time to lie here and think about it this morning," said the old man. "She came in bang on nine o'clock—I'm sure of that because the news was starting." He nodded at a portable television set on a table pushed against the wall. "And she left a few minutes after it ended, say at nine thirty. I know that's so because I always like to listen to the news and it used to annoy me that she came just then—she always did, when Marion was out."

"Couldn't you have asked her to come earlier, or later?"

"I did hint, but to no avail. It was her mother, I believe. Like an alarm clock, that woman was. Though heaven knows, I shouldn't complain about that. When one's in this sort of situation it's all too easy to be thrown when one's little routine is disturbed. You wouldn't believe how easy it is to sin lying here in bed! The temptations are endless—to bad temper, self-pity, lack of consideration... It's so easy to justify one's lapses, you see, to think you have every right to indulge in them..." He grinned wickedly at Thanet. "Confidentially, I do allow myself the occasional self-indulgence, just for the pleasure of feeling guilty afterwards. It convinces me I'm still alive!"

Thanet laughed out loud. "I must remember that, the next time I'm tempted."

"But I mustn't waste your time, Inspector, must I? It's just that it's such a pleasure to see a new face, have a new audience.... You see how easy it is to slip? I'm doing it now! Please, do go on with your questions."

"I'd be very interested to know what you thought of Miss Birch."

"What did I think of her," said the old man ruminatively. Like his daughter, he looked away, out of the window, as if to recapture an image already blurred by the passage of time. Or was he simply trying to gain time while he thought up a suitable answer? Thanet waited with interest.

The reply, when it came, was a disappointment, echoing Marion Pitman's.

"Quiet. Unobtrusive. A good worker, and reliable. I don't know what we'll do without her."

And Mr Pitman had the same reservations as his daughter, Thanet noted. He tried again. "But . . . ?"

The old man did not evade the question nor did he answer it satisfactorily. "But I never really warmed to her. Mind, she had a very bad time with that mother of hers, so it's not surprising that she was so . . . reserved."

"What did you talk about, when she was here?"

"We didn't talk, not really. She had work to do, but apart from that our conversation was strictly about practicalities— what I wanted, needed and so on."

"Did she have any close friends, do you know?"

"Not to my knowledge. She led a very circumscribed life, you know. Whenever she wasn't working she was dancing attendance on her mother. I shouldn't think she'd ever been further away from Nettleton than Sturrenden in her whole life."

Thanet was being distracted and he knew it. But he didn't want to alienate Mr Pitman. An old man like this, with a lively, enquiring mind and considerable local knowledge, might be a valuable ally. There were already questions crowding into Thanet's mind, but he wasn't ready to ask them yet. He wasn't certain that they were the right ones. Those, he knew, would emerge as the case progressed and then he would enlist Mr Pitman's help openly. He was sure that the old man would be delighted to cooperate. There was just one point, though . . .

"Was she honest?" he said, suddenly.

Mr Pitman looked startled. "Did she steal, you mean? Not to my knowledge. If she did, I've never heard a whisper of it."

There was something about that reply that was interestingly off-key, but Thanet decided not to query it. He rose. "Well I think that's all for the moment, Mr Pitman. May I come and see you again, if I think of anything else I want to ask you?"

The old man grinned. "I didn't think you'd need my permission. But in any case, I'd be delighted. I'll be keeping my eye on you all, of course."

Now it was Thanet's turn to look startled.

Mr Pitman nodded at the wall behind Thanet. On it there was a large convex mirror which reflected the road outside. Thanet half squatted until his head was on a level with Mr

Pitman's and alongside it, then looked at the mirror. The area which it reflected was surprisingly extensive, stretching from the new vicarage gate on the left to well past the entrance to Church Lane on the right. As Thanet looked, a familiar figure, slightly distorted by the curvature of the mirror but readily recognisable, emerged from the front gate of number five and started to walk down the lane toward the road: Lineham, his interview with Miss Cox over.

"So I see," Thanet said, straightening up.

A pity, he thought as he took his leave, that it had been dark last night when Carrie left the Pitmans' house. Mr Pitman would not only have seen where she had gone, he might even have seen the murderer.

4

The exterior of the Plough and Harrow in Nettleton was unprepossessing, its car park almost empty.

"Just our luck," said Thanet to Lineham. "The food'll be terrible, the beer unspeakable, by the look of it. Still, at least it should be quiet." He pushed open the door and they went in.

The two men had left their cars parked in front of the church and had walked down to the pub, which was at the other end of Nettleton on the main Sturrendon to Maidstone road. Thanet had enjoyed the short stroll. The temperature had risen several degrees and the sun was doing its best to break through the dense bank of cloud which earlier had so depressed him. His mood had lightened considerably now that he had something on which to focus his energies.

On the way he had filled Lineham in on the interviews with the Pitmans. Now he was eager to hear how Lineham had got on.

They bought pints of beer and the soggy tomato sandwiches which were all that the pub had to offer in the way of sustenance and settled themselves in a corner of the bar. The only other two customers were a middle-aged executive type in a dark blue suit, striped shirt and floral tie, and a pretty girl of about twenty. One thing about a place like this, Thanet thought—if you wanted to conduct a clandestine love affair, there wasn't much danger of being spotted.

He put his paper plate down on the red formica table and took a long swig of beer. Just as he had expected. Tasteless. He should have stuck to bottled.

"Well," he said. "What about you? How did you get on?"

"Nothing," said Lineham with a grimace. The Davieses had watched television all evening apparently, and had heard nothing, seen nothing, outside the walls of their living room. Lineham had been unable to rouse anyone at number three. "If Gamble was there, he must sleep like the dead," he said sourly.

"I believe they do. Nightworkers, I mean. The seasoned ones, anyway. They just switch off. What about the old girl next door on the other side?"

"Mmmm?" Lineham's eyes were on the electric clock behind the bar and it seemed an effort for him to re-focus on Thanet. "Oh, Miss Cox. Nothing there, either." Lineham's eyes wandered back to the clock. It was twenty past one.

"Mike," said Thanet, "do you think you could keep your mind on the job, if it's not too much effort?"

Lineham started, flushed. "Sorry, sir. Look, would you mind if I just slipped out and made a quick phone call? There's a phone box outside, I noticed as we came in."

"Go on," said Thanet with resignation. "But be quick about it." Perhaps then he would have Lineham's full attention. He refrained from saying so with difficulty, watched the younger man as he half ran towards the door. Then he smiled, indulgently. Lineham probably wanted to give Louise a ring. Thanet well remembered how vital it had once seemed, when they were courting, to hear Joan's voice just for a few seconds, how the need would obsess him to the exclusion of all else. The thought of her, however, reminded him of his present dilemma and he frowned, took another swig of the

flat beer. He would have to let her go, of course, but he
didn't like the idea one little bit.

"All right?" he asked when Lineham came back, transformed.

"Yes, thanks. It's mother," Lineham went on, clearly feeling that some sort of explanation was necessary. "She wasn't
feeling too well this morning and I just wanted to catch her
before she goes up for her rest at half past one, to see how
she is."

So his guess had been wrong. Nevertheless, Thanet could
sympathise. With the wedding on Saturday and two fiascos
already clocked up, Lineham must be watching his mother as
if she were a time-bomb about to explode.

"You were saying, about Miss Cox," Thanet said.

This time Lineham gave his mind to the matter. "Ah yes.
Funny old bird. Pathetic, really. She was in a real state when
she opened the door. Shaking, all over."

"Perhaps she thought you'd come to arrest her," said
Thanet jokingly.

"No," said Lineham, apparently taking him seriously. "I
think she was just upset about Miss Birch and alarmed by all
the activity. And I expect she's worried about how she's going
to manage—she's got one leg in plaster and I gather that Miss
Birch had been doing her shopping for her."

"If I know Marion Pitman," Thanet said, "she'll be making
arrangements for someone to take that job over. Do you want
another of those?" He nodded at Lineham's glass.

"No thanks. Do you?"

"Not on your life," said Thanet. "Let's go, shall we? No,"
he went on as they left the pub and began to walk back
through the village, "I expect Miss Cox is just scared stiff,
poor old thing. If you live alone and you've got one leg in
plaster and the woman next door gets murdered, you're
bound to wonder if you're going to be next, I should think.
Anyway, she couldn't tell you anything useful?"

"Not a thing. She was in all evening, but she was listening
to the radio—wireless, she called it. Would you believe, she
hasn't got a television? And she had her machine going last
night too, she said."

"Machine?"

"Sewing machine. That's how she makes her living, I
gather. Making loose covers for Barret's."

Barret's was the largest department store in Sturrenden.

"Surely someone, at some point, must have seen or heard *some*thing," said Thanet in exasperation.

"I don't know. It's not like a town out here. I get the impression everything closes down when it gets dark."

"Except the pubs, of course." Thanet stopped dead. "That's an idea. It's just possible that someone going either to or from the pub might have seen something. Send someone back down to the Plough and Harrow this afternoon to find out if any of last night's customers came from this end of the village. The landlord'd be sure to know the locals by name. What do you think, Mike, d'you think our man—or woman, of course—is a local?"

"Oh, definitely," said Lineham at once.

"You sound very sure about it."

"Only a local would have known about that disused toilet," said Lineham with conviction.

"But if he was a local, why bother to hide the body at all? He must have known that Carrie would be missed by her mother within a very short time, and have realised that any sort of search would find her."

Lineham frowned. "A need to get her out of sight, fast, for some reason? Or panic, perhaps, because if he'd left her where she was the place would have given away his identity."

"Not so much *cherchez la femme* as *cherchez l'endroit*," said Thanet, who rather prided himself on his French.

"Er . . . yes," said Lineham, who had abandoned French after O level with a sigh of relief. "You mean, if we could find out where, we'd find out who . . . ?"

"Precisely."

"Of course, it could have been a straightforward mugging."

"But in that case, why hide the body at all? Besides, if it had been muggers, they might have hit her on the head but I can't see why they would have bothered to finish her off afterwards, as Doc Mallard thinks likely."

"Unless she had recognised them. Which she probably would have done, in a small place like this, if they'd been locals."

Thanet shook his head. "I can't see it. It just doesn't feel right, somehow. Though I suppose we'll have to keep it in mind. You'd better get some of the men to check up on the whereabouts of the local talent last night."

"Right."

"She looked such an inoffensive little thing," mused Thanet.

"And yet, there was all that money... I think we'll go and take a look at the other people she worked for, the Selbys. Though I imagine he'll be out at work at the moment. He's a local big-wig. He's standing in the County Council elections next month. Now *he*'d be a good subject for blackmail. He'd have a lot to lose—prestige, position..."

"What about the Pitmans, sir?"

"Most unlikely blackmail victims, I would have thought. Though I did feel that they were both holding something back, as I told you. Perhaps Marion Pitman had her fingers into church funds...we'll just have to keep an open mind at present."

They were passing the Pitmans' bungalow now and Thanet raised his hand.

"Who're you waving at?" said Lineham, puzzled. No one was visible at any of the windows.

"Old Mr Pitman." Thanet explained about the mirror. "He's as sharp as a needle, doesn't miss a thing. I've a feeling he may be very useful to us, when I've a better idea of where we're going. Ah, here we are. Let's hope someone's in."

Neatly tacked up on a wooden notice board beside the front gate of the Old Vicarage was a blue-and-white Conservative election poster exhorting the population of Nettleton to vote for Henry Selby. Thanet and Lineham paused to study it. Selby had thinning hair, a toothbrush moustache and gimlet eyes. Only the eyebrows defied discipline, sprouting luxuriantly forward as if to compensate for the lack of hair on the top of the head and giving Selby the air of an aggressive Jack Russell.

Lineham voiced Thanet's thought. "He looks an awkward customer."

Was this the face of his adversary? Thanet wondered as they moved on.

Well screened from the road by densely planted trees and shrubs, the house stood at the end of a short but immaculately kept gravel drive which curved away around the side of the house, presumably in the direction of the garage. It was typical of the many vicarages which have been abandoned by England's clergy in favour of smaller, more convenient dwellings—big, rambling, not particularly attractive and no doubt very expensive to heat. Not, by the look of it, that the latter consideration would much concern the Selbys, Thanet thought. The place had the unmistakable aura of money: well-manicured lawns, weedless flower beds, shining windows, gleaming paintwork and a general air of well-fed smugness.

Thanet rang the bell and the succeeding silence was broken by the crunching sound of wheels on gravel. After a few moments around the corner of the house came a man pushing a loaded wheelbarrow. He was small and bent and had what Thanet felt was a distinctly appropriate resemblance to one of the gnomes beloved of suburban gardeners.

"You'll have to go round the back," he said, jerking his thumb and peering up at the two men from beneath the rim of a cap which looked as though it had been bought third-hand at a jumble sale many years ago. "Bell's out of order and She won't have heard you."

Interesting, thought Thanet, how he had managed to invest the pronoun with a capital letter.

Thanet thanked him and they made their way around the corner of the house to a door at the far end of the side wall. Thanet knocked once, twice and then, when there was still no response, put his head into the kitchen and called, "Mrs Selby?"

Here again there was evidence of money: streamlined units built of solid wood, ceramic hob, battery of electrical gadgets, ceramic tiles on walls and floor. The place, however, was in a mess, littered with dirty saucepans and unwashed dishes.

Thanet took a step inside and called again.

This time there was a response and a few moments later footsteps could be heard. A woman came into the kitchen, frowning.

"Mrs Selby?" Thanet said quickly. "Detective Inspector Thanet, Sturrenden CID."

"Oh," she said. "I thought I heard someone."

Thanet studied her as he introduced Lineham. She was small and fair, with a face in which middle age was definitely winning the battle against youth. The skin beneath the eyes was slack and puffy and the frown which Thanet had thought directed at himself and Lineham was a permanent feature, deep vertical creases scored between her eyebrows. And yet, he thought, she must once have been a pretty woman and she certainly hadn't given up on her appearance; her hair had clearly been freshly set and her clothes, a well-cut tweed skirt and matching cashmere sweater, were casually elegant. He shook the surprisingly large, strong hand she proffered and followed her along a wide corridor, through a spacious drawing room dominated by a grand piano and into a glass conservatory which had been built along one side of the house.

"Do sit down, Inspector." She waved a hand at the cane armchairs and began to transfer coffee cups and glasses from the low bamboo table on to a wicker tray. "If you'll excuse me, I'll just get rid of these. I shan't be a moment."

She disappeared through the door by which they had entered and the two men examined their surroundings. Joan would love this room, Thanet thought. It was all light and air and growing things. Against the house wall was a wide, raised flower bed edged with brick and overflowing with plants. Above them was trained an exotic climbing plant with variegated foliage and apricot-coloured, bell-shaped flowers.

"What a delightful room, Mrs Selby," he said, when she returned.

"Yes, isn't it? It's my favourite room in all the house. My husband says he thinks I would be quite happy to live in it all the time." She seated herself opposite him. "Now, what can I do for you, Inspector?"

Now that he had a chance to study her closely, Thanet could detect signs of tension. The knuckles of the hands clasped in her lap were white and there was a tiny, uncontrollable tic in her left eyelid. As he spoke she put up her hand as if to brush it away.

"We are investigating the murder of Miss Birch, of course," he said. "And naturally we are asking everybody in the neighbourhood if they noticed anything suspicious last night."

"You mean lurking strangers, that sort of thing," she said, with an attempt at a smile.

"Anything at all unusual," Thanet said.

She was shaking her head, a curiously regular, clockwork motion. "I'm sorry, I can't help you, Inspector. I didn't go out last night and as you will have seen when you came in, we are well screened from the road."

"Miss Pitman had to go to a PCC meeting last night and she arranged for Miss Birch to look in on Mr Pitman during the evening. Some of your upstairs windows overlook the Pitmans' garden and there is a street lamp outside their house. Did you by any chance see her arrive or leave?"

"I'm afraid not. I was in here, watching television." She nodded at a small portable colour set which stood on a low table in one corner.

"Alone?"

"Yes. My husband arrived home just after ten—he'd been away on a business trip since last Thursday—and my daughter a few minutes before that." The eyelid twitched. "She spent the evening with a friend, in Sturrenden."

"And neither of them mentioned having seen anything out of the ordinary?"

"No. Certainly not."

"Is your husband at home now, by any chance?" Thanet was remembering the coffee cups.

"No. Though you've only just missed him, as a matter of fact. He came home for lunch, today."

"I should like to have a word with him, just in case he did notice anything unusual last night," Thanet said. "Will he be at home this evening, do you know?"

"I think so, yes."

"Good. Now, about Miss Birch. She worked for you two afternoons a week, I believe?"

"That's right. She should have come today, as a matter of fact. Hence the mess you will no doubt have noticed in the kitchen. Usually she sees to that."

"What was she like?" asked Thanet softly.

"Like?" Something moved in the depths of the blue eyes and was quenched. Mrs Selby made a vague gesture. "Oh, mousy. Insignificant. A good enough worker. She was a bit heavy-handed, but with a place this size one's grateful for any help one can get."

"Did you like her?"

She shrugged. "Well enough, I suppose. I can't say I ever gave much thought to the subject."

"You had no reservations about her, then?"

"Reservations? Well no, of course not. Why should I?"

But like Marion Pitman, Mrs Selby was lying. Thanet was certain of it.

"Oh, no reason," he said. "No reason at all. I'll call again this evening, if I may, to see your husband. Say, nine o'clock?" He rose and Lineham followed suit.

"By all means." Her air of relief was unmistakable and she stood up with alacrity. "I'll see you out."

"Well, what did you think of that?" said Thanet as he and Lineham walked away down the drive.

"Like a cat on hot bricks, wasn't she? Couldn't wait to get rid of us."

"I wonder why," said Thanet thoughtfully.

People on the whole do not enjoy being caught up in a murder investigation, and a certain degree of tension is understandable. Nevertheless, he thought . . .

"You think the Selbys are involved, sir?"

Thanet shrugged. "Too early to tell, yet. What puzzles me is that I have this feeling that they're all holding back about Carrie Birch, for some reason. And I just can't get a clear picture of her. She's like a negative that's too thin for printing." He made up his mind. "Look, I think I'll just nip down to Sturrenden General and have a word with the mother. You stay here. Send someone down to the pub, as I suggested, and get some enquiries organised about the local yobs, just in case it's a simple case of mugging after all. Try the Gambles again and then see if anyone's at home there." He nodded at the large modern house between the Pitmans' bungalow and the church. "I shan't be long, an hour at the most, I should think."

Perhaps, he thought as he drove towards Sturrenden, Mrs Birch might be able to enlighten him about Carrie. Or perhaps he was looking for something that simply wasn't there. Perhaps Carrie really had been as uncomplicated as people seemed to want him to think. He shook his head, a fierce, involuntary movement. No—muggers apart, simple, uncomplicated people just didn't get themselves knocked on the head and then suffocated.

And then, there was the money. . . .

No, there was something about her that they were all covering up, he was sure of it. And he was going to find out what it was if it was the last thing he did.

5

"I'm afraid she's a bit disorientated," said the nurse as she led Thanet into the ward.

"What, exactly, is the matter with her? Medically, I mean?" he asked.

"A combination of things. Weak heart, diabetes... She had to have a foot amputated a few years ago. She really is not capable of looking after herself. As soon as there's a place at The Willows, she'll go there."

This was the first time Thanet had ever been in a geriatric ward. His father had died a mercifully swift death from a heart attack and his mother, at the age of sixty-five, was as sprightly as ever. He had seen much of the stuff of human tragedy in his work, but this place shocked him. These old people were sick, of course, any natural liveliness they might possess quenched by illness, but even those who were sitting out in armchairs beside their beds looked but half alive. Only their eyes moved, following Thanet and the nurse as they walked down the ward, and he felt that even this degree of interest arose only from the fact that they were moving objects in an otherwise stationary world.

It was unnerving, and he was relieved to reach his destination. Mrs Birch was seated in a wheelchair with a rug over her knees and Thanet's first reaction as he looked at her was one of astonishment. He had seen her before, of course, from a distance, when she had been wheeled out to the ambulance, but it had not been obvious then just how monstrously fat she was. Little piggy eyes sunk in deep folds of flesh peered out venomously at him as the nurse introduced him, and although he could feel pity for the woman's physical state it nevertheless aroused an unexpected revulsion in him; he could not help remembering Carrie's thin, bird-like body and he suppressed with difficulty the macabre thought that in some way Mrs Birch's bloated flesh had fed upon the dessicated body of her daughter, draining it of life and vitality. Certainly, unlike the other old women in the ward, Mrs Birch was very much alive.

"'Ave you found 'im yet then?" she demanded, when he was settled upon the stool which the nurse pulled from under the bed.

"Not yet, no," he said, consciously gentle. He reminded himself that personal dislike was irrelevant, could only get in the way, warp his judgement and cloud his ability to think clearly. Besides, there was genuine cause for compassion in the woman's physical condition. Nevertheless, he found it difficult to believe what he was hearing.

"Trust Carrie to go and get 'erself killed like that," she said. "Typical. Born useless, that girl was." The bright little eyes dared to disagree.

It was pointless to waste time arguing. He plunged straight in.

"Could you tell me what time she went out, last night?"

"Five to nine, wasn't it, same as usual when she goes to visit the old man."

"You're sure?"

The eyes sparked malevolence at his daring to challenge her.

"'Course I am. Always like to be settled in me bed by five to nine, don't I? Light out at nine, on the dot."

"Did you hear her come back?"

Her eyes told him that she considered this a stupid question. "Asleep, wasn't I? Took me tablets, as usual. Asleep, always, by half past."

"So when your daughter went across to the Pitmans' house in the evenings, you never heard her come in?"

"No." A glint of satisfaction. "Trained her to be quiet, didn't I? Don't like me sleep to be disturbed."

Thanet subdued with difficulty the spurt of anger he felt on Carrie's behalf. Trained her, indeed! As if she were an animal! He had a brief, unpleasing vision of the dead woman creeping through the silent house, easing open the staircase door beside the head of her mother's bed, terrified to make a sound, while this monstrous woman lay snoring soundly only inches away from her.

"So you had no idea that she was missing until she didn't appear this morning?"

"S'right. Eight on the dot she used to come down to make me tea. Well, by half past I was wondering what was up. Rang me bell, shouted, not a sound. Thought she'd overslept, didn't I? In the end I banged on the wall with me stick and that Jenny from next door come over. Took long enough about it, too. Dead loss that lot are, noisy, you wouldn't believe. Telly going till all hours, pop music blaring..."

"You don't like them?"

"They're all right, I s'pose, apart from the noise. Keep themselves to themselves, that's all."

Scarcely surprisingly that the Gambles hadn't been exactly eager to be on close terms with a woman like this, Thanet thought. Who would?

"Noisy last night?" he said hopefully.

"Not too bad. Told you. Went to sleep. No, it was the other one who woke me up last night."

"Other one?" said Thanet, suddenly alert.

"Old maid next door."

Miss Cox, presumably.

"Calling that blasted cat of 'ers, fit to wake the dead."

Not the happiest of analogies in the circumstances, Thanet thought. "What time was that?"

"'Ow should I know? Woke me up, that's all. And if I'm woke out of me first sleep I 'ave terrible trouble getting off again."

"Did you do anything about it?"

"What, f'r instance?" She gave him a withering glare. "What d'you expect me to do, like this?" And a pudgy hand reminded him of that overweight, diseased mountain of flesh.

"Call your daughter?" he suggested.

"Well I tried, of course I did. But she didn't answer. Stands to reason, don't it? She wasn't there. Thought she was asleep. Always did sleep soundly."

Or, thought Thanet, had developed a necessary deafness to her mother's night-time demands.

"So you really have no idea what time it was, when you heard Miss Cox calling her cat?"

"Told you. No. Didn't put the light on—thought it would wake me up even more."

A thought struck him. "Where was the calling coming from?"

She looked at him as though he were out of his mind. "Next door, of course."

"Was Miss Cox inside or outside?"

"Outside."

"You're sure?"

Again that withering glance. "Dead certain. That's why she woke me up, see. Must've been going down the garden path after 'im. Mad about that cat, she is. Went on and on and on."

"She can get about with that leg of hers, then?"

"When she wants to," said Mrs Birch darkly. "Of course, that didn't stop 'er getting Carrie to do 'er shopping. And ungrateful!" Mrs Birch leaned forward. "D'you know, with all that Carrie did for 'er since she broke 'er leg, she still didn't let 'er over the threshold!"

"Really?" Thanet was genuinely interested.

Mrs Birch shook her head ponderously, so that her jowls wobbled. "Typical, that is. Real old 'ermit, that woman is."

"Has she always been like that?"

"Far back as I can remember. Ever since that kid brother of 'ers was killed in the war. Doted on 'im, she did. Still, you gotta go on living, 'aven't you, no matter what happens." Mrs Birch scowled around at the ward, as if to say, Look at me, I'm surviving, aren't I? "But I did think when she got Carrie to do 'er shopping that she'd at least ask 'er in for a cuppa tea or something. I mean to say, it's only common politeness, isn't it?"

It was a real grievance, Thanet could see. No doubt Mrs Birch had been longing to know all the ins and outs of her neighbour's life.

"As if Carrie didn't 'ave enough to do, what with me to look after and all 'er other jobs and all."

"Other jobs?"

"Pitmans every morning. Selbys two afternoons, church two evenings. Peanuts she got paid for that, too."

"For cleaning the church, you mean?"

"Yer."

"Which evenings did she go there?"

"Tuesday and Thursday. But them Pitmans was worst of all. Thought that just because 'e'd been 'er old 'eadmaster, she could always be at 'is beck and call."

"Mr Pitman?"

"Yer. 'ead of the village school 'e was, until 'e retired."

In that case, Thanet thought, as well as Carrie herself Mr Pitman would have known some of the other people involved, way back. . . . "Well," he said, rising, "thank you very much, Mrs Birch. You've been most helpful."

The currant eyes looked vaguely affronted, as though his thanks were anything but gratifying. What did I tell him that was so interesting? she seemed to be asking herself as she gave an ungracious nod and said goodbye.

Disorientated was a charitable way of describing her condition, Thanet thought.

The many eyes watched him dully all the way back down the ward and it was with a sense of relief that he left the hospital and took deep breaths of fresh air again. In the car he did not start the engine immediately but sat staring sightlessly out across the hospital car park which was now filling up. Visiting time was approaching, he supposed.

That woman! What a miserable life poor Carrie must have had, always dancing attendance on her mother. It must have been one long round of cleaning, running to and fro for her mother and more cleaning. No wonder she had needed that little pile of paperback romances to provide her with a temporary escape from the unremitting grimness of it all. But would that have been enough? Could Carrie, in some as yet undiscovered way, have needed to seek further excitement?

Thanet thought again about the money, and wondered.

He realised that he hadn't had a pipe since early morning and began to fill one, absently, as his mind ranged back over the people he had met so far. Would any one of them be a good candidate for blackmail? He wouldn't have thought that the Pitmans were sufficiently well off to be suitable subjects, but of course the money could have been paid over quite a long period. The Selbys seemed much more promising. As he had said to Lineham, Major Selby had more to lose and, on the face of it, more money available. Thanet was looking forward to meeting him.

Meanwhile, there was work to do. He set off again for Nettleton. He wanted to see Miss Cox, partly because his curiosity had been aroused, partly because he wanted to check the time at which she had made her sortie into the back garden to look for her cat. She might very well have seen or heard something of which she did not realise the significance.

First, however, Thanet wanted to talk again to old Mr Pitman, fill in a little background information on all these people. Why hadn't the old man mentioned that he had been Carrie's headmaster, that he had known her since childhood?

This was the first question he put to Mr Pitman when he had settled himself in the armchair beside the bed. He tried not to sound too accusing but he needn't have bothered; the old man was quite unabashed.

"Because I knew you'd find out soon enough, Inspector," he said, a wicked glint in his eye. "And that then, of course, you'd have to come and see me again. Why should I deny myself the pleasure of a second visit by telling you everything I know at our first meeting? Just as a matter of interest, who told you? No," he added quickly, "let me guess." He was silent for a moment. "Could it have been the ravishing Hilda?

Carrie's mother," he explained. "Ah, I thought so. What did you think of her, Inspector?" But it was clear that he didn't expect an answer.

"So you've known Carrie ever since she was a child? What was she like?"

"Plain, I'm afraid. Plain and not very bright. A most unprepossessing combination. And, of course, completely under her mother's thumb, as always." Mr Pitman sighed. "Poor Carrie, the dice were loaded against her right from the beginning."

"What happened to her father?"

"A rather nasty accident with some machinery at the farm—he worked for Mr Martin. Did you know that there is an exceptionally high risk factor in working as a farm labourer? Strange, isn't it?"

"No, I didn't. That's interesting. You'd think that a peaceful, rural existence would guarantee a long and healthy life, wouldn't you? How old was Carrie at the time?"

"Oh, quite young. Seven or eight, I suppose."

"How did she get on with the other children at school?"

"She didn't. They just didn't like her. She was always the one who would be standing on the sidelines, watching. Pathetic little thing, really. And, as I said, so unprepossessing. Scrawny, unattractively dressed, hair in two little plaits so thin I'm afraid they always made me think of rats' tails. Not surprising, really, that the other children didn't take to her. And the situation was made worse by her attitude. Somehow you felt that she expected to be ignored, left out of things. It was that mother of hers, I'm sure of it. I expect Carrie was so used to being belittled at home that she didn't expect anything different at school."

"You really do paint a pathetic picture of her, don't you? Strange, you know, earlier on I wouldn't have said you were, how shall I put it, quite so sympathetic to her."

"Oh?"

"No."

A brief silence. Then Thanet went on. "In fact, I felt that you had distinct reservations about her."

"Did you now?"

"I did."

Another silence. The old man obviously wasn't going to relent, Thanet decided. He sighed, tried a different tack.

"I suppose you knew the Coxes, too. I gather they've lived here all their lives as well."

Mr Pitman pounced upon the change of subject with a relief he couldn't quite conceal. "The Coxes. Ah, yes. Now there's another unhappy case. Mrs Birch told you about it, I suppose?"

"Only the barest outline," said Thanet. "I'd be very interested to hear more."

"Yes, well, Matilda Cox—Matty as we always call her—was ten when her brother Joseph was born, and her mother died giving birth. It must have been a very bad time for her, poor kid. This was back in nineteen twenty-five, you understand, a couple of years after I came to Nettleton as Assistant Teacher."

A swift calculation told Thanet that Miss Cox must now be sixty-six.

"Anyway," Mr Pitman went on, "she seemed to compensate for her mother's death by turning all her capacity for love on to the baby. Her father was not a particularly affectionate man and God knows what he would have done with the baby if Matty hadn't been around. Anyway, she took the child over. Even brought the baby to school with her! There were several neighbours who offered to have him during the day, but she wouldn't agree and we all felt so sorry for her that the Headmaster agreed, providing that the child wasn't a nuisance."

"Extraordinary," said Thanet. "It could never happen today."

"System's so much more impersonal," agreed the old man. "Anyway, it seemed to work out very well. Matty looked after the house and the baby, left school at the earliest possible moment and devoted herself to bringing Joseph up. Inevitably, of course, she was over-protective and he had a hard time of it when he started school. Kids always know when one of their number is weak and it seems to bring out the worst in them. I'm afraid poor Joseph suffered badly from their teasing— and worse than teasing on occasion, too. It didn't do him any good, just made him retreat more and more into himself and that's how he grew up—shy, nervous, withdrawn. Disaster struck, of course, when he was called up in 1943." Mr Pitman broke off. "I'm sorry, perhaps I'm boring you. Is this the sort of thing you wanted me to tell you?"

"Exactly the sort of thing. Do go on, please."

"I was away at the time, in North Africa, but my wife told me about it. Matty's father was out in Africa too, but he was less fortunate than me. He was killed that year, and it was only a couple of months afterwards that Joseph got his papers. As you can imagine, Matty nearly went mad trying to get him exempted but she failed and off Joseph went. Into the RAF. And you can guess what happened next."

"Shot down?"

"Yes. In the Berlin raids, just before Christmas. Missing, believed killed. Everyone thought that Matty would go berserk, but she took it very calmly. Said she didn't believe he was dead. My wife said it was heartbreaking. Matty lived in daily expectation of his coming home. His room was kept ready at all times and week after week, month after month Matty would do her best on her miserable rations to keep up a supply of Joseph's favourite food in preparation for his homecoming."

Thanet pulled a sympathetic face. "I expect there were a lot of women who behaved like that."

"No doubt. And in some cases, of course, their patience was rewarded. But not in Matty's. And with her it was an obsession. Anyway, in the end she stopped, quite suddenly, about a year later. Mary, my wife, was surprised, thought that she would have kept it up until all the men had finished trickling back from the prisoner-of-war camps, but Matty didn't. Mary thought that perhaps it was some sort of defence against disappointment—better to hope for nothing and be overjoyed than to live on a knife-edge all the time and be doomed to perpetual disillusion. But it changed her—Matty, I mean. She just withdrew into her shell and she has scarcely emerged from it since. Never goes out, except to do her shopping, never, ever asks anyone in. Not that she ever was a particularly sociable type but now, well, she's a total recluse. I just don't know how anyone can live like that."

"My sergeant says she's very shaken, over the murder."

"She would be. Not that she was on close terms with Carrie or with anyone else, for that matter. But an event like that, happening right next door, must have a pretty cataclysmic effect on a life like hers, withdrawn as she has been from reality for, oh, it must be nearly thirty years now."

"Have you any ideas about who might have killed Carrie?"

The old man shook his head. "But then, you see, if it was someone local—and I think it must have been, don't you?—I wouldn't, would I? After all, one is bound to find it near-impossible to suspect people one has known for years."

"What makes you say it must have been someone local?"

The old man sighed, then listed all the arguments which Thanet had already worked out for himself.

"But you really have no suspicions?"

Mr Pitman folded his lips in a stubborn line.

"You said you found it near-impossible to suspect people you had known for years. Who were you referring to?"

The old man described a tight circle in the air with one of his misshapen hands. "Carrie's life was very circumscribed, you know."

"Yes. So you're talking in particular about...?"

A shake of the head. "It's no good, Inspector. This is where I dry up. Facts, past history I will give you, yes. But gossip, speculation about my neighbours, no."

"But if you do think of any relevant facts... you will let me know?"

"I won't lie to you, Inspector. But I can't guarantee to volunteer information if I am not sure of its relevance."

"But if you are sure?" Thanet said, quickly.

"Then I'd have to think about it. I do realise that this is a murder investigation, that it is my duty to help you in any way I can."

And with this assurance Thanet had to be content.

6

Thanet watched appreciatively as the driving door of the scarlet MGB opened and a pair of long, slim legs appeared. Not many women could extricate themselves as gracefully as this from a car like that, he thought with admiration.

The rest of the woman matched his first glimpse. She was,

he thought, a real stunner: curves in all the right places, long, very dark hair which curled with disciplined abandon about the pale oval of her face, delicately modelled nose, really beautiful dark eyes and white, even teeth which were now revealed in the tentative half-smile she gave Thanet as he advanced upon her.

As he had reached the gate of the Pitmans' bungalow, the MGB had turned into the driveway of Latchetts, the modern house next door, and he had followed it up the drive. If the woman had been out, Lineham might well have missed her when he called earlier.

"Detective Inspector Thanet, Sturrenden CID," he said. "Did my sergeant call to see you, this afternoon?"

"Joy Ingram," she responded, the smile a shade more positive now. "I'm afraid I've been out since mid-morning."

Now that he was closer he could see that her beauty was marred by the frown lines on her forehead and that she was considerably older than he had originally thought: in her late thirties, probably, he decided.

"You will have heard about the murder?" he said.

"Yes," she said, and the frown lines deepened. "Poor Miss Birch. What a terrible thing. Who on earth could have wanted to kill an inoffensive little creature like that?"

"Naturally we are asking everybody in the area if they saw her at all last evening."

She shook her head, slowly. "I'm afraid not."

"She must have passed your house, you see, twice. Once at about nine, on her way to the Pitmans' next door, and again when she left there, at nine-thirty. You're sure . . . ?"

"No." Her voice was firmer now. "We didn't see her, I'm sure of that."

"Your husband was at home?"

"Yes. Yes, of course. Why do you ask?" It was as if her concentration had suddenly sharpened by several degrees.

"You said, 'We'."

"Oh . . . oh, I see. Yes." She turned, stooped to reach for handbag which lay on the passenger seat. Then she slammed the car door with an air of finality. "Well, if that's all, Inspector . . ."

"What about your husband?" he persisted.

"What about him?"

"Could he have seen anything?"

"I'm sure he didn't." She slung the bag over her shoulder, half turned, as if to walk towards the house.

"You're certain he didn't look out? Either then or later?"

"Inspector." She swung back to face him squarely. "My husband and I were in all evening. Together. The curtains were drawn and after dinner we watched television. Then we went to bed. I'll leave the rest to your imagination. Now, if you'll excuse me. . . ." And without waiting for an answer she marched towards the front door, did not look back as she took the key from her handbag, let herself in.

After the door had closed Thanet stood gazing thoughtfully after her for a moment or two before crossing the road to Church Cottages. Her reaction at the mention of her husband had been distinctly interesting. He was content to let the matter rest for the moment, but he thought that a visit to the Ingrams this evening might perhaps be fruitful. He had to come out to Nettleton anyway, to see Major Selby; he could kill two birds with one stone—no, three, he corrected himself. If the Gambles were out all day, he would probably have to see them this evening too.

He walked up the front path to number five with a certain degree of anticipation. Matty Cox was an eccentric and he enjoyed eccentrics. Obviously she couldn't care less about appearances. All the other gardens of Church Cottages were trim and well kept but this one had long been neglected. The bricks in the path were green with algae and many were broken, clumps of grass thrusting their way up through crumbling mortar. A few sad daffodils almost obscured by long grass still struggled vainly to brighten the sour little plot but otherwise nothing flourished but grass and weeds.

Nor did Miss Cox bother with the exterior of the house; the paintwork couldn't have been washed in years and the windowpanes were thick with the winter's grime.

There was no immediate response to his knock and he waited several minutes before knocking again. Matty Cox, after all, had a leg in plaster and he must allow her time to get to the door. There was still no sound within, however, and this time his knock was more peremptory. Come on, my beauty, he thought, I know you're in there.

With a roar the red tractor turned into the lane from the main road and rattled past on its way back to the farm, the driver lifting a friendly hand. Thanet waved back, then turned to knock again, only to find that the noise made by the tractor had drowned the sound of the door opening.

Miss Cox did not fit his image of her. He had expected someone small, plump, motherly; a shy, retiring little woman with a disillusioned, embittered face. But this woman was tall, almost as tall as he. And very unfeminine. Her face was square, her jaw heavy and her coarse grey hair was short and straight, held back on one side by a hairgrip. She probably cut it herself, he decided, noting its uneven length, rather than expose herself to the cheerful chattiness of a hairdressing salon. She wore no make-up and her clothes heightened the masculine effect—baggy brown corduroy trousers and checked shirt. Only the heavy, drooping breasts straining against the buttons of the shapeless cardigan betrayed her sex.

"Miss Cox?"

The woman did not reply, merely waited, leaning heavily on a walking stick held in her left hand. Her right gripped the edge of the door, effectively barring any move he might have made to enter the house. Intentional or not? he wondered, his curiosity whetted. To think that no one had entered this house for almost thirty years...

"Detective Inspector Thanet, Sturrenden CID," he said. "I believe my sergeant came to see you this morning."

She nodded, opened her mouth. Thanet waited but still she did not speak and after a moment he said, "I'm sorry to trouble you again, but there is one small thing... I went to see Mrs Birch at the hospital this afternoon, and she tells me that she heard you calling your cat last night. She thought the sound came from outside the house... Were you outside last night, looking for him?"

Her hand on the door slipped an inch or two and the stick wobbled as she shifted her position slightly. She cleared her throat.

"It was the wind," she said. Her voice was hoarse. From disuse, he wondered?

"The wind?" he repeated blankly.

"It blew the door to, shut Tiger in the shed."

As if on cue a large tabby cat emerged from the house, sat down at Miss Cox's feet and fixed Thanet with an unwinking stare.

It was almost, thought Thanet fancifully, as if it had decided that its mistress needed some moral support.

"I see," he said. "What time was this?"

"Ten o'clock."

"It was ten o'clock when you put him out?"

A little, impatient shake of the head. She seemed to be more at ease now. "Ten o'clock when I missed him. I always puts him out at five to ten, see. He's out five minutes, then I opens the door and he comes back in. Last night he didn't." For her, it was a long speech.

"So what did you do?"

"I calls for another minute or two, then I puts on me coat and goes to look for him."

"And you found him in the shed?"

"S'right."

"Where is this shed?"

"Bottom of the garden."

"You managed all right, with your leg?"

"I got me stick. I managed."

"And it would have taken you how long, to go down the garden, find him and get back to the house?"

The effort of standing was clearly beginning to tell upon her. The knuckles of the hand gripping the stick were white with strain. She frowned. "Dunno."

"Try to think, please. It could be very important."

She looked at him sharply, then down at the cat. Tiger appeared to have lost interest in the proceedings. He was now washing himself, one leg stuck up in the air in a position which looked anatomically impossible. "Ten minutes?" she said, at last.

"Now," he said, "I want you to think very carefully indeed. While you were out in the garden, did you hear anything? Anything at all, I mean?"

It was a long shot, of course. Carrie had been killed between half past nine, when she had left the Pitmans' house, and eleven—give or take a little. It was too much to hope for, that the murder should have taken place during the only few minutes when someone in the neighbourhood was actually outside the house, not glued to the television set. Still . . . he awaited her answer eagerly.

"What sort of thing?"

"Anything. Anything at all."

She frowned. "It was too windy. I told you, it was blowing hard."

Damn that wind, he thought, remembering how blustery it had been last night.

"You're sure?"

She nodded, clearly hoping that the interview was at an end. Thanet sighed inwardly. Another blank. "Well, thank you very much, Miss Cox. If you do remember anything you might have heard, though, please let me know. My men'll be about all day and would be glad to take a message."

Already Tiger had whisked inside and the door was closing. Thanet turned away. So even that slender hope was now gone. He really seemed to be getting absolutely nowhere. It was all vague suspicions, feelings. . . . What he needed was some satisfyingly positive lead, something he could really get his teeth into.

He scowled, looking about him for a focus for his irritation. Where were all those men he had mentioned to Miss Cox, anyway? There wasn't a policeman in sight. Thanet set off down the lane, at a brisk pace. At the corner he almost collided with Lineham.

"Where the devil have you been?" he snapped. "And where are all the others?"

"Sorry, sir," said Lineham defensively. "But we've only been carrying out your instructions. Bentley and Carson are checking up on the local yobs and the others are split between doing a house to house and searching the back gardens of Church Cottages."

"No sign of the weapon yet?"

"None, sir, so far. Nor of the handbag. I've been up to Church Farm to see Mr Martin—you wanted to know if he owned the Cottages."

"And does he?"

"Yes, sir. But it looks as though he's in the clear for last night. He was at a charity dinner in Sturrenden and we can easily check on that."

"Ah well," Thanet said. "It was a very long shot anyway. I can't really see a prosperous farmer bumping off the daughter of a crippled tenant just to gain vacant possession, can you? Look, let's go and sit in the car for a few minutes."

They waited while a laden articulated lorry went grinding past them.

"Ridiculous allowing monsters like that on roads like these," said Thanet. "The truth is, Mike," he went on as they crossed the road towards the church, "I just don't feel we're getting anywhere. It's all bits and bobs of information." Quickly, he gave Lineham a summary of what he had learned from Mrs Birch and old Robert Pitman.

"Miss Cox didn't say anything to me about going out last night to look for her cat," Lineham said, when Thanet had finished.

"I suppose she didn't think it sufficiently important. Anyway, she swears she didn't see or hear anything unusual while she was in the garden and I really can't see that there's any reason to disbelieve her. Did you go down to the pub, by the way?"

"Yes. The landlord says that the only person he remembers coming in from this end of the village was Mr Ingram. He . . ."

"Ingram?"

"Yes." Lineham raised his eyebrows at the surprise in Thanet's voice. "He lives in that . . ."

"Yes, yes, I know where he lives. It's just that I saw his wife just now—I gather she was out when you called earlier—and she swears that they were both in all evening."

"Does she, now?"

"The landlord's sure of this?"

"Certain. Apparently the pub was fairly empty last night—the weather wasn't good, if you remember. It was very windy. He says Ingram came in at around ten—he couldn't be more precise—and stayed for about half an hour. He was in a pretty grim mood apparently. Had four double whiskies and was very unsociable."

"More and more interesting," mused Thanet. "I think I'll pay Mr Ingram a little call this evening."

"Will you need me, sir?"

"I should think I could just about manage without you holding my hand," Thanet said with a grin. "Why?"

"Well I had promised Louise to give her a hand with a bit of decorating we wanted to finish off before Saturday, but of course if you want me . . ."

"So long as I know where to find you," said Thanet. "You go ahead with your plans. You only get married once." If you manage to get married at all, he added silently. "How are the others getting on with checking the whereabouts of the local talent last night?"

"They're waiting for them to get home from school," Lineham said. "There are four possibles, apparently, and they all go to Littlestone Comprehensive and come home on the school bus. It gets to Nettleton about four, so Carson and Bentley should be finished some time in the next hour."

"Good. Well I think I'll go back and get started on reports. There's not much more I can do here at the moment. You hang on until you've heard what they've got to report. If there's anything interesting, I'll come back out. If not, you can get off home."

"Right," said Lineham, getting out of the car. "Thank you, sir."

Thanet was still hard at work on his reports when Lineham rang an hour later to say that it looked as though all four youths were in the clear. They had, they claimed, been to a disco in the next village where they were all well known. Their story would be checked, of course, but it didn't look too hopeful.

The news didn't surprise him, thought Thanet as he put the phone down. For local youngsters, Carrie Birch would scarcely have seemed a fruitful target. Unless there had been any rumours about money in the house? But no attempt had been made to break in. No, Carrie's death had been no random killing, he was sure of it, and sooner or later the real reason for her murder would become clear.

He hoped.

7

Bridget and Ben were already in bed but the sound of Thanet's key in the front door brought them both thundering

down the stairs with demands for a story and in the resulting
confusion any constraint between Thanet and Joan passed
unnoticed.

"Go back up to bed this minute!" said Joan, emerging
flushed from the kitchen.

"Up you go," said Thanet, with a playful slap on each small
bottom. "I'll be up in a minute." He gave Joan a kiss. "Hullo,
love."

"Better go straight away," said Joan, disappearing into the
kitchen. "Supper's nearly ready."

After an instalment of *Paddington* for Bridget and one of
Mister Clumsy for Ben, Thanet returned downstairs.

Supper, as usual, was first-rate: chicken fricassee with
savoury rice and french beans, followed by home-made
blackberry ice cream. How long would it be, Thanet
wondered gloomily, before such delights were a thing of
the past?

They talked, as usual, about their day's activities. Thanet
had always been careful not to exclude Joan from his work.
His theory was that the resentment and bitterness felt by
many police wives over the demands of their husbands' work
could be avoided if they felt that they were not being
excluded from it. For Joan and himself this approach had
always seemed to work but now he found himself questioning
its value. Clearly, it left her unsatisfied. She listened as
eagerly as ever to his account of the day's progress, asked
pertinent questions, as usual, but underneath Thanet was
aware of new reservations in her. Or were they in himself?
He wasn't sure. The fact was, they were there.

"What about you?" he said at last. "What have you been up
to?"

"Oh, nothing much." Her mouth tugged down at the
corners. "Ironing, cleaning. Took Ben to the playgroup this
morning, fetched him home again." She shrugged. "Just the
usual."

Not a very inspiring list of activities, he thought guiltily,
assessing them in the light of Joan's projected foray into the
world of work. Especially when one considered that they
were repeated over and over again, day after day, week after
week, year after year. Many of them, naturally, were centred
around the children, especially Ben, and for the first time he
really thought about how it would be for her when Ben went
to school.

Boring, he decided guiltily. Condemned to such an existence himself he would have gone quietly mad.

"Look, love," he said. "I've been thinking about what you said last night..."

The eagerness in her face as she looked up heightened his guilt.

"Yes?" she said.

"I meant it, you know. You go ahead, sound out the position. Make enquiries, find out the sort of thing you'd enjoy." But the false heartiness in his tone did not deceive her and she bit her lip, glanced away from him.

She shook her head. "It's no good, Luke. I can see you don't like the idea."

He could not bring himself to lie again, knowing that in any case he could not do it with conviction. "Look," he said, leaning across the table to take her hand, "all right, it's true, I can't say I'm keen. At the same time I know it's unreasonable to expect you to stay cooped up in the house for the rest of your life. So I mean it. You go ahead."

But her hand beneath his lay lifeless, unresponsive and again she shook her head. "What's the point, if you're so much against it?"

"But I'm not so much against it, as you put it," he said, withdrawing his hand in exasperation. "I just like things the way they are, that's all. Is that so wrong of me?"

"No of course not," she said quickly, "but—oh, darling, don't you see? I just don't want to do it if you're not wholeheartedly behind me."

"So what do you want me to say?" he cried. "You want me to lie, is that it? To say, Yes, go ahead, marvellous, I'd love to have a working wife, to come home to an empty house and have latch-key children. Is that what you want? Well, I can't and that's that. Go ahead if you wish, and I'll back you to the hilt, you know that. But don't expect my approval because in all honesty I can't give it."

She stared at him for a moment, eyes dilated and then, with a little choking sound of distress, she got up and ran from the room.

Thanet half rose to follow her and then sat down again. What was the point? He'd been honest with her, hadn't he? Told her how he felt? And told her to go ahead when it was the last thing in the world he wanted. What more did she expect?

Scowling he rose, began to clear the table. He carried some of the dishes into the kitchen, put them down on the table and then, with a sigh, started up the stairs.

As he had expected, she was lying face down on the bed, still in tears. Suppressing a sigh of exasperation he sat down beside her, put his arm across her shoulders. "Joan," he said. "Come on, love, cheer up. It's not the end of the world, you know. I'm sure we'll work something out." He thrust a handkerchief into her clenched fist. "Here, blow," he said.

Obediently she raised herself on her elbows, mopped at the tears, blew her nose. Then she rolled over on to her back. She avoided looking at him, however, covering her swollen eyes with the back of one hand.

"That's better," he said, smiling.

"It doesn't solve anything, though," she muttered.

"But honey, what do you want me to do? I can't change my feelings, can I?"

"Nor can I," she said, with a touch of defiance.

"I know."

"There you are," she said.

"What?"

"It's going to be a barrier between us." And to his dismay, the tears began again.

"Darling," he said, putting his arms around her and lifting her up to hold her close against him. "Don't. It'll only be a barrier if we let it."

"But how can we prevent it?" she murmured into his shoulder.

"There'll be a way," he said, with a confidence he did not feel. "You'll see."

She pulled away from him then, tried to smile. "I only hope you're right," she said. She swung her legs over the side of the bed, stood up and walked to the dressing table. "What a mess!" she said, peering into the mirror. She picked up her hairbrush, began to tug it through her mass of fair curls. "What time do you have to go?"

"Now, I'm afraid," he said, glancing at his watch. It was almost half past seven. "I've got three calls to make this evening." He crossed the room to stand behind her, put his arms around her. "Feeling better?" he said, dropping a kiss on the nape of her neck where the hair curled softly into a little point.

She put down the brush, turned. "Yes," she said. "Sorry."

They kissed with the ardour of a sincere desire for reconciliation, but Thanet was aware that underneath nothing was resolved. The problem would rear it ugly head again and again until...what? Mentally he shrugged. Time would no doubt bring some sort of resolution, some compromise equally unacceptable to both. Shocked at his own cynicism he released her. "I'd better be off, then," he said. "I shan't be too late, I hope."

It was equally shocking to experience a sense of relief as he shut the front door behind him. Usually, if had to go out in the evening, he left Joan with reluctance. As he drove back to Nettleton, however, he managed, with an effort, to slough off his domestic problems and focus his mind on the evening ahead. He found that he was looking forward to it, and particularly to the interview with the Ingrams. True, there was no reason whatsoever to show that either of them had been involved with the murder, but Mrs Ingram's lie had somehow made him feel fractionally more optimistic. It was only a tiny lever, but if he could wield it correctly, he might just manage to open up a crack in the wall of silence which he felt these people were building around Carrie Birch.

There were already several cars parked in front of the church and the lights were on in the building itself. It was a clear but moonless night and after locking the car Thanet stood quite still for a few minutes, adjusting to the darkness. There was a dim light on the lychgate and a little street lamp in front of the Pitmans' bungalow, but to Thanet's town-oriented gaze it was practically pitch dark. Across the road the footpath at the rear of Church Cottages was in total darkness. Had there been a moon last night? He ought to check.

Pausing only to note with satisfaction that the lights were on in number three, where he hoped later to see the Gambles, Thanet picked his way carefully up the drive of Latchetts. He wanted to tackle the Ingrams first.

The curtains were drawn across the huge front windows but as Thanet approached the front door he could hear the sound of angry voices. He soon traced their source: a tiny window set into the wall at eye level in the shallow portion of wall which projected forward at right angles to the front door. It was obviously used for ventilation and someone had forgotten to close it. Thankful now for the concealing darkness Thanet pressed himself against the house wall and listened.

". . . bloody stupid!" That must be Ingram. And furious, by the sound of it.

His wife's response was only a murmur, her words, muffled probably by thick curtains, indistinguishable. By her tone of voice, though, she was on the defensive.

"Well of course they're bound to find out," said Ingram angrily. "This is a murder investigation, isn't it? And in a murder investigation everyone but everyone even remotely connected with the victim is put under the microscope."

Mrs Ingram obviously protested, for her husband went on, "*I* know there wasn't any bloody connection, *you* know there wasn't, but *they* don't, do they? And you can be damned sure they'll try to find out. And if anyone's caught lying—don't you see? Even if they're innocent, it looks bad. Why the hell couldn't you simply have told him the truth?"

"How could I, when I didn't know what it was?" This time Mrs Ingram's voice was audible. She, too, was getting angry.

"And just what the hell do you mean by that?"

"What I said!" she snapped. "That I didn't know what the truth was. All I know is that we had a row, you stamped out of here at about a quarter to ten and you didn't come back until about half past. Oh, I know you *said* you'd been to the pub . . ."

"And what the devil do you think I'd been doing? Bumping off that poor little woman across the way?"

Her reply was inaudible, but he was obviously dissatisfied with it.

"No, come on, tell me. Just tell me, will you? Precisely what do you think I was doing in that three quarters of an hour?" His anger had reached its zenith now and inevitably his wife's flared up to match it.

"How should I know?" she screamed at him. "Having it off with that cow Marion Pitman, probably!"

From the dead silence which followed Thanet deduced that Ingram's astonishment matched his own.

Then, unexpectedly, came laughter. "Marion Pitman . . ." Ingram spluttered. "Marion Pitman . . ."

"I've been watching the pair of you for months," Mrs Ingram went on, her voice still raised to make herself heard over his continuing laughter. "Don't think I didn't know what you were up to!"

The laughter stopped abruptly. "Look, Joy," said Ingram, his voice suddenly very cold, "you'd better stop this nonsense at once. There never has been, is not and never will be anything between Marion Pitman and myself."

"Amen," mocked his wife. "You expect me to believe that?"

"Believe it or not," he said. "It's true. I like Marion well enough, she's a very nice woman, but that's as far as it goes."

"What about all the little trips next door?"

"What little trips?"

Thanet had heard enough. He wasn't interested in a purely domestic quarrel and it was all too obvious now where it was leading. By the sound of it Mrs Ingram, despite her beauty, suffered badly from the disease of jealousy.

He rang the bell. At once the voices stopped and a moment or two later the light went on in the hall and Ingram opened the door.

"Yes?" He had himself well under control, Thanet was interested to note. A cool customer, then. He was tall, well built and as fair as his wife was dark. One lock of hair flopped boyishly over his forehead and he brushed it away with what was clearly an habitual gesture as he absorbed Thanet's self-introduction. At once he was all affability.

"Derek Ingram," he said, holding out his hand and shaking Thanet's vigorously. "Come in, come in, Inspector. This way."

The room into which he shepherded his visitor was all glass and stainless steel, angles and geometric patterns in pale, bleached shades of cream, off-white and beige. Mrs Ingram, intentionally no doubt, was a stunning contrast in a flame-coloured floor-length dress in some soft, clinging fabric which moulded itself to her beautiful body as she stood up and held out her hand. Her smile was dazzling.

"Inspector," she said, with an emphasis on the second syllable, as if he were the one person in the world above all others that she wanted to see. "What a surprise! Do sit down."

Having overheard their earlier conversation it was easy for Thanet to interpret the looks which flashed between them. What do we do now? said hers. Leave it to me, his responded.

Mrs Ingram subsided gracefully on to the long, low couch of blond leather and Ingram sat down beside her. The curious-looking contraption of tubular steel and strapped leather into which Thanet gingerly lowered himself was, he found, surprisingly comfortable.

"I'm afraid," said Ingram, taking the initiative with a deprecating little laugh, "that first of all I must clear up a

slight misunderstanding. When you saw my wife this morning she rather misguidedly, perhaps, but understandably, I'm
sure you will agree, misled you."

"So I gathered," said Thanet dryly. "The window's open,"
he went on, inwardly amused at their blank faces. "And I'm
afraid you were talking rather loudly. . . ." There was a moment's silence while they assimilated this and he could see
that they were frantically trying to recall exactly what had
been said.

"I gather you went down to the pub last night?"

Ingram nodded eagerly, clearly relieved, now that the
initial shock was over, to be saved the trouble of explaining.
"That's right."

"And—correct me if I'm wrong—you left here at about a
quarter to ten, returned at about half past."

"Yes."

"So, I would be most grateful if you could cast your mind
back and try to recall if you saw anyone or heard anything on
the way there, or the way back."

"Inspector," broke in Mrs Ingram. "May I just ask a
question?"

"By all means."

"What . . . do you know what time Miss Birch was . . . killed?"

"I'm afraid I can't tell you precisely, but the period in
which we are particularly interested is between nine thirty
and eleven o'clock last night. I really must stress how vital it
is that people should be frank with us. If you have nothing to
hide, you have nothing to fear."

The rebuke was gentle but she bit her lip, flushed, glanced
at her husband.

He, however, ignored her. Clearly, he was thinking. Eventually, "I'm sorry, Inspector, but I simply don't remember
seeing anybody either on the way down or on the way back.
It wasn't a very nice night, if you remember, blustery and
rather chilly. Needless to say, I wish I had seen somebody, if
only because they would presumably be able to vouch for
me."

"Quite," said Thanet. "But you're sure?"

Ingram shook his head slowly. "I'm sorry."

"Can you by any chance remember if there was a moon?"

"Intermittently, yes. At times it was quite bright, then the
clouds would blot it out completely."

"Any cars parked in front of the church?"

"Oh yes, a number. I assumed there was a meeting at the vicarage."

"The PCC, I believe," said Thanet. "What about when you came back?"

"None. I remember thinking that the meeting must be over."

A sudden clamour of bells made Thanet start. Joy Ingram rose and reached behind the curtain to shut the little window and at once the sound receded to a distant tintinnabulation.

"Bellringing night," she said with a grimace.

Thanet rather liked it but refrained from saying so. Perhaps, if he lived next door to the church and had to put up with it once a week as the Ingrams did, he would feel the same as she.

"Well," he said, rising, "I think that's all for the moment. I'd be grateful though, Mr Ingram, if you would try very hard to think back to last night, see if you can remember anything which might be useful to us."

"Certainly," said Ingram, leading the way to the door.

Outside the air vibrated with the clangour of the bells pealing out into the night. Thanet walked down the path to the Ingrams' front gate and then stood listening, his face turned up to the stars which out here in the country shone with an unfamiliar clarity. He felt strangely uplifted, exhilarated by the cascades of sound rippling through the darkness. The bellringers, whoever they were, were very good indeed.

Enjoyable though the experience was, however, it would not advance him in his task and reluctantly he dragged his attention back to the matter in hand. Could there by any truth in Mrs Ingram's astonishing accusation? Could her husband be having an affair with Marion Pitman? Thanet tried to visualise the two together, but somehow they didn't match up. In any case, it was a pointless exercise. The attraction of one person for another is frequently, to the outsider, a mystery. But if it was true...

Could Carrie Birch have found out, have threatened either Marion or Ingram with exposure? Say, for instance, that she had approached Marion first and that Marion had given her money to keep quiet, but had said nothing to Ingram for fear that he would react violently. And that Carrie had become greedy, that Marion had been unable to step up the payments, that Carrie had then decided to approach Ingram. Say that she had done so last night, had perhaps lurked outside the Ingrams' house in the hope that he might come out. Ingram had a temper, as Thanet had heard for himself this evening. He might well have lashed out at the blackmailer and then have been forced to finish her off in order to prevent exposure. . . .

There was a streak of brightness across the sky, so swiftly gone as to have been almost invisible. A shooting star! Thanet had never seen one before and he blinked, his concentration broken, trying to recall the superstitions attached to seeing one. If he made a wish, would it be granted? Or had it marked someone's death?

He shook his head impatiently. What on earth was he doing, mooning over church bells and shooting stars! He must find some way, he told himself briskly as he set off across the road towards the Gambles' cottage, to check this story about Ingram and Marion Pitman. But how, without starting a rumour which might be completely false? He needed someone with absolute discretion.

It was at this moment, as if Fate had for once decided to give him exactly what he needed at the precise moment he needed it, that he became aware that someone was crossing the road parallel to him some ten yards away to his left. Dim though the light was Thanet could see that this person was wearing some sort of long dress which flapped about its ankles. The figure marched purposefully up to the vicarage gate and pushed it open and at once Thanet realised: not a dress, but a cassock.

"Excuse me. . . ."

The figure turned, waited as Thanet approached.

"Yes?"

"We've not met before, Mr . . ."

"Ennerby."

". . . Mr Ennerby. Inspector Thanet of Sturrenden CID."

"Of course. Poor Miss Birch. A terrible thing. . . ."

Thanet found himself shaking the warm, strong hand which was extended to him.

"There is a rather delicate point on which I would very much appreciate your help, Mr Ennerby."

"By all means. Come along in, won't you?"

Thanet followed the tall figure with its billowing robe to the front door. A light had been left on in the shallow, open porch and as they reached it Mr Ennerby stooped, picked something up. The front door, the policeman in Thanet noted disapprovingly, was not locked—was not even latched, for the vicar pushed it open with his foot before leading the way inside.

"We'll go into the kitchen," Ennerby said. "It's warmer in there."

He was right. The room was bright, modern, well-equipped, with a Raeburn cooker which gave forth a comforting heat. Thanet had not realised just how chilled he had become standing out there by the Ingrams' gate and he moved towards the stove, extending his hands to the warmth.

"My parishioners are convinced that if I'm left to my own devices I shall starve," Ennerby said, carefully setting down on the table the object which he had collected from the porch. It was, Thanet now saw, a large earthenware casserole. Ennerby, then, must be either a bachelor or a widower. An unmarried parson was no doubt the object of much solicitude, particularly from the unattached women of the parish, a perfect focus for the attentions of romantic and maternal alike.

"Do sit down, Inspector," Ennerby said, removing his cassock and flinging it over the back of a chair.

The two men seated themselves on opposite sides of the formica table.

"Now," said the vicar. "How can I help?"

Thanet looked at him carefully before broaching the subject, for vicars after all are only human and although confidentiality is supposed to be their strong point he would like to be sure of this one's discretion before continuing.

He liked what he saw. Ennerby was not good-looking in the conventional sense but there was strength in the lines of face and jaw and his steady grey eyes evoked a sense of confidence. Here, one felt, was a man who would listen and understand without judging, one who looked as though he himself had suffered. He was, Thanet guessed, in his early fifties.

"As I said, it's rather a delicate matter. That is why I wanted to approach someone who would respect a confidence."

"Don't worry, Inspector, I can keep my mouth shut, I assure you." The man's grin showed that he had appreciated the hint.

"As you can imagine, in an investigation of this kind one turns up all sorts of rumours and naturally one has to look into them. The one I am concerned with at the moment concerns Miss Pitman and Mr Ingram."

The vicar's reaction was interesting. He was clearly astounded and a faint colour crept up into his cheeks. His voice, however, was level enough as he said, "Are you suggesting that there is some kind of attachment between them?"

"I had heard something of that kind, yes."

Ennerby gave a little laugh. "Absolute nonsense, I can assure you, Inspector."

"You're sure of that?"

"Quite, quite sure. You can take my word for it. I can't imagine who..."

"It doesn't really matter," Thanet said. "So long as you're certain. And I don't think the person concerned is going to spread the rumour any further, so..."

"I do hope not. If there had been any truth in it I would have heard, I'm sure of it. It is a sad fact that people are always only too anxious to let me know if one of the church members is suspected of backsliding."

"Fine," said Thanet, "I'm quite happy to accept that. Now, while I'm here... I understand that there was a PCC meeting here last night. Could you let me have a list of those who attended it?"

"By all means." Ennerby rose, left the room and came back a few moments later with a sheet of paper. "Here you are. This is a complete list of PCC members, so I've crossed out the names of those who weren't able to attend the meeting last night."

Thanet glanced at it. Selby's name was there, he noted, duly crossed out.

"Thank you," he said, rising.

"I must confess," Ennerby said, opening the door and leading the way into the hall, "I'm at a complete loss to imagine who on earth could have wished to kill an inoffensive person like Miss Birch."

"You knew her well?"

"Not well, no. She wasn't a church-goer. But she's always been about and I'd occasionally see her in the church on the evening she cleaned it, have a little chat with her, you know..."

"The *evening* she cleaned it, did you say?" Thanet stopped with his hand on the front door jamb.

"Yes. She always came on Tuesdays."

"Only on Tuesdays?" Thanet wanted to be quite sure.

"Yes, why?"

"I had been given to understand," Thanet said carefully, "that she cleaned the church on two evenings a week."

"At one time she did," Ennerby said. "But about, let me see, three years ago we had to have an economy drive and we cut it down to one."

Interesting, Thanet thought as he headed once more for the Gambles' house. Mrs Birch had been very positive about it. What could Carrie have been up to on Thursday evenings, if she had not been innocently engaged in scrubbing the church floor?

Whatever it was, she obviously hadn't wanted her mother to know about it.

8

Thanet's knock at the door of number three was answered by a girl of about twenty. Her jeans and baggy mohair sweater suited her rather gamine good looks—neat features, pointed chin and shining cap of short, dark hair.

She led the way into a sitting room which was all warmth, colour and noise; a gas fire was heating the room to suffocation point, a bright green carpet patterned in yellow fought with an orange three-piece suite and the television was turned up several decibels too high for comfort. There were two other people in the room, a plump middle-aged woman toasting her toes in front of the fire and a good-looking young man a little older than the girl who had answered the door.

"The Inspector, Mum." The girl had to shout to make herself heard above the noise of the television.

"Eh?" The woman turned a puzzled, tired face towards Thanet.

"About . . . you know," said the girl. "Her. Miss Birch."

Comprehension flooded into the woman's face and at once she began to struggle to her feet. "Chris, turn that thing off, for goodness sake," she said to the young man, flapping her hand at the television set. "We can hardly hear ourselves think. Take a seat, Inspector, do."

Welsh, decided Thanet. And now, looking at her more carefully, he could see the Celtic strain: small stature, sallow skin, dark hair and eyes, all reproduced in her daughter. The son, though, was of a different type; stocky, yes, but with much lighter hair and hazel eyes. Took after his father, no doubt. Thanet was not concerned that Gamble was not here. Lineham had checked with the factory this afternoon and had been satisfied that last night Gamble had been working right through the period during which Carrie had met her death.

"A terrible thing," went on Mrs Gamble. "Terrible. I could hardly believe my ears when I heard about it."

"When was that?"

"On the bus. On the way home from work. Full of it, they were. Strangled, they said, and in her own back garden."

Although they lived next door to the Birches, the Gambles knew very little about the tragedy, Thanet realised. Mrs Gamble and her son had already left for work when the alarm was raised. Mr Gamble had slept right through the commotion and even Jenny Gamble, who had gone to Mrs Birch's aid, was unaware of the details of what had happened later; as soon as she had handed over responsibility to Marion Pitman she had had to leave for work.

"It wasn't quite like that," he said. "You can't believe all you hear, in a case like this." And then, because the details would become public soon enough and these people, after all, had as much right as anyone to know the facts, living next door to the victim as they did, he went on, "As a matter of fact someone hit her on the head and then hid the body in the outside privy of number two."

"Duw," breathed Mrs Gamble. "D'you hear that, Jen, Chris? There's terrible."

She was genuinely shocked, no doubt about that, Thanet thought.

"What time did it happen?" she said.

He told her.

"Between half past nine and eleven," repeated Mrs Gamble. "But . . . but we was *here*, wasn't we, Jen? And to think that right next door . . ." She shuddered and reached for her daughter's hand.

"You were in, you say. All of you?"

"Well my hubby was at work, of course. He left about a quarter to eight. He's on the night shift, you see. And Chris was out, at the pictures. What time did you go, Chris?"

"Caught the quarter to seven," said her son, speaking for the first time.

"And you came back . . . ?" asked Thanet.

"On the twenty-five to ten."

"Rather early, surely, if you'd been to the cinema?"

"No choice, is there?" Chris Gamble scowled. "Twenty-five to ten's the last bus out from Sturrenden, unless you want to walk." It was obviously a sore point.

"He's saving up for a car," said Mrs Gamble fondly. "They're looking out for one for him, at the garage."

"The garage?"

"Where he works. He's a mechanic, aren't you, love? But he doesn't want any old rubbish, do you? He's waiting till he sees a really good bargain."

"Oh Mum," growled the boy, looking embarrassed. "The Inspector don't want to hear about cars."

"I'd have thought a lad like you would've got himself a motor bike," said Thanet.

"That's his dad," said Mrs Gamble quickly, as the boy opened his mouth to speak. "Don't hold with them. Dangerous things, they are."

"Still . . ." said Thanet. Boys of twenty-one didn't usually refrain from doing things they wanted to do just because their fathers didn't approve.

"Didn't have much choice, did I?" said Chris bitterly. "Not if I wanted to go on living at home. And how much would I have had left from me pay packet, if I'd had to pay for digs?"

Thanet saw that he had unwittingly touched on a long-standing bone of contention. "Anyway," he said hurriedly, before Chris and his mother launched into a full-scale argument, "you say you caught the twenty-five to ten home last night?"

"Yeah."

"What time does it get into Nettleton?"

"Between ten and five to ten."

"Good," said Thanet. "Now look, Chris, the murder was, as I said, committed between nine thirty and eleven last night, so it's just possible you might have seen or heard something useful. Could you think back very carefully and tell me exactly who you saw and what you heard on the way back from the bus stop—where is it, by the way?"

"Opposite the post office," said Mrs Gamble. "You all right, Chris?"

He ignored her. Thanet doubted that he had even heard her. His eyes had glazed and he was frowning a little in concentration. They all watched him expectantly.

"It's no good," he said. "I just can't remember."

"Start from further back," suggested Thanet. "Were there many other Nettleton people on the bus?"

"A few."

"Anyone else from this end of the village?"

Chris hesitated and his sister, who was sitting on the arm of Mrs Gamble's chair, stirred uneasily.

"I don't think so," he said.

"But you're not sure?" Thanet was convinced that Chris was lying. But why?

"I told you, I'm not sure." But he avoided Thanet's eye.

Mrs Gamble opened her mouth, then closed it again as Thanet looked at her expectantly.

"But if there were only a few Nettleton people on the bus," Thanet said, "surely you can remember whether or not any of them were from this end of the village?"

"I wasn't really paying much attention," mumbled Chris.

Thanet decided not to press the point any further at the moment. Perhaps it would be a good idea to try to get hold of the boy's mother or sister at a time when he was not there. By the look of it, they both knew what he was holding back. Whatever it was, Thanet had a feeling that it was irrelevant to his enquiry—or at least, that all three Gambles considered it to be so.

"Did you see anyone on the way home?"

Chris considered. "There was several cars parked in front of the church," he volunteered.

"Did you recognise any of them?"

"Mr Waley's Rover three thousand five hundred, Mr Martin's new Range Rover, Mrs Dobson's Mini, Mr Parson's old Cortina . . . I think that's the lot."

Predictably, Thanet thought with resignation, a young mechanic would notice cars rather than people.

"There was a PCC meeting at the vicarage," he said. "Did you see any of the people coming out?"

Chris shook his head. "There was lights on in the vicarage, I noticed. But I didn't see nobody."

"Which way do you come in, front or back?"

"Back in the day, front at night. Back door's locked at night and I got a front door key of me own."

Pity, Thanet thought. "Now think very carefully. As you passed the entrance to the footpath last night, did you see or hear anything, anything at all?"

It was obvious that all three members of the family were aware of the importance of this question. Chris frowned fiercely, his mother clamped her teeth over her lower lip and watched him tensely and his sister raised her free hand to her mouth and began to gnaw at the quick of her first finger.

"I dunno," he said at last. He ran one hand through his hair. "I've just got this feeling there was something, but . . ."

His audience of three watched him with total concentration. Suddenly he snapped his fingers, making them all jump.

"Got it!" he said. "It was Miss Cox from number five, calling her cat."

The sense of anticlimax in the room was almost tangible.

"You saw her?" Thanet asked.

Chris shook his head. "Heard her, that's all. Must've been in her back garden."

"Nothing else?"

"Nope. Sorry."

Thanet switched his attention. "What about you, Mrs Gamble? And Jenny?"

The two women looked at each other, but there was no complicity in the glance they exchanged.

"In all evening, wasn't we, Mum?" said Jenny, entering into the conversation for the first time.

"Had the telly on, I'm afraid," said Mrs Gamble.

"The entire evening?"

They nodded in unison, like two clockwork dolls.

"Good film on," said Jenny.

"Oldie," said her mother. "*For Whom the Bell Tolls*. Didn't finish till eleven. Chris watched it too, after he come in."

"Neither of you went upstairs for any reason, looked out of the window?" Stupid question anyway, Thanet thought. It had been pitch dark at the relevant time.

"Toilet's downstairs," said Mrs Gamble primly.

"Well, thank you," Thanet said. "I think that's about it, for the moment. No need for me to tell you to be careful about locking up. . . ."

The television blared behind him as he stepped out into the night. The church bells were silent now but only temporarily; before Thanet reached the road they began to ring again.

Who else, from this end of the village, had been on that bus, Thanet wondered, and why should Chris Gamble wish to protect him—or her, of course? Thanet's pace faltered as a possible answer came to him. The Selby girl! Mrs Selby had said that her daughter had spent the evening in Sturrenden with a school friend and had arrived home just before ten. So, unless she had used her mother's car—assuming that Mrs Selby had one, and that her daughter could drive—she must have come home on the same bus as Chris Gamble. And if so, Chris's lie aroused interesting possibilities. Suppose that he and the Selby girl were going out together . . . a man of Major Selby's position and status might well not approve.

Thanet clicked his tongue in exasperation. That was the trouble with police work. People lied, evaded, prevaricated for the most irrelevant of reasons, afraid, presumably, that their little secrets would be made public. The problem was, trying to sort out which lies or evasions were relevant and which were not—always a frustrating waste of time.

The light from the little street lamp in front of the Pitmans' house did not penetrate the dense shrubbery which fronted the Selbys' garden and the first section of the curving drive was very dark. Ahead, however, was some kind of illumination and when he rounded the bend Thanet could see that a lamp outside the front door had been switched on, perhaps in expectation of his visit. The door opened almost at once in answer to his knock.

"Inspector . . . ?"

"Thanet. That's right. Miss Selby?"

She nodded, stepping back. "Come in."

A real honey of a girl, this one, thought Thanet: tall and slim, her unconscious elegance lifting her outfit of tight jeans and ruffled blouse into the eye-catching class. Her colouring was pure English Rose—fair complexion, eyes the colour of a summer sky, long, silky blonde hair.

"This way," she said. "Daddy's expecting you."

Major Selby was planted squarely in front of the hearth in the drawing room with his hands clasped behind his back, feet slightly apart. Behind him, a cheerful fire crackled. He was shorter than Thanet and of slender build, but he gave the impression of a whip-cord strength. He was expensively dressed in a well-cut tweed suit of lovat green, tattersal check shirt and shoes which shone like ripe chestnuts. Perhaps the poster had made him look more aggressive than he really was. Certainly his greeting was affable enough.

"Ah, Inspector . . . ?"

"Thanet."

"Inspector Thanet. Of course, of course. Sit down, won't you?"

The two men shook hands and Thanet complied, irritated to find, however, that Selby did not follow suit but returned to his original position in front of the fire, thereby giving himself a slight psychological advantage.

"Drink, Inspector? It would have to be something soft, I'm afraid. We're teetotal. Or we could offer you coffee, or tea . . . ?"

"Thank you, no."

Selby's daughter had been hovering at the door and he now gave her a dismissive nod.

"Just one moment, Miss Selby, if you don't mind," said Thanet quickly.

She hesitated, clearly torn between responding to Thanet's request and obeying her father's unspoken command. Selby was frowning.

"I don't see . . ." he began.

"I understand Miss Selby came home on the twenty-five to ten bus from Sturrenden last night," said Thanet.

"So I believe," said Selby. "But quite what . . ."

Thanet sighed inwardly. Clearly he was going to have to fight for any scraps of information she could give him. "Please, Major," he said politely, and turned to the girl.

She hesitated a moment and then, as her father did not intervene, said, "That's right, yes."

Thanet had already decided not to risk compromising her in front of her father. If she and young Chris Gamble had indeed been out together the previous evening, it was none of his affair. So he merely said, "Could you tell me, do you think, whether or not you saw or heard anything suspicious on the way home from the bus stop? Particularly in the region of Church Cottages?"

He thought he detected a flicker of relief in her eyes before she replied, "I've already thought about that. Mummy thought you'd want to know. And no, I'm afraid I didn't. There were some cars parked in front of the church, that's all."

"PCC last night," said Major Selby testily. "And now, if you've finished with Susan... She has some prep to do, I believe."

Thanet had no choice but to let her go. Privately, however, he made a resolution to try and catch her on her own. She looked a bright, intelligent girl but it was pointless to try to get her to talk freely with her father present. He turned his full attention to the man before him.

The Major seemed to relax a little now that his daughter had left. He turned, picked up the poker and prodded the fire into a brighter glow.

"Mrs Selby well?" Thanet surprised himself by saying. He had no intention of putting questions to a man's back, but even so.... Unwittingly, he seemed to have touched some kind of tender spot. Unmistakably the Major's hand hesitated and his back stiffened slightly before he stooped to replace the poker.

"A little tired, that's all," he said as he turned back to face Thanet. "Naturally, today has been rather a strain for her. She knew Miss Birch—Carrie, as we called her—quite well, of course."

"She had been working for you long?"

"Ever since we came here, about five years ago." And now, at last, Selby relaxed sufficiently to sit down.

"And they got on well together?"

The Major stared. "I presume so." The woman, his gaze said, had not been here to "get on" with his wife, but to work.

"What did you think of her?"

Selby considered. "Never had much to do with her really. She was usually here only when I was out, of course, during the day."

"But you must, over the years, have seen something of Miss Birch, have formed some opinion of her."

The Major waved his hand. "She was a little mouse of a thing. Did what she was paid to do well enough, I suppose, but she never had much to say for herself."

"You arrived home just after ten last night, I believe," said Thanet, giving up.

"As I'm sure my wife will have told you. Yes."

"And did you by any chance . . ."

"See or hear anything suspicious? No. Come, Inspector, I was tired after a long trip, thankful to get home. I merely drove into the garage, parked the car and came indoors. The road is invisible from the house, as you will no doubt have noticed and in any case I used the kitchen door, which is closer to the garage."

It was pointless to go on, Thanet thought. He thanked the Major and left.

Half way back to Sturrenden he suddenly remembered the money under Carrie's mattress. He really ought not to leave it there all night. He'd look an absolute idiot if by any chance it were stolen. Cursing, he did a three-point turn on the deserted road and headed back once more to Nettleton.

It was now a quarter to ten and lights were still on downstairs in numbers one, three and five. Thanet fumbled the unfamiliar key into the lock of number four and stepped into the small living room, closing the front door behind him and groping along the wall for a light switch. He found none. Perhaps it was on the far side of the room, near the kitchen door. The room smelt musty, as if its occupants were already long departed and it had been shut up for some time. There was, too, the unmistakable odour of sickness and old age, overlaid with a faintly medicinal smell reminiscent of hospital corridors.

The room's dreariness struck him anew as he found the switch and clicked the light on. The overhead bulb encased in its dreary shade was of too low a wattage and drained out of the room the little colour it possessed. Thanet did not feel inclined to linger and he pushed open the door into the old woman's bedroom, using the light filtering through from the front room to locate the switch for the staircase.

Upstairs in Carrie's room he heaved the mattress aside once more and quickly counted up the packets of pound notes. There were twenty. He began to stow them away in his raincoat pockets, his movements slowing as he became aware of a feeling that there was something he had left undone. When he had finished he lingered, looking around the room, trying to pin down the source of his unease, but it was no good, his mind remained obstinately blank.

And God, he was tired. It had been a long day, not as long as many he had known but long enough, nevertheless. At the beginning of a case there was always so much to absorb and there was work yet to be done before he would be free to go home. He still had to get this money counted and checked into the office safe and write up his reports on tonight's interviews. He had found from past experience that if he procrastinated on these they would pile up into unmanageable proportions with unbelievable speed. Besides, irritating though it was to have to spend so much time on paperwork, it frequently helped to have to get it down in black and white, the act of writing it down forcing him to reassess what he had learned, to clarify his impressions and try to be objective about them.

He looked about him once more at the cheerless little room and shook his head. Perhaps, if he stopped thinking about it, the elusive reason for that nagging doubt would surface of its own accord.

Stubbornly, however, it refused to do so. It was one o'clock by the time he got to bed and he was still no nearer understanding it.

Consciously, he tried to relax, to empty his mind of the crowded impressions of the day. But for a long time this proved impossible and endlessly, obsessively, he retraced his steps, relived jumbled snatches of conversation.

Just before he slept the first two lines of Blake's poem floated irrelevantly through his mind.

"Tyger! Tyger! burning bright
In the forests of the night . . ."

9

When Thanet arrived at the office next morning Lineham was already at work.

"Finish your decorating?" said Thanet, giving his raincoat a shake before hanging it up. Overnight the sky had clouded over and it was a grey, cheerless morning with intermittent showers borne on a blustery March wind.

"Yes, thanks. Most of it, anyway."

"Interesting?" Thanet nodded at the report Lineham was studying.

"The path. report," said Lineham, handing it over. "Doc Mallard was right, as usual. She was hit on the head and then suffocated."

Thanet scanned the report quickly and then read it again, brooding over certain passages. "Yes, he's quite definite about it, isn't he? 'Cause of death: asphyxia.' So the blow on the head—there was only one, I see—would just have knocked her out."

"That's right," said Mallard, who had entered the room as Thanet was speaking. "It certainly wouldn't have killed her."

"And our old friend the blunt instrument was used."

"Yes. Poker, stick, length of piping..."

"Arnold—the builder—would be using copper piping for the plumbing work on number two," Lineham said.

"I shouldn't think he'd leave it lying around," Thanet said. "It's valuable stuff these days. But check, anyway. So," he went on thoughtfully, "she was knocked out by a not-very-hard blow on the head, and then suffocated."

"By something handy, I should guess," Mallard said. "Pillow, cushion..."

"Indoors, then?" Lineham said eagerly.

"...coat, blanket, travelling rug," intoned Mallard.

Thanet and Lineham grimaced.

"Could have been anywhere," Thanet said.

"Well, mustn't sit about here doing nothing." Mallard stood up. "Should have started a clinic half an hour ago." At the door he paused, peered over his half-moon spectacles at Lineham. "You look as though you could do with a good night's sleep. Build up your strength for Saturday." And with a wicked grin he was gone, leaving Lineham pink about the ears.

Thanet glanced sharply at Lineham. Mallard was right. The sergeant was looking distinctly drawn. The skin beneath his eyes was shadowed and the rounded lines of cheek and jaw seemed to have sharpened, adding years to his appearance.

Thanet opened his mouth to speak but Lineham said hurriedly, "Did you find out anything interesting last night?"

If Lineham didn't want to talk about his private life, that was his affair, Thanet thought.

"There were one or two intriguing suggestions. That Marion Pitman is having an affair with Derek Ingram, for instance."

"Any truth in it, you think?"

Thanet shrugged. "The vicar doesn't seem to think so."

"He would know, surely, living smack across the road like that."

"Quite. All the same, I don't think we ought to dismiss the idea out of hand."

"Who suggested it?"

"Mrs Ingram herself. Oh, not to me directly. When I went to see them last night I happened to overhear a conversation between her and her husband. There was a window open. . . . Odd, how often the jealous ones are absolute knockouts. Have you seen her?"

"Mrs Ingram?" Lineham shook his head.

"She really is something. Nobody'd ever think, looking at her, that she could possibly be jealous of anyone. But she is . . . which is very interesting from our point of view."

"I don't see what you mean, sir."

"Well, what happens when his wife accuses an innocent man of having an affair with another woman?"

"He denies it, I suppose."

"Yes, but does she believe him?"

"If she's the jealous type, presumably not."

"Then what? Put yourself in his position. Year after year you are falsely accused. At first you love your wife, protest your innocence, but you get tired of all the suspicion, the arguments, the tears, the rows, the fact that you can't even look at a woman let along speak to one without your wife thinking you're ready to hop into bed with the poor girl. . . ."

"I don't know," Lineham said. "I suppose if it went on long enough and I got fed up enough, I might think, well, I'll give her something to complain about. . . ."

"Exactly," Thanet said. "And we have one unfaithful husband who if he'd been left in peace might never have strayed at all. She drives him to it, don't you see, and in the end she herself brings about the very situation she has been afraid of all along. Now, suppose that at just this stage a third person intervenes . . ."

Sudden understanding dawned in Lineham's eyes. "You mean..."

"Carrie. Yes."

"If she'd found out," Lineham said excitedly, "threatened to tell Mrs Ingram..."

"We'd have a neat explanation for all those nice little piles of pound notes."

"Yes...!" breathed Lineham.

The two men sat in silence for a while, contemplating this theory which did at least have the merit of fitting all the known facts. Ingram had left the house at a quarter to ten on the night of the murder. Suppose that Carrie had been blackmailing him, and had arranged to meet him that evening, that the quarrel with his wife had been manipulated by Ingram in order to give him an excuse for stamping out of the house at the appropriate time.... Suppose that Carrie had then stepped up the pressure, had demanded more money.... There would just have been time for Ingram to kill her and dump her in that convenient little outhouse before hurrying down to the Plough and Harrow. The landlord had said that Ingram had arrived around ten.

"It could fit, sir," Lineham said.

"I agree. But 'could' is the operative word, I think. We'll keep an open mind at present. One thing I would like you to do is to try to find out if Ingram had a girlfriend in Sturrenden."

"You don't think he is having an affair with Miss Pitman, then?"

"I don't think he's her type. Nor she his, for that matter. I could be wrong, but I'd guess that he would go a little further away from home for consolation. Carrie could still have found out about it."

"But how, if the girlfriend lives in Sturrenden? So far as we can gather, Carrie never seems to have left the village, not even to go shopping. Though I suppose she must have, occasionally."

"I think there was more to Carrie than meets the eye. I forgot to tell you that there was another interesting little fact I gleaned last night." And Thanet told Lineham what the vicar had said about Carrie and the church cleaning. "So you see, there was one evening a week when nobody, not even her mother, knew what she was up to. She may have spent it somewhere in the village, of course, and if so, no doubt the fact will emerge eventually, but she might well have gone into Sturrenden. Make enquiries about Thursday evening buses, see if you can get hold of the drivers."

"Well, well, well," Lineham said, grinning. "Good for her. I'm glad she managed to put one over on that horrible old woman." Then, abruptly his smile vanished and his eyes grew bleak.

Thanet hesitated and then said gently, "What's the matter, Mike?" He could guess, of course. Mention of Carrie's mother had made Lineham think of his own. "Look," he went on, as Lineham pursed his lips and shook his head, "I know I've no business to interfere, but . . . it's your mother, isn't it?"

"Yes," Lineham admitted miserably. "She's not well again this morning and . . ."

"You're afraid the wedding'll have to be called off again. Right?"

Lineham nodded.

Thanet stood up abruptly and walked to the window, looked down into the street. It was pouring with rain and there were few people about. It wouldn't be very pleasant out at Nettleton this morning.

"Look," he said, turning, "perhaps I've no right to say this, but you're going to have to make up your mind what to do, if she is taken ill again."

"I won't have any choice, really, will I?" said Lineham grimly. He had been fiddling with a ball-point pen and now he stabbed viciously at the blotting paper in front of him before throwing the pen down in disgust.

"Won't you?" Thanet said softly.

Lineham's head came up with a jerk. "What do you mean?"

"Well," Thanet said carefully, "there *is* a choice, isn't there?" He would have to be very tactful.

"You mean, I should go ahead with the wedding regardless?"

Thanet returned to his desk, sat down again. "Look, Mike, I don't like to interfere, as I said, but you can't go on like this. If you have to put up with much more of it you'll be a nervous wreck. What does Louise feel about it?"

Lineham grimaced. "She's fed up, naturally. But she says I have to make up my own mind."

"Very sensible of her. If she put pressure on you, you'd only resent it later, if anything went wrong."

"That's what she says."

"So what are you going to do?"

"I don't know. What do *you* think I ought to do?"

Thanet considered. He was treading on dangerous ground and he knew it. If he told Lineham to go ahead and Mrs Lineham had a fatal attack, he, Thanet, would feel responsible for her death. On the other hand, in Thanet's experience, people only took advice if it was what they really wanted to do anyway. Perhaps Lineham simply needed some moral support in order to go through with what amounted to outright rebellion against his mother.

"If you really want to know, I think you should plan to go ahead."

"Regardless?"

"Regardless. But as Louise so rightly says, you are the only one who can really decide. And it's a miserable position to be in, really miserable, I know that. But try to look at it objectively. Twice, already, you've had to postpone the wedding. Now this can't go on indefinitely. From what I know of her, Louise isn't the sort of girl, however much she loves you, to be prepared to play second fiddle to your mother for ever. I know it's hard, but it seems to me that sooner or later you'll have to choose between them. And the longer you put off that decision, the more likelihood there is that you're going to lose Louise in the process. How much does she matter to you? That's what you have to ask yourself."

Lineham was obviously thinking hard and Thanet waited for a minute or more before going on.

"And if that happened," he said eventually, "how would you feel about your mother? My guess is that you'd be bitterly resentful and you'd end up by being on bad terms with her too. So what I would suggest is this—and remember, it is only a suggestion—that you go to her, tell her that although you are naturally worried about her health, you feel that you have no right to keep Louise dangling like this. Say that you therefore feel that whatever happens you have to go ahead with the wedding arrangements this time. And see how she reacts. You never know, if she sees that you really have decided, she might just accept it. . . ."

"You think so?" said Lineham bitterly.

Thanet shrugged. "I wish I could say yes, Mike, but I can't. I just don't know."

Lineham looked away, out of the window. "We've even thought of slipping off quietly to the registry office, without saying anything to anyone, even to mother. That way, we thought she might not have time to get worked up about it and if she knew it was done, over, she might get used to the idea in time."

"But?"

"We just didn't like the idea of being so underhand about it. And Louise especially wants a church wedding—oh, not for the fuss and bridesmaids and so on but because she goes to church regularly and won't feel properly married, she says, if it's just a civil ceremony. So it just wouldn't do." He looked thoughtfully at Thanet. "I might just try what you suggest, sir."

"Well, as I said, it's your choice. But if you do tell her you're going to go ahead regardless, make sure you do just that. Otherwise . . ."

"Yes," Lineham said. "There'd be no end to it, would there? Well, thank you, sir," he added stiffly. "I'm sorry to bring my problems to work with me."

"We all do," Thanet said, "from time to time."

Twenty minutes later, after briefing the others, he and Lineham made a dash across the car park to their respective cars, heads lowered against the driving rain. Thanet had handed over to Lineham the list of PCC members which the vicar had given him, with instructions to cross-check their stories and also find out if any of them had seen anything of interest when leaving the vicarage on Monday evening.

The sudden flurry of movement, the sting of rain on his face, exhilarated him and as he swung out of the car park and headed for Nettleton he found himself looking forward eagerly to the challenge of the day ahead. Whom should he see first?

He wanted to check up on his hunch about Susan Selby and Chris Gamble and he also wanted to dig a little further into the rumour about Marion Pitman and Ingram just in case his instinct was wrong; but most of all he wanted to try to deepen his understanding of Carrie herself. In a case like this it was essential to get to know the victim and it was extraordinarily, really, how little he felt he knew about her. He had now talked to all the people in her claustrophobic little world and she herself still remained shadowy, elusive, a pathetic ghost hovering in the wings. Perhaps she would stay that way. Perhaps she really had been such a nonentity, had had so negative a personality, that there was nothing of real interest to be discovered.

And yet, he thought once more, there was that money. . . .

Perhaps it was time for a change of tactics. Perhaps he ought to stop pussy-footing around and try a little bull-dozing instead. But he'd never found that that sort of approach worked for him. He had always found patience and subtlety infinitely more effective. Perhaps he had just been too *busy*, had not given himself sufficient time to absorb, think, weigh. . . . A leisurely talk with old Pitman was what he needed. The man was no fool and Thanet was convinced that there was a great deal yet to be learned from him about his unlovable former pupil. Poor Carrie. After such a life, to have met such an end . . .

Thanet frowned, remembering his certainty, the previous evening in her bedroom, that there was something he had failed to do. What *was* it? He still hadn't pinned it down but it was very near the surface now. He could feel it hovering there, on the very fringe of his awareness.

As he turned into Nettleton he made up his mind. Before seeing Robert Pitman he would go and take one more look at Carrie's room.

He was suddenly convinced that it had not yet yielded up all its secrets.

10

There were no chairs in Carrie's room so Thanet took off his dripping raincoat, hung it on the end of the curtain rail, and perched on the bed. The wan, grey light filtering through the half-net curtains did nothing to enhance the dismal little room. The hands of the old alarm clock still stood at twelve fifteen and indeed time itself seemed to have stopped here.

The very air of the place seemed as devoid of life as its former occupant.

Thanet sat with shoulders slumped and hands clasped between parted knees and gazed aimlessly about him. The sense of urgency which he had experienced in the car, the impetus which had sent him hurrying up the narrow staircase, had dissipated the moment he had stepped into the room. He must have been crazy to expect otherwise. He and Lineham had searched the place thoroughly enough the first time, after all. And yet . . . this had been Carrie's own domain, the one tiny corner of the whole world in which she could have been assured of complete privacy. Even her mother had not been able to penetrate up here: those steep, narrow stairs had been as effective as a drawbridge. Once up here, had Carrie really been satisfied with nothing more than a cupboard full of cheap romantic fiction?

And why not? he asked himself impatiently. Having so little in her life outside this room, why should she not have been contented with very little more inside it?

Thanet stood up and began to pace restlessly about in the narrow corridor of space between the bed and the window. The point was, Carrie had got herself murdered. He didn't, couldn't believe that hooligans had killed her and therefore there must have been something about her, something in her character, knowledge, habits, behaviour, that set her apart, something that had ultimately provoked that final act of violence.

Surely it was therefore not unreasonable to expect to find traces of that something here, in the only place which had been truly hers?

Unnoticed by Thanet his cracked and slightly distorted reflection advanced and receded in the mirror of tiles as he passed to and fro, scowling down at the worn brown linoleum with its herringbone pattern of imitation wood blocks. Absorbed in his thoughts as he was it took some time for him to register that one small area of this shabby flooring seemed more scuffed than the rest of it. At once he stopped. Why should that be? Enlightenment came swiftly. The spot was about eight feet from the tile mirror. Here Carrie must have stood whenever she wished to study her full-length reflection.

Thanet frowned. A Carrie who lingered to admire herself in the mirror did not fit the image of the Carrie he had seen. She had looked to be the sort of woman sho would use a mirror only in the most cursory fashion, to check quickly on over-all neatness.

A Thanet neatly divided into squares advanced to meet him as he approached the mirror. He had seen these tiles in the shops. Six inches square, with a self-adhesive backing, they were a quick and easy way for an amateur to achieve the effect of a full-length mirror. Also, of course, they were both small and portable. If Carrie had wanted to install a long mirror up here without her mother knowing, then they would have provided her with the perfect solution. Smuggling them up a few at a time would have presented no difficulty. She had made a good job of sticking them up, too, Thanet conceded. He ran his fingers over the satin-smooth surface. If only mirrors could talk, he thought fancifully, what tales they would have to tell. . . .

He swung away, impatient with himself. The question was, why should it have been important to desiccated little Carrie Birch to have a full-length mirror on the wall of her bedroom? Thanet squatted to look more closely at the worn patch on the linoleum. It was roughly circular, and within there were a number of tiny indentations. Thanet's eyes opened wide in astonishment as understanding came.

Carrie Birch in high heels?

A sudden, vivid image of Carrie's feet in their sensible black lace-up shoes flashed into Thanet's mind and sent him hurrying across to the curtain behind which Carrie had kept her clothes. He drew it aside, stared down at the floor, where Carrie's shoes were lined up neatly: cheap, sensible and low-heeled, every one.

Perhaps the marks on the floor dated from long ago? Perhaps Carrie had once been young and glamorous, high heels her normal foot-wear? Thanet shook his head. It was possible, of course, but he couldn't somehow believe it—though it was certainly more credible than that Carrie should have worn them recently. He went back to the worn patch, squatted once more and ran his fingers over the crescent-shaped depressions like a blind man reading Braille. He pursed his lips. Comparatively recent, he would say.

Thanet stood up abruptly, wincing as he did so. At incautious moments like this the spectre of his former back trouble tended to raise its ugly head. Testingly he eased his pelvis this way and that, gave a sigh of relief. No harm done this time, it seemed. He looked about him once more. How could

he and Lineham have missed something as distinctive as a
pair of high-heeled shoes? Perhaps Carrie had got rid of
them?

His gaze travelled methodically around the room, lingering
on each of the few items of furniture before quartering the
walls. Then he turned his attention to the ceiling.

His stomach gave a great lurch of excitement. There it was,
so normal a feature of at least one room in every house that
until now its presence had not registered: an oblong trapdoor
set into the ceiling to provide access to the roof space.

Surely he remembered seeing a step ladder leaning against
the wall just inside the door of the back bedroom? Castigating
himself for not having thought of the loft before, Thane
hurried across the landing and into the other bedroom. Yes,
there was the ladder. He seized it, hastened back to Carrie's
room and set it up beneath the trapdoor. Climbing on to the
third step he raised both arms and pushed. The door swung
back easily. It was hinged on one side and Carrie—for who
else could it have been?—had kept the hinges well oiled.
Eagerly, he climbed two more steps.

The bedroom ceiling was low and his head and shoulders
were now projecting up into the roof space. Despite the
gloom he saw at once the row of carrier bags ranged around
the sides of the opening. Treasure trove indeed! One by one
he seized them, eased them through the opening and lowered
them to the floor. Behind the furthest one he found a tiny
suitcase. Like a small boy prolonging the anticipation of a
treat, he waited until he had removed them all before
descending the ladder and carrying the first across to the
bed.

Each bag had been encased in a larger, plastic one, presumably as a protection against dust—though there was very
little of that, he noted. He slid the inner bag clear of the
outer one and peered inside. On top was something soft,
black and silky and he pulled it out, his eyebrows climbing
his forehead as he realised what it was.

A woman's slip made of black satin, trimmed with lace. . . .

A matching pair of panties followed and then bra, suspend-
er belt, sheer black stockings. Beneath this complete set of
lingerie was another, in pale blue silk and then a third, in
peach-coloured satin. Thanet laid them all out neatly on the
bed and stood staring at them for a moment before arranging
them in three neat little piles and turning to the next bag.

Dresses, this time. Day dresses, he supposed they would be called, all of them expensive, made of the highest-quality materials—wool, cashmere, crêpe and silk.

Bag after bag yielded up its treasure: sweaters, blouses, skirts, evening dresses, suits, nightdresses and negligees, cocktail dresses. Finally, there was a bag of shoes, all of them made of the finest leather, shoes for every occasion: high-heeled sandals and court shoes, walking shoes (but how different from those in Carrie's official wardrobe!) and even a pair of calf-length boots in soft grey suede.

By now the bed was heaped with finery. Thanet stood looking at it, struggling to relate such luxurious elegance to the insignificant, unpretentious little woman who had been the public Carrie. He couldn't ever recall feeling so truly astonished.

He stepped back, as if distance could give him a better perspective on his discovery and almost tripped over the little suitcase, which he had left to last. Carrying it to the end of the bed, he cleared a small space in which to sit. Then he laid it across his knees and clicked open the locks.

Make-up this time, the lot. This was a vanity case, with fitted compartments for everything. Thanet picked up one of the bottles: Elizabeth Arden.

But the most interesting discovery was still to come. As he removed the tray Thanet saw human hair. He plunged his hand into its silkiness and lifted it out. A wig, blonde, short and softly curling. He shook his head in amazement, trying—and failing—to visualize Carrie wearing it.

So she had had a complete disguise, an entire transformation kit for her fantasy persona. Had she been satisfied with dressing up behind closed doors, he wondered—or could she have, *had* she ventured forth into the outside world? Truly, the imagination boggled.

Thanet tucked the wig back beneath the tray, snapped shut the lid and set the little case gently on the floor. He stood up and contemplated Carrie's secret wardrobe once more. There must be hundreds of pounds' worth of stuff on that bed—thousands, perhaps. He couldn't wait to see Lineham's face when he saw it.

Well, Thanet thought as he made his way reflectively down the stairs and let himself out of the house, he had been looking for another dimension to Carrie's character and he had certainly found one. The question was, how did it affect

his thinking about the case? And where—where, and *how*—
had she come by all that money?

Engrossed in speculation, he was at the gate before he
realised that old Miss Cox had, for once, emerged from her
self-imposed isolation. She was sweeping the front path, or
trying to; crutches under armpits, with the cat Tiger weaving
around her feet. If she wasn't careful, she'd end up breaking
the other leg, thought Thanet as he said good morning,
offered to complete the job for her.

"I've just finished, thank you," she croaked in that rusty
voice of hers. Then she just stood, not looking at him, not
speaking, the cat rubbing against her legs, the steady rain
slicking down her hair and dripping into the upturned collar
of the old raincoat she was wearing. Clearly, she was expecting
something.

Thanet realised that she had probably been lying in wait
for him, that she must have seen him go in the Birches' house
and, despite the rain, had decided to sweep the path so that
she should not miss him when he came out. No doubt she
was longing to know what progress he had made. Her chosen
isolation must be cold comfort at the moment, with an empty
house next door, her leg in plaster and a murderer at large.

But what reassurance could he give her? He certainly felt
no nearer at the moment to discovering the identity of
Carrie's killer and even if he had he could not have divulged
the information. However, the degree of pressure which her
unspoken demand was making upon him was extraordinary.
He could feel her willing him to speak and the intensity of
her need both aroused his pity and stiffened his resistance. It
was all too easy in a situation like this for compassion to lead
to indiscretion.

"You're getting very wet, Miss Cox," he said gently. "I
should go in now, if I were you."

She gave him a quick, puzzled glance as if he had been
speaking a foreign language and then, as he turned to leave
she said, "Please..."

He paused, reluctant yet unable to ignore her plea, raising
his eyebrows in hypocritically polite incomprehension.

"Please," she said again. "Have you found out yet...?"

He shook his head. "Not yet, no."

She stood staring at him, her eyes dark with fear, her lips
working as if she were trying to bring herself to ask him some
further question.

Thanet waited and when she did not speak said firmly, "We shall, though, I promise you."

She let him go then, abruptly turning back towards the house, the cat running ahead of her and disappearing through the half-open door.

Thanet hunched deeper into his raincoat and set off down the lane. So certain was he that she must be watching from her doorstep that in front of the Gambles' house he turned, half-raised his hand in a farewell salute. But her door was shut. Perhaps she was standing at the window, invisible behind the net curtains.

He shrugged and was about to continue on his way when he caught a flicker of movement in the front room of the Gambles' house. Now who could that be? Mr Gamble, unable to sleep? Or one of the others, home from work for some reason?

He set off up the path to the front door.

It was Jenny Gamble who answered his knock, eyes watering and with a handkerchief to her nose.

"Don't come too close," she said. "I've got a shocking cold."

"If I had a penny for every cold germ I'd met in the course of my work," Thanet said with a grin, "I'd be a billionaire."

She opened the door wider. "Suit yourself," she said.

Once again the sitting room was suffocatingly hot. Jenny plumped down into the armchair next to the gas fire, which was on full blast, and blew her nose. "It came out overnight," she grumbled.

"It's a streamer all right," said Thanet. It made his eyes water just to look at her. All the same, he wasn't going to allow sympathy to deflect him from his purpose. "Why didn't you tell me your brother was going out with Susan Selby?" he said casually.

She fell right into the trap. Her eyes flicked open wide with shock and she became very still. After a moment, "How d' you find out?" she said. "Did . . . it wasn't Major Selby, was it?"

Thanet shook his head.

"Thank God for that," she breathed. "Chris would've done his nut."

"Is that why you didn't tell me last night? Because you were afraid Major Selby would find out?"

She nodded. "It's supposed to be a deadly secret." Her eyes narrowed. "How *did* you find out? Susan didn't tell you, surely?"

"No. Never mind how, I just did. But that's not the point. The point is, it's dangerous not to be frank in a murder investigation. It could give us all sorts of odd ideas."

"Such as?" she said, warily.

"That you didn't want us to know because there was some connection with the murder."

"But that's stupid!" she burst out. "How could Chris and Susan going out together have anything to do with . . . what happened?"

"Well now, let me see," said Thanet thoughtfully. "Say your brother was determined that at all costs Major Selby shouldn't find out about him and Susan. Then say Miss Birch saw them together somewhere, threatened to tell . . ."

He saw at once that she had remembered something which frightened her. She was staring at him aghast. "No," she breathed and then, more vehemently, "No! You can't believe that, surely! Chris just isn't. . . . He'd never hurt a fly, let alone an old woman like Miss Birch. He *couldn't*. . . ."

"You'd be astounded if you knew how often we hear the families of young offenders say that."

"I don't care what other people say! I know Chris and I just don't believe he could ever do a thing like that, no matter how desperate he was. Anyway," she went on, as Thanet remained silent, "I'm not sure they'd mind all that much if Major Selby did find out."

"That wasn't what you said two minutes ago," Thanet said gently.

Jenny sneezed rapidly four or five times in succession before blowing her nose and mopping at her streaming eyes. "I know," she said at last. "But that's because that's what they *say*. They both *act* as though it'd be the end of the world, too, but I'm not sure."

"What do you mean?"

"Well, Chris hates all this hole-in-the-corner business. He just falls in with it to please Susan, I know that. But Susan . . . I can't really make her out. . . ." She stopped.

Thanet waited in what he hoped was an encouraging silence.

"I'd go mad if my dad carried on like hers," Jenny said. "He's a real pig. She mustn't have any boyfriends, she's not allowed to go to discos, she's always got to be in by ten o'clock at night, and she always, always has to let her parents know exactly where she is at all times. I mean, you can understand her going behind their backs, can't you? After all, she is seventeen! But I've sometimes wondered . . . I mean, she's really something, Susan, isn't she? Have you seen her?"

Thanet nodded.

"Then you'll know what I mean. So, what I wonder is, why Chris? He's my brother and I'm fond of him but let's face it, he's no oil painting and he's not all that brilliant, either."

"I'm not quite sure what you're getting at."

"Well, just lately I've been wondering if she's after some kind of show-down with her father. And she's kind of using Chris. The way I see it is, if she does something awful—awful in her father's eyes, like having a boyfriend who's a motor mechanic—and her dad finds out, she might be able to wangle herself a bit more freedom."

"You mean she'd say, 'I'll give him up if you let me go to discos with my girlfriends', that sort of thing, so he'll feel he's choosing the lesser of two evils?"

She nodded.

"It's possible, I suppose," Thanet said. Though even if that were so, he reflected, and Susan really wouldn't have minded too much if her father found out, Chris wouldn't have been aware of the fact. If Carrie had tried a spot of blackmail he might well have felt it his duty to protect Susan. But, to the extent of killing for her? Frankly, Thanet doubted it. And as far as long-term blackmail was concerned, a young motor mechanic certainly wouldn't have been able to come up with the kind of sums Carrie had been amassing. Perhaps—perish the thought!—she had had more than one victim?

"Where did Miss Birch see Susan and your brother together?" he asked softly.

Jenny shook her head, a fierce little shake as if repudiating both the question and the necessity of answering it.

"Oh come on," Thanet said. "She did, didn't she?" And then, when Jenny still said nothing, "Remember what I said just now," he said gently, "about being frank with us? And just remember this, too: to solve a crime like this we need every scrap of information we can collect, every bit of help we can get. If your brother is innocent, you may be helping to clear him by telling us everything you know, even if on the face of it the information seems to incriminate him. Now, where *did* Miss Birch see them together?"

She hesitated a moment longer and then, with an air of resignation, said, "In Sturrenden."

"Exactly where? Do you know?"

"Catching the last bus home."

"This happened more than once?"

"Every week."

"On Thursday evenings, I presume?"

"Yes, but how did you...?"

"It figures," Thanet said.

So, he thought, as he thanked Jenny for her help and left, while Mrs Birch thought that her daughter was innocently engaged in cleaning the church, Carrie had been living it up in Sturrenden.

It was still raining hard. Turning up his collar against the relentless downpour, Thanet hurried down the lane and crossed the road towards the Pitmans' bungalow. With his hand on the gate, however, he hesitated. He didn't feel quite ready to talk to old Mr Pitman yet. He'd like a few minutes in which to assimilate what he had learned this morning. There was only one place to go: the car.

What could Carrie have been doing in Sturrenden every Thursday evening? he wondered, staring through the streaming windscreen at the blurred outline of the church. Briefly, he had a wild fantasy of Carrie dressed up in some of those glamorous clothes, blonde wig gleaming, soliciting on the pavements of Sturrenden or besporting herself on the floor of the town's one and only dancehall. Don't be ridiculous, he told himself. You're letting yur imagination run away with you. But was he? If anyone had told him what he would find in Carrie's attic he would have laughed at him. And wouldn't prostitution explain away the hoard of cash?

He caught a glimpse of himself in the car mirror. He was grinning like an idiot. Just wait till Lineham hears this one, he thought. He'll think I've flipped!

All the same, could it be possible? Carrie would only have had to put her gear into an old carrier bag and change her clothes in a ladies' lavatory somewhere in the town and she'd be all set. He'd heard Joan say that nowadays any woman could be attractive if she took enough trouble over her appearance, and miracles could be achieved with make-up. The old, conventional ideas of prettiness were gone forever. Nevertheless, it required a superhuman leap of the imagination to transform poor duck-like Carrie into the swan appropriate to those glamorous clothes.

Nonetheless, it had happened—if not in public, then at least in the privacy of Carrie's bedroom. Thanet was convinced of that. He pictured her waiting until she was certain

that her mother's sleeping pill had taken effect and then
stealthily setting up the step-ladder, taking the carrier bags
down from the loft and emptying them of their contents,
gloating over the quality and texture of satin, silk and lace,
cashmere and lawn, standing in front of the mirror and
holding the dresses up against her body one by one, selecting,
discarding, making her final choice and then, finally, dressing
up, preening in front of her transformed image. . . .

Suppose that for a while this secret satisfaction had been
enough for her, but that there had come a time when she
wanted to test out this other, glamorous self in the world
outside, emerge from her chrysalis as the butterfly she might
have felt herself truly to be. . . .

A knocking at the car window aroused him from his rever-
ie. Lineham was peering in, his face distorted like that of a
drowned man under water by the rain-washed glass.

Thanet wound down the window.

"You all right, sir?" Lineham was frowning anxiously.

"Think somebody'd bumped me off?" said Thanet with a
grin. "No such luck, I'm afraid. I was merely engaging in the
noblest activity known to man. Thought," he explained to
Lineham's blank look. "Stand back, will you, I'm coming out."

He leaned across to take his torch from the glove compart-
ment, then wound up the window and got out of the car.

"Come on," he said, anticipation filling him with boyish
glee, "I've got something to show you."

11

"I've come to throw myself on your mercy," Thanet said.

"Really?" Old Robert Pitman's eyes sparkled. "You give me

an agreeable sense of power, Inspector, an unfamiliar sensation for me these days, needless to say. Sit down and tell me
more."

Thanet sat. He and Lineham had spent the lunch hour
chewing over Thanet's find. Lineham's reaction to Carrie's
cache had been most gratifying. Together he and Thanet had
climbed up into the loft and searched it thoroughly; it had
occurred to Thanet that if Carrie had been indulging in a spot
of blackmail she might possibly have hidden away evidence of
some kind up there. But they had found only dust and
cobwebs. Now, he was determined to tap the reservoir of
Robert Pitman's knowledge. He settled back comfortably into
his chair.

"A murder investigation is a fascinating affair," he said
discursively. "I'm not talking about gang warfare or terrorist
activity, of course, or about the random killing for gain.
Domestic murder is something quite different."

The old man's attention was fully engaged, Thanet was
pleased to see. Robert Pitman was sitting quite still, his eyes
fixed unwaveringly upon his visitor's face.

"So often," Thanet continued, "we find that it has been
committed by the victim's nearest and dearest—husband,
wife, son, brother and so on. But sometimes, as in this case,
the victim's closest relation could not possibly be responsible.
Quite apart from the fact that Mrs Birch had everything to
lose in terms of physical comfort by her daughter's death, as
you know she had to have a foot amputated some years ago
and it would have been quite impossible for her to have
dragged her daughter's body as far as that privy.

"So then, of course, we have to look a little further afield,
widen the area of investigation. And I always find that it
helps enormously to understand the victim himself—or, as in
this case, herself. Somewhere in his or her character there
always seems to be some quality which has—how shall I put
it?—interacted with the character of the murderer in such a
way as to provoke him to violence. It may be something
which other people would find merely irritating. We all vary
so much in our reactions to other people's quirks. But the
murderer, on one particular occasion, finds that quality truly
intolerable, so intolerable that he cannot endure its continued existence. So he destroys it." Thanet glanced at the old
man, who was still listening with rapt attention. "I'm sure
you can see where I'm going," he said.

"Fascinating," said the old man. He settled back deeper into his pillows and folded his swollen hands together gently, as if every tiny movement was painful. "So you want to pick my brains about Carrie," he said.

"Who better?" Thanet said. "You've known her nearly all her life."

Robert Pitman nodded gently, then his eyes went out of focus and he seemed to withdraw into himself, gazing away perhaps down the long corridor of time which led to himself as a vigorous young schoolmaster, and Carrie as the scrawny, unprepossessing child he had described the last time Thanet had come to see him.

Thanet sat still, relaxed, legs stretched out before him, hands clasped loosely in his lap, prepared to wait as long as was necessary.

Finally the old man stirred and his gaze returned to Thanet.

"Bowed but not broken," he said.

Thanet raised his eyebrows.

"That's how I'd describe Carrie." Mr Pitman hesitated. "I told you before, she was a little mouse of a creature, unobtrusive, always creeping about so you'd hardly notice she was there. And yet, somehow, you always did."

"What do you mean?"

The old man sighed. "I don't like talking like this, you know. There's always that 'mustn't speak ill of the dead' feeling. Which is perhaps why I was less than frank with you last time. But I do see that such an attitude can be highly obstructive. Someone, after all, has been killed, and you have to try to find out who did it. All the same, that doesn't alter my feelings."

"I can understand that," said Thanet.

"I know," Mr Pitman said. "Otherwise I wouldn't be talking to you like this." He sighed again, looked down at his hands. "The truth of the matter, I suppose, is that I couldn't stand the woman." He cast a quick, shamefaced glance at Thanet.

Thanet's immediate feeling was one of profound relief. At last a crack had opened up in that wall of silence. But he said nothing.

"There was something disconcerting about her," Mr Pitman went on. "I've been thinking about her a lot since it happened, of course, trying to work out what it was. And I've come to the conclusion that she had, as it were, gone underground. It's very difficult to explain what I mean, exactly. You see, there she was, the quiet, cowed little woman I've described to you and yet underneath you felt that she was, well, not exactly laughing at you, but gloating in some way. And although up *here*," the old man painfully lifted his hand to point at his forehead, "you knew you ought to feel sorry for her because of what she had to put up with from that awful mother of hers, down *here*," and the hand crept down to lie gently against the old man's heart, "you felt quite differently about her. Perhaps I'm not putting this very clearly, but you seemed to react to her on two different levels simultaneously, and the result was that you felt very confused about her. Or at least, I did." He stopped, his eyes begging Thanet for understanding.

"Yes. Yes, I see," Thanet said slowly. "I do see, exactly what you mean." He paused, thinking. "So when you said, 'bowed but not broken', you meant that although on the surface she had apparently given in completely to her mother's, what shall I call it, tyranny, underneath there was something rebellious that had never quite been subdued."

"Yes. That's exactly right. That's what I meant by 'gone underground'." The old man appeared more relaxed now. "Occasionally you'd catch a glimpse of it in her eyes, just as one might catch sight fleetingly of a wild animal in the jungle. One second it's there, the next it's gone, and you're left wondering if you really saw it at all."

"But you really do feel that as far as Carrie was concerned, it was there?"

"Oh yes. It was there all right."

"And was it ever more than a feeling on your part? I mean, did you ever see any evidence that this hidden self of Carrie's ever surfaced?"

"Ah, there speaks the policeman! Give me evidence, sir, he says. Oh, I'm sorry, Inspector, I suppose that wasn't really fair. After all, you are a policeman, and evidence you must have."

"Evidence would be useful," Thanet said with a grin. "It always is. But make no mistake about it, Mr Pitman, what you have just told me is immensely valuable to my understanding of the case."

"Good." The old man beamed. "Excellent, in fact. I can feel I haven't bared my soul in vain."

"But it *would* be useful..."

". . . if I could also produce something a little more concrete. Yes. Well, I suppose I might as well go the whole hog and tell you the worst. To put it bluntly, Carrie was a snooper of the first water."

"Ahhh . . ." It was a long exhalation of satisfaction. So that was why everybody had been so reticent about Carrie. Together with the effect that she had had on people, which Mr Pitman had just described . . . Yes. Thanet was experiencing a steady beat of excitement. "You caught her at it?"

"Hardly." Mr Pittman grimaced down at the inert body beneath the neatly folded sheets. "Though always, when she was dusting in here, I had the feeling she didn't miss a thing. But Marion was sure of it. Oh, it was only little things—a letter replaced the wrong way around in an envelope, things slightly displaced in drawers, that sort of thing—but after a while Marion got into the habit of making sure she never left lying around anything she wouldn't want Carrie to know about."

"But why go on employing her, if you were so sure that she was snooping?"

The old man lifted his hands in a hopeless gesture. "What alternative did we have, with me like this? It's not easy to find someone reliable, to do Carrie's job. And she was at least that. Marion often talked of giving up her work, staying at home permanently to look after me. And if it had just been the money, well that wouldn't have mattered so much. It's nice to have it, of course, but we don't have expensive tastes and we could easily have retrenched a bit. But I was dead against it. It's bad enough for me to know what sort of limitations I put on Marion's life as it is, without having to feel I'd cut her off completely from any personal satisfaction. She loves her work, you know, she's really devoted to those children. So we decided we'd grin and bear it." The old man gave Thanet a rueful grin. "Not the ideal situation, but there we are."

"I can see that," Thanet said with sympathy. "Do you think," he went on, carefully, "that she would ever have been tempted to use anything she might have learned in that way?"

The old man's eyes narrowed. "Blackmail, you mean? Now there's a thought. . . ." He considered. "I just don't know," he said at last. "But if so . . ."

"Exactly," Thanet said. "And I don't need to ask you to keep that idea under your hat."

"No, but... I've often asked myself what she got out of it, why she did it. And I came to the conclusion that it was the sense of power it gave her. To know people's secrets, and think they didn't know she knew."

"Nasty."

"Quite." The old man's tone was dry.

"I don't suppose you happen to know where she went on Thursday evenings?" Thanet asked casually.

"To clean the church I think. Why?"

"Just wondered." So old Mr Pitman didn't know everything that went on in the neighbourhood.

"Well," Thanet said, standing up and walking to the window, "it looks as though it's stopped raining at last." The unbroken mass of grey cloud which had earlier obscured the sun was beginning to break up, and a little wind was teasing the shrubs in the front garden. As Thanet watched, some forsythia blossom drifted down on to the bare brown earth in the border against the low front wall.

He turned away from the window, went to pick up his raincoat. He still had to ask the most delicate question of all. He liked the old man, didn't want to upset him, but it had to be put. If Mr Pitman thought him insensitive, it couldn't be helped.

"Your daughter never wanted to marry?" he inquired, in as casual a tone as possible.

He could see at once that he had underestimated the old boy. The blue eyes sharpened at once.

"Come now, Inspector," the old man said. "I know you better than that. What are you getting at?"

Thanet gave a rueful smile. "Just a rather unpleasant rumour I heard, that's all," he confessed. "I didn't want to mention it, but I have to check up, you understand."

"Stop pussy-footing," said the old man testily. "What was it?"

"That your daughter is having an affair with Mr Ingram next door."

Mr Pitman's reaction took Thanet completely by surprise. The old man threw back his head and laughed. Thanet's eyes narrowed. Did he hear the unmistakable timbre of relief there?

"With that jackass? Credit her with more sense, Inspector, for heaven's sake!"

"I should think he could be very attractive to women," Thanet said stiffly.

"To some women, maybe. But not, I'm afraid, to Marion.

nd I can guess where the rumour came from. The delecta-
le Joy has been at it again. Don't look so surprised, Inspec-
r. We do live next door to them, you know. And in the
mmer you'd be surprised what floats in through my open
indows. I'm afraid, to put it crudely, she gives him hell."

"Jealous," Thanet said.

"That poor fellow," Pitman continued, "has been accused of
aving affairs with just about every woman under the age of
fty in this village. And with a lot more besides."

"I'll be off then," Thanet said. "Thank you for your help.
nd don't forget."

"I know," said the old man, laying one misshapen forefinger
gainst his lips. "Mum's the word. Oh, Inspector," he added
s Thanet turned towards the door, "there is just one thing."

Thanet waited, one hand on the doorknob.

"Have you talked to Marion since yesterday morning?"

"Not properly, no."

"Only, she said that you'd been asking about Carrie's
utine and that she'd forgotten to mention that whenever
ajor Selby was away, Carrie used to pop in to the Selbys'
ouse morning and evening."

"What for, do you know?"

The old man shook his head. "No idea. To be frank, I've
ften wondered, myself. All I know is that the length of time
e stayed there used to vary enormously. Sometimes it would
e a matter of minutes, sometimes as much as an hour."

"Really?" Thanet was intrigued.

"And that she had a key to let herself in on such occasions."

"You mean, she didn't normally have a key when she went
ere to work during the day?"

"No. I only know this because on one occasion when Carrie
ame in here in the evening before going on to the Selbys'
e got into a terrible tizz because she'd lost the key. She
und it, in the end. It had fallen out of her handbag when
e'd dropped the bag in the hall on the way in. Anyway, I
appened to mention this to Marion, later, and she was very
urprised—said that she knew Carrie didn't usually have a
ey to the Selbys'. It's the sort of thing next-door neighbours
et to know about, especially in a small village. I remember
e thought it quite a little mystery."

"One to which you never found the answer?"

"I'm afraid not." The old man's eyes were twinkling. "So if
ou do uncover it, don't forget to let me know, will you,

Inspector? It's not good for me, in my condition, to be pre
to unsatisfied curiosity."

Thanet grinned. "So on Monday evening, after leaving yo
Carrie would have gone around to the Selbys'?" Why hadn
the Selbys said so, he wondered.

But Robert Pitman was shaking his head. "No. She nev
used to go on the evening Major Selby was expected back.

More and more interesting, Thanet thought.

Marion saw him to the front door. He realised that he ha
forgotten to mention Miss Cox's plight to her, and did so. H
needn't have bothered, however. Marion had already a
ranged for someone to do her shopping for her.

"I only wish it was as easy to find a replacement fo
Carrie," she said, with a worried frown.

"Try Mrs Gamble," Thanet said, with a sudden stroke
inspiration.

"But she's already got a job, in Sturrenden."

"When I saw her last night she looked dead tired," Thane
said. "It might be worth a try."

"It'd be marvellous if she could," Marion said wistfully. "But
couldn't pay her anything like what she'd earn in a full-time job."

"You never know. She wouldn't have bus fares and lunches t
offset against her earnings. You'd have nothing to lose by asking.

"Perhaps I will," she said. "Thank you, Inspector. You'r
very kind."

Social-worker Thanet at your service, he said to himse
wryly as he left. It was the old, old problem: how to tread th
tightrope between entering too fully into the lives and mind
of the people he came across in the course of his work, an
remaining too detached from them. He had constantly to b
on his guard against the emotional involvement which woul
he knew, cripple his judgement.

Outside, he stood for a moment breathing in the smell o
wet earth, the faint fragrance of rain-washed flowers and the
he walked thoughtfully down the path, turning at the gate t
wave to Mr Pitman who would, he was sure, be watching hir
in the mirror. Had he imagined the note of relief in the ol
man's laughter at the suggested liaison between Ingram an
Marion? And if not, what was the reason for it? Had he com
close to a truth which Mr Pitman had not wanted him t
discover? If so, the implication was that Marion might not b
involved with Ingram, but she was with someone else.

Who?

Outside the gate Thanet hesitated, unable to give his attention to the question of where he wanted to go next. Perhaps he shouldn't have talked so freely to the old man. If Carrie had discovered that Marion had a lover, had threatened her with exposure. . . . Thanet shook his head impatiently. He couldn't believe that the Pitmans would have been able to find the sort of money Carrie had been raking in. All the same, it was extraordinary the lengths that people would go to, to scrape blackmail money together. Perhaps Marion had come to the end of her resources and, unable to meet Carrie's demands, had decided to kill her?

It was no good, he couldn't believe it. He just didn't see Marion as a murderer. Nevertheless the annals of crime are well stocked with murderers whose guilt astounded those who knew them best. He would not entirely rule out the possibility. Who might the man be? Someone at the school where she taught, perhaps? Lineham would have to do a little discreet checking.

Thanet glanced at his watch. Half past two. He had already decided to try to catch Susan Selby as she came out of school at ten to four. So, he had another hour or so in hand. Perhaps he would pay another call on Mrs Selby.

Those twice-daily visits of Carrie's, whenever Major Selby was away, intrigued him. He walked briskly along the road and up the Selbys' drive.

12

There was no sign of the little gnome of a gardener today, but someone—Mrs Selby, he presumed—was in. Music floated down the drive to meet him. A piano recital on Radio Three, he decided as he approached the front door, listening with pleasure to the great arching ripples of sound. Then, with his hand on the knocker, he became quite still. Had that been a wrong note? Could it possibly be Mrs Selby who was playing? Almost at once there was a crashing discord, as if someone had brought his hands down with despairing anger upon the keyboard. Thanet stood motionless, listening. Silence.

Eventually he knocked at the door and waited, knocked again and then a third time. If she didn't answer, he decided, he would go around and try the back door. Just as he was about to turn away, however, he heard footsteps and Mrs Selby opened the door, blinking at him as though she had never seen him before. Her clothes were just as expensively elegant as yesterday—a pale green woollen dress with softly draped skirt and long full sleeves—but there was an indefinable difference in her. Thanet studied her closely as he spoke, trying in vain to pinpoint it.

She was clearly reluctant to let him in but she did, standing back and setting off down the hall without a word. Once again she lead the way to the conservatory. In the big drawing room the grand piano stood open and there were sheets of music scattered around the floor. The grate had not been cleared and the room looked untidy, neglected. Clearly, Carrie's absence was making itself felt.

Warmth and the damp, slightly musty odour of plants growing in a confined space enfolded them as they stepped into the conservatory.

"Sit down, won't you," said Mrs Selby, waving him into one of the cane armchairs. "Will you excuse me for a moment?"

Without waiting for a reply she left, crossing the drawing room towards the hall with a purposeful yet curiously hesitant stride. Thanet watched her out of sight, frowning, then strolled around the conservatory while he waited, thinking once again how Joan would have loved it. The plants which climbed the walls and scrambled along the roof, filtering the light, imparted to the little room an air of natural grace, and created an atmosphere of restfulness which soothed the spirit. Thanet had never been in a room quite like it before yesterday and he felt that he could now understand the Victorian addiction to such places. A green oasis such as this would provide its owner with a unique solace.

The plants in this one were many and varied in shape, size

nd habit, but all of them had one thing in common: beautiful
oliage. Gold and silver, plain and variegated, delicate, feath-
ry or heavily sculptural, they stood stiffly upright, arched or
crambled according to their nature. It was early in the
eason and there were as yet few flowers, but there was one
lant in bloom and Thanet strolled towards it.

He had noticed it the other day. It was trained against the
vall and had now reached head height. Its foliage was grace-
ul, trilobate and stippled in random patterns and speckles of
yellow on green. The flowers which adorned it were unlike
ny Thanet had seen before: bell-like, their petals were of
palest apricot, fragile as tissue paper. Delicately, Thanet put
up a finger, tilted one to look inside and was astonished to see
hat depending from one of the petals was a tear-drop. He
ouched it with a fingertip and it rolled on to his skin, but
sluggishly. Not water, then? He bent his head, cautiously put
ut his tongue. Honey! No, he corrected himself. Not honey,
nectar. He licked again. This, then, was the food of the Gods.

He stooped once more, to see if all the flowers had this
extraordinary quality and it was at this point that he caught
he glint of glass in amongst the dense foliage at the base of
he shrub. He bent down and parted the leaves. It was a
ottle, three-quarters empty. He picked it up, looked at the
abel: gin. Beside it, planted in the moist, warm earth, was a
glass. *We're teetotal, I'm afraid*, Major Selby had said.

It was one of those moments when the tumblers whirr and
everything clicks into place. If Mrs Selby was a secret drinker, perhaps even an alcoholic . . .

Hearing the tap of her heels in the hall he wheeled around,
sat down hastily in the chair she had indicated. He observed
her closely as she entered the room, watching with new eyes
that careful pacing, the tic beneath her eye, the beginnings of
disintegration in her face.

"Forgive me for asking," he said as she sat down, "but was
that you, playing the piano as I came up the drive?"

He had thought to put her at her ease by introducing a
neutral topic and was astonished at her reaction. Those
surprisingly large, capable hands—pianist's hands, he could
see it now—curled involuntarily into fists and she closed her
eyes briefly, as if in pain. Her smile, as she replied, was little
more than a grimace. "I'm afraid so, yes."

"Afraid so? But you play wonderfully well," Thanet said,
sincerely.

"You should have heard me when . . ." Abruptly she stopped
"But you obviously haven't come to talk about my prowess a
a musician, Inspector. What did you want to see me about?"

On the alert, now, Thanet could detect the meticulou
enunciation of the secret drinker. She was holding hersel
under a tight rein, every muscle stiff with tension. He had ne
doubt, however, that her self-control would hold. She had ;
long way to go before she reached the stage when she woulc
fall apart. He might as well come straight to the point.

"I understand that when Major Selby was away, Miss Birch
used to call here morning and evening."

Once again, her reaction surprised him. Almost at once she
rose, her movements curiously stiff, as though she were ;
marionette. She walked jerkily to the windows overlookin;
the garden and stood looking out, her back to Thanet. Was i
that she didn't trust herself to look at him, for fear of what he
might read in her face?

"Yes, that is so," she said, and her voice had a waiting
quality. He could hear the dread in it.

"Major Selby was away on Monday," he said. "I wondered
if Miss Birch had called in here on the way home from the
Pitmans'?"

"Oh," she said, turning around, lightness in her voice now
face transformed. "I see. Oh . . . no, of course not. We knew
that my husband was expected home that evening, so there
was no need."

"No need?" he said, seizing the opening he had hoped for

Had he imagined the flash of panic in her eyes? She
crossed the room in a sudden, unsteady flurry, sitting down in
her chair and gripping the armrests as if she were clinging or
to them for safety. Then suddenly, bewilderingly, her manner
changed. She looked coyly down at her lap, positively fluttered
her eyelashes at him.

"It's my husband," she said confidingly. "He fusses so
When he's away. . . . He just likes to be sure that someone is
keeping an eye on us . . . on our safety, that is. Susan's and
mine. A house like this, you know, such a temptation to
burglars . . ."

Thanet listened incredulously. A more unlikely watchdog
than Carrie he could not conceive of.

"Oh, I can see what you're thinking," Mrs Selby went on
"You're thinking Carrie wouldn't have been much protection
And it's true, of course, she wouldn't. But my husband had

given her instructions to ring him immediately if she suspected that there was anything wrong. He always made sure she knew where to contact him. As long as there's an outside person keeping an eye on the place he can go away with an easy mind, he says." She stopped, looked at him hopefully and he could almost hear her thinking, *Does he believe me?*

And of course, he didn't. He could see, of course, that there was some kind of sense in what she was saying, but it wouldn't have been necessary for Carrie occasionally to stay up to an hour if she had only been checking to see that Mrs Selby and Susan were safe. A knock at the door and a moment's conversation would have told her that. No, Thanet now had a much more credible explanation of Carrie's visits. But one thing was certain: if his theory was correct, Mrs Selby was never going to admit it.

"Yes, I see," he said, watching the relief in her face with compassion. Irene Selby would never have made an actress. "And you're certain she didn't call in last Monday?"

"No, she didn't. I told you, Henry was due back on Monday evening. There would have been no point."

"Thank you then, Mrs Selby," Thanet said, rising. "I'm sorry to have troubled you again."

Relief made her almost gay. "That's quite all right, Inspector. I know you have to get to the bottom of this awful business and anything we can do to help . . . any time . . ."

Through the dusty drawing room, down the hall in the front door her voice flowed on, babbling platitudes. Thanet left her with relief. It was now almost half past three; time to be on his way, if he wanted to catch Susan on her way home from school.

En route he thought about the Selbys. Major Selby must be worried sick about his wife's problem. He was the kind of man to whom position, status in the community, would matter very much indeed. So, where did Carrie come in? Working in the house as she did it was more than likely that she had long ago discovered Mrs Selby's secret. The point was, how had she used the knowledge? From what he knew of her and of Major Selby, Thanet could not imagine the subject ever having been directly broached between them; but he could see how, by hints and sly glances, Carrie could have communicated her understanding of the situation to her employer.

And then?

A meek request for higher wages, perhaps, granted by a secretly fuming Major Selby. How he would have hated being in the power of a nonentity like Carrie Birch.

And those visits while he was away? Thanet could see the situation having arisen in which, much as he would have loathed being beholden to Carrie, Major Selby could have decided to turn Carrie's knowledge of his wife's secret to his own advantage. Those business trips must have been a source of tremendous anxiety to him, for how could he keep his eye on his wife from a distance? Carrie must have seemed the perfect watchdog.

Thanet grimaced in distaste as he imagined Carrie, with licence to search, ferreting about for undetected bottles. In such a situation, Irene Selby could have swung violently between humiliation and anger; nothing infuriates an alcoholic as much as having his supplies taken away from him.

Suppose, then, that after leaving Robert Pitman on the night she died, Carrie had for some reason—misunderstood instructions, perhaps?—gone to the Selbys' despite Major Selby's return? Suppose that she had found Mrs Selby belligerently drunk and had tried to remove her store of alcohol . . . Here, indeed, was a potentially explosive situation. Thanet could imagine the whole distasteful scene, picture only too well Carrie's sly satisfaction, her sense of power as her employer pleaded with her. Driven by desperate need, Irene Selby might well have attempted to seize the bottle by force; might have struggled with Carrie, knocking her over perhaps and causing her to bang her head as she fell. And then, aghast at what had happened she might have panicked...

And this was where the theory foundered, thought Thanet. He could visualise everything up to this point, but he could not then imagine Irene Selby picking up the nearest cushion and cold-bloodedly finishing Carrie off. Why should she? She would have achieved her object, retrieved her bottle.... Unless, of course, her hatred of Carrie had by then been such that the opportunity to get rid of her for ever had been irresistible?

He was now driving past the tall hedge which marked the boundary of Sturrenden High School. In a moment he would come into sight of the main entrance. Rounding the bend in the road he was relieved to see that he was in good time. A long line of parked cars stretched down the drive and out on to the road: mothers, waiting to ferry their daughters home. Sturrenden High was a single-sex school, fee-paying and with

an excellent academic reputation. Some of its pupils boarded
but most came daily, travelling sometimes quite considerable
distances from outlying villages. Thanet parked on the opposite side of the road, on the bus-station side of the school.
From here he had a good view of the school gates and a
reasonable chance of catching Susan as she went by.

A bell rang somewhere inside the building and almost at
once the tranquil scene became one of swarming activity. The
trickle of girls issuing from the building became a stream,
then a flood. The cars crept steadily forward, picking up their
passengers and then sweeping around the curve of the one-
way drive to emerge on to the road some fifty yards away.
Thanet began to worry in case Susan had had a lift or was
perhaps staying on for some after-school activity. It was stupid
of him, perhaps, not to have come earlier and asked for her to
be brought out of lessons for an interview. But he hadn't
wanted either to alarm her or to cause gossip. For the nth
time in his career he told himself that he was too soft, that he
would have to toughen up, stop being so ridiculously consid-
erate of other people's feelings.

Then he saw her. By now the flood had dwindled to a
trickle again. She was with two other girls, but even from this
distance she was unmistakable. That silken curtain of blonde
hair, the eye-catching figure and elegant, swaying walk—she
would stand out anywhere. Susan Selby, Thanet reflected,
would be able to earn a living as a model any day. As soon as
the girls turned out of the gates he started the engine, pulled
across the road and into the kerb a little way ahead of them.
Then he got out of the car and stood waiting.

She recognised him at once and her step faltered. Then she
said something to the other girls and they smiled, nodded,
flicked their fingers in economical gestures of farewell and
walked on without her, casting inquisitive glances at Thanet
as they passed.

"I wondered if you might like a lift home," he said, smiling
at her as she came up to him.

"The third degree in comfort?" she said, arching her
eyebrows. She gave a slight shrug. "OK."

She waited until they had pulled out in the traffic and then
half turned to face him, resting one arm on the back of her
seat so that her fingers were brushing his shoulder.

"Fire away," she said.

13

Thanet did not immediately respond to her challenge. The afternoon traffic was building up and he waited until they were clear of the worst of the congestion and out on the Nettleton Road. Once they started to talk he wanted to be able to give her most of his attention. Meanwhile, he thought about what he was going to say. Some of it could be distinctly tricky.

He began blandly enough.

"I just wanted to talk to you about Monday night."

"Surprise, surprise! But I really haven't anything to tell you, Inspector."

"You were out that evening, though."

"Yes."

"In Sturrenden?"

"Right!"

"At the cinema, with Chris Gamble."

Silence. Then, "If you damn well know it all, why bother to ask?"

She didn't deny it, though. He wondered what she was trying to hide behind that flippant, half-cynical manner. Thinking of her parents, it wasn't difficult to guess: a rampant insecurity, a bitterness which could poison her life if she weren't careful. He would have to be gentle with her.

After a moment she said sulkily, "Who told you, anyway?" And then, "I suppose you're going to tell my father?"

He ignored the first question. "Why should you assume that?" he said.

She shrugged. "Isn't that your job? Stir us all up and see what crawls out?"

"That's not how I see it. There's no virtue in causing unnecessary distress. I simply want to catch a murderer."

A quick, sideways glance showed that she didn't believe him; she was staring out of the window, lips set in a stubborn line, arms folded defiantly. He sighed inwardly. This was going to be difficult.

There was a lay-by ahead and he signalled, pulled into it, switched off the ignition. Then he turned to face her. She really was a beautiful girl, he thought, with the kind of good looks that would improve with age: a smooth oval of a face and a classic bone-structure.

"Did either of you see or hear anything unusual on your way back from the bus stop?"

She lifted her shoulders. "I don't know about Chris. I didn't."

"You're sure?"

"I told you, no."

No point in pursuing the subject. "What did you think of Miss Birch?"

"Oh, *her*." Her mouth twisted and she looked away, out of the side window.

"You didn't like her." It was a statement, not a question.

"She was a creep, a real creep."

"In what way?"

She looked at him then, a long, considering look. He could hear her thinking, *How much shall I tell him?*, almost as clearly as if she had spoken the words aloud. At last, "She snooped," she said. "Poked her nose into everything." Indignation made her expansive. "I'd get home and find she'd even been through my underwear drawer, for God's sake!" Her nose wrinkled in distaste. "I didn't fancy wearing it, I can tell you, when I knew she'd been pawing it. She thought I didn't know, of course, but she never put things back in exactly the right way. You wouldn't believe how tidy I got, laying little traps for her. And she fell into them every time. If I could have locked up everything I owned, I would have."

"You never tackled her about it?"

"What was the point?" Susan said scornfully. "She would simply have denied it. There was never any proof, you see. And she never actually took anything."

"To know that you knew might have been enough to stop her."

"Not on your life. She loved it, you see. Poking and prying. I bet that's what finished her off in the end."

"You mean, she found out something...?"

"That someone couldn't afford to let her know."

"Who, for example?"

"Mr Casanova Ingram, perhaps, and his fancy woman. I bet he wouldn't want his wife finding out about her."

"You know who she is?"

"The girlfriend? Sure. Works in that glam hairdressing salon in Turtle Street. Blonde and very painted."

Useful information, if true. As it probably was, for it could easily be checked. But why was Susan being so free with it? Diversionary tactics?

"I heard your mother playing the piano this afternoon," he said. "She's very good, isn't she?"

She looked at him warily. "Very." She hadn't been fooled by the apparent inconsequence of his remark, he could see.

He would have to come out into the open, do it as gently as he could. She was painfully vulnerable and he didn't want to hurt her, but he had to find out exactly what part Carrie had played in the Selby household.

"Susan," he said gently, "I'm sorry, but I know... about your mother."

She didn't pretend to misunderstand him, just stared at him for a moment, eyes stretched wide.

"My God," she said, "you're despicable, d'you know that? You're as bad as *her*, aren't you, poking about in other people's lives, turning over the stones and gloating over the nasties that crawl out. How can you do it? What sort of satisfaction do you get out of it?" She was shouting at him now, her face distorted with anger.

He bowed his head, waiting for the storm to pass, recognising the pain that lay beneath. He was only too familiar with the agonies of distress and humiliation experienced by the families of alcoholics and Susan was, despite her veneer of sophistication, only a child.

Her anger suddenly fragmented and she began to cry, arms folded across her body, hugging herself as if to try to contain her distress. Thanet pushed a handkerchief into her hand and waited in silence.

When, finally, her sobs had abated she blew her nose and whispered. "You don't know what it's like. You can't imagine."

He said nothing.

"It's him, you see. My father." She blew her nose again. "He's.... You're right, you know. Mum *is* a fine pianist, but she's nothing now to what she was. I've read her press cuttings. She could have been really first-rate—world-famous, even, perhaps. And *he* stopped her. Wanted a meek little wife to cook his meals, warm his carpet slippers and generally run around him in circles. God knows why she was prepared to do it. I suppose she was in love with him, wanted to please him, and before she knew where she was it was too late to change things. He's a tyrant, d'you know that? A real tyrant. D'you realise, he won't even let me go out in the evenings unless he knows exactly where I'm going, who I'm going with.... No boyfriends.... I haven't been to a party since I was thirteen.... So I'm not making any excuses about deceiving him over Chris. And, believe me, once I'm eighteen, he won't see me for dust."

She glanced at Thanet, looking at him properly for the first time since her anger erupted.

"Oh, I know what you're thinking," she said. "You're wondering what'll happen to Mum then, if I do go. You're thinking I'm a selfish bitch. Well, maybe I am, but if so, then it's him that's made me so. As for Mum...." Her face crumpled and for a moment Thanet thought she was about to start crying again. She regained control, however, and looked down at her hands, twisting his handkerchief into a long, tight spiral. "I've just got to save myself, you see. It's too late for her, he's ruined her, so I've just got to get away. It's the only way I can survive...."

She looked at him again then, a surprised, assessing look. "No," she said. "You weren't thinking that at all, were you?"

Thanet shook his head gently.

The compassion in his eyes made hers fill with tears. "What am I going to do?" she said. "Oh, what am I going to do?"

Thanet reached out to take her hand, squeezed it briefly before releasing it, and laid it back in her lap. It would need far more time than he could give, to help her. "Isn't there anyone you could talk to, in confidence?"

Her mouth twisted. "Who, for example?"

"One of the teachers at school, perhaps?"

"Not really. Well, perhaps there is one..."

"Why not think about it? Or there's a youth counselling service in Sturrenden."

She gave a quick, vehement shake of the head. "I couldn't talk to a stranger."

"I'm a stranger, and you're talking to me," he said. "People say it's often easier, to talk to strangers. They're not part of your life, you see. You don't have to face them, afterwards."

"I hadn't thought of it like that." She was much more composed now and she pulled a rueful face. "Wow, look at the mess I've made of your handkerchief. I'll have to buy you a new one."

"Forget it," he said. "Losing handkerchiefs is an occupational hazard."

She smiled, then, for the first time and Thanet caught his breath at the transformation. "Susan," he said, "before we get back to what we were discussing, let me just say this. Try not to let your relationship with your father poison your life. After all, if you think about it, that really would be letting him win, wouldn't it?"

She bit her lip, frowned, looked away.

"And now, back to business," he said.

It was much easier, this time. And he had been right, he discovered. It had been impossible to hide Mrs Selby's sickness from Carrie and Major Selby had decided to use the fact to his own advantage, to employ her as a watchdog during his frequent absences on business. Her job during those morning and evening visits had been to hunt out Mrs Selby's hidden reserves of alcohol and pour away the contents of any bottles she found.

"Can you imagine what it was like," Susan said bitterly, "knowing that she knew, feeling that she had Mum at her mercy, so to speak? And what was the point anyway? Mum always managed to hide it away somewhere..." She stopped, clearly torn between loyalty to her mother and dislike of the cleaning woman. "It's an illness, you know," she said, defensively. "Mum just can't help herself. I've read up about it. And it can be treated, there are places.... But Dad could never look at it like that. He sees it as a simple matter of will-power.... *Simple!*" She gave a bitter little laugh. "I tried to persuade him to get her some proper treatment, but he would never listen. He's too afraid it'll get out, that his precious social standing would be smirched, if people knew. He'd rather sacrifice his own wife. . . ." She gave Thanet a shamefaced little glance. "I did try to help her, but he wouldn't have it. I wanted to give up school after my O Levels, stay at home with her, but he wouldn't allow me to. He preferred to use that woman, instead."

"He wasn't afraid she'd talk?"

"Oh, he paid her well, believe me. No, she knew which side her bread was buttered."

How well? Thanet wondered, remembering the bundles of notes, the carrier bags of expensive clothes. And had Carrie become greedy, put pressure on him? Major Selby wouldn't have like that. Nor, for that matter, would he have enjoyed being beholden to her. Perhaps he had begun by finding it the lesser of two evils, ended by finding it intolerable.

"You arrived home before your father on Monday evening, I believe," he said.

She looked at him with quick understanding. "Yes, I did. And if you're thinking what I think you're thinking, you can forget it. Carrie had left even before I got home."

"She was there on Monday night?"

"She must have been. She always came when Dad was away."

"But not on the evening he was due home, surely?"

"No. But he came home early this time. He wasn't really due until Tuesday. He got through his business more quickly than he had expected, I gathered."

"Would he have let your mother know that he was coming home early?"

"Probably."

"In that case, she would surely have got a message to Carrie, saying that it was unnecessary for her to come?"

"I suppose so. You'd have to ask her."

Thanet didn't say that he already had, that Mrs Selby had lied over her husband's expected time of arrival. And why should she have done so? Because she didn't want Thanet to know that there had ever been a possibility of Carrie having been in the house on Monday evening? Could she suspect her husband of the murder?

"Where was your mother, when you got home?"

"In bed." Susan grimaced. "Well, not exactly. She was, to be precise, lying on top of it. . . . And if you're thinking she

could possibly have had anything to do with Carrie's death,
you can forget it. Mum was out for the count. Had been for
some time, by the look of it. I went straight up to her room
when I got in and I'd just managed to get her under the
covers when Dad arrived. So I could just pretend she was in
bed and asleep, thank God."

But, thought Thanet, what if Major Selby was at that point
arriving home for the second time? What if he'd come home
earlier, while Carrie was there, and found his wife in a
drunken stupor? Might he not then have accused Carrie of
incompetence, have lost his temper? Thanet could just imagine the scene: the Major purple in the face, Carrie meek,
submissive yet all-powerful—just the sort of situation to
provoke a man like Selby beyond endurance.

"You heard your father's car come into the drive?"

"No, just the back door shutting."

So it was possible. Selby's car could already have been in
the garage at the back of the house when Susan arrived
home. Perhaps it would be possible to trace someone who
had actually seen the Major's car turning into the drive?

Thanet had learned as much as he could from Susan for the
moment so he thanked her, started the car and drove her
back to Nettleton in thoughtful silence. Just as she was
getting out, however, he thought of something he had forgotten to ask.

"I believe that on several occasions you saw Miss Birch on
the last bus back from Sturrenden? Always on Thursday
evening, I understand?"

Susan turned back, stooping to talk to him through the
open door. "That's right, yes. I wondered if she'd tell Dad
about Chris and me, but she never did. She'd just give me
that sly, knowing look of hers. It seemed enough for her, to
know that you knew she knew, if you see what I mean."

"Can you remember how she was dressed on those occasions?"

Susan's eyebrows rose. "Sure. Same as usual. Drab old this
and that. As if she'd just walked into a jumble sale and
grabbed the first dreary things that came to hand."

"Did you happen to notice if she was carrying anything?"

Susan considered. "Just a handbag I think. Nothing very
bulky, anyway."

"Did you ever run into her earlier in the evening, in the
town?"

"No, never."

"And she never gave you any indication of where she had
been, on those Thursday evenings?"

"'Fraid not." Susan's attention had strayed now and she
was looking over her shoulder at the house, wondering no
doubt what sort of state she would find her mother in today.

It was with compassion that Thanet said goodbye and
watched her walk away up the drive towards her expensive
home and her daily purgatory.

14

"What the hell has it got to do with you?" snarled Ingram.

Dennis Ingram was the owner of the largest employment
agency in Sturrenden and his office was as modern and
expensive as his house: thick carpets, chrome and leather
chairs, smoked glass tables and paintings to which Thanet
wouldn't have given house room. Its one enviable feature in
his opinion was the view of the river, framed in a window the
length of Thanet's living room.

"Nice view you've got here, sir," Thanet said, crossing the
room to look out at the broad expanse of water, shimmering
in the late afternoon. The inconsequence of the remark was,
he knew, deliberately provocative. When people were angry
they were often indiscreet. And he was comfortably sure of
his ground. After dropping Susan he had called in at the
hairdressing salon in Turtle Street before coming here. Ingram's
"blonde, very painted" had freely admitted her involvement
with him—which was evidently more than Ingram was prepared to do, the other way around.

"Never mind the bloody view. I don't see what right you

have to come poking about in my private life." Head down, colour high in cheeks, Ingram looked like an angry bull about to charge. There was no doubt about it, he was over-reacting. Because he was afraid that his wife would now find out about his girlfriend, or because he had been involved in the murder? Thanet was determined to find out.

"Mr Ingram," Thanet said in a world-weary tone, "your private life is, I can assure you, of no interest to me except insofar as it touches upon the murder I am investigating. No," he said, holding up a hand as Ingram opened his mouth to interrupt, "please, let me finish. The young lady in question has already admitted her involvement with you. I am merely asking you to confirm it. If that involvement has no bearing on the case, I can assure you that my interest in the matter will cease forthwith."

Ingram stared at him, eyes narrowed. "You mean," he said at last, "that my wife doesn't necessarily have to know about this?"

"What would be the point in my telling her? Assuming, of course, as I said, that there is no connection with the murder."

"But what possible connection could there be?" said Ingram. He had relaxed a little now and was sitting back in his chair. He picked up a pencil and began to slide it through his fingers from one hand to the other in a smooth, rhythmic movement that Thanet guessed was habitual.

Thanet found this reaction interesting. Hands were often a give-away, less easily controlled than facial muscles. It really began to look as though Ingram's main concern was his wife.

Thanet shrugged. "At this stage I'm casting around amongst Miss Birch's acquaintance, seeing what turns up. Seeming irrelevancies can often prove to be of vital significance."

"Well, this one won't," Ingram said. "It's true that I have been . . . involved . . . with Miss Parker, but I really do fail to see how that fact could have even the remotest connection with the death of Miss Birch."

"You knew Miss Birch, and. . . ."

"So did the postman and the dustman," Ingram cut in with a little laugh. "And are you investigating them? Seriously, Inspector, my acquaintance with Miss Birch was no closer than theirs. I passed the time of day with her when I saw her and that was as far as it went."

Ingram was still slightly on the defensive but that could be perfectly natural. Thanet knew that even innocent people feel obscurely threatened when being questioned by the police. He was becoming more and more convinced that Ingram was telling the truth.

On the other hand, he reflected as he drove back to the office for the daily stint of reports, Ingram might simply be a superb actor. He must, after all, have had plenty of practice in lying to his wife and, if he was guilty, the fear of being found out could be enough to inspire the finest performance of his life. If so, Thanet could only hope that sooner or later some kind of clinching evidence would surface. It was surprising how long it sometimes took for this to happen. People hesitated, forgot, did not realise the significance of some piece of information and it could be days or even weeks before they came forward.

Meanwhile, he began to hope that Lineham or one of the others might have turned up something interesting today.

No such luck, however. Lineham was just completing his reports when Thanet arrived and he shook his head gloomily in response to Thanet's question.

"More or less a blank, I'm afraid," he said. "It's all here," and he tapped the little stack of papers beside him, "but briefly, there's still no sign of the weapon or the handbag, no news of Ingram's girlfriend, if he had one, and none of the PCC members saw or heard anything of interest on the night of the murder. They all left the vicarage together at ten, except for Miss Pitman. She's the treasurer and stayed behind to have a word with the vicar about something."

"Yes, she told me. She didn't see anything either, I'm afraid."

"The only interesting fact we've gleaned all day," said Lineham, "is that Miss Birch used to catch the last bus home from Sturrenden on Thursdays."

In view of all the unfruitful work the others had put in today, Thanet felt a twinge of guilt that he had already learnt this for himself, but he told himself not to be so sensitive. That was, after all, police work: hours, days, weeks, sometimes months of dreary slog, only to find when you finally turned up something interesting, that the other chap had beaten you to it. "So I heard," he said. "Jenny Gamble told me, and Susan Selby confirmed it. Tomorrow you'd better get the men on to trying to find out where she went in Sturrenden. Incidentally, Susan also put me on to Ingram's girlfriend."

And briefly, Thanet gave Lineham an account of his afternoon's activities.

Lineham left shortly afterwards and Thanet settled down to his own reports. By the time he had finished it was eight o'clock and his brain felt as though it were stuffed with cotton wool. He rubbed his eyes, stretched, then relaxed, consciously trying to empty his mind. What he needed now was a peaceful evening and a good night's sleep.

A peaceful evening! Inwardly, he groaned. Not much prospect of that. In his absorption in his work he had temporarily forgotten about Joan's back-to-work campaign. As he drove home he hoped devoutly that she would not broach the subject again that evening. He really didn't have the mental energy left to discuss it. Today he had seen so many people assimilated and assessed so much information that he didn't think he could manage anything more taxing than an evening sunk in stupor in front of the television set.

For once it was a relief to find that the children were in bed and asleep. Thanet sniffed appreciatively as he stepped into the hall: some sort of savoury casserole, he decided. With herb dumplings, perhaps? Mouth watering, he made his way into the kitchen and gave Joan an enthusiastic kiss. As he did so, he felt a pang of regret. Would this kind of welcome soon be a thing of the past?

Joan must have sensed the sudden reservation in him. "What's the matter?" she said.

"Nothing," he lied. "Wearing day, that's all."

She wasn't sure whether to believe him or not, he could see. Always sensitive to his moods, she was probably interpreting his behaviour towards her at the moment solely in the light of his attitude to her problem. Correctly, as it happened.

"Supper's all ready," she said. "I'll dish up. Why don't you go and have a drink, while you're waiting?"

The stiff whisky helped and by the time they sat down at the table he was a little more relaxed. Even so, he found himself on his guard, waiting for her to bring the subject up again. She did not do so until they were seated peacefully by the fire, drinking coffee.

"Darling..." she said diffidently. Here it comes, he thought.

"...what you said last night..." She was still hesitating.

"Mmmm?" he said, head resting against the back of the settee, eyes closed. Even this non-committal response managed to sound irritated, long-suffering, he realised.

". . . about me going ahead," she finished. "Did you mean it—really?"

"Honey," he said wearily, "can't we leave it, just for to-night? I'm whacked."

She said nothing and he opened his eyes to look at her.

She was staring into the fire, her lips set in a mutinous line. Guilt and anger warred within him, the latter flaring up as she said tightly, "Luke, we have to get this sorted out."

"But why now, for God's sake?"

She turned her face towards him and he caught his breath a little at the unhappiness in it. "But that's the trouble, don't you see?" she said. "It never is the right time. That first evening, when we started to talk about it, I told you I'd hesitated to broach the subject because I didn't know how you'd react. But I didn't tell you just how long I'd been hesitating, did I? Almost a year, d'you know that? And do you know why? Because it's never the right time. Because you're always too busy, too tired or too late, too *some* damn thing!"

The unfamiliar, mounting anger in her voice suddenly faded and she turned away, staring miserably into the fire again. "Oh, I'm sorry . . . I didn't want to say all that. I hoped it wouldn't be necessary, that you'd just say whole-heartedly, 'Go ahead.' But don't you see, Luke, it's time now for me to have something of my own to work for. All these years . . . I've tried hard to be the sort of wife you want, and I've even hoped that would turn out to be enough for me. But it isn't, and there's no point in pretending otherwise. So, don't you see, we can't just go on shelving the problem, hoping that it'll go away. It won't. And I can't go ahead without your approval, I just can't. I'm not that sort of woman. It's not simply that, if I do get an interesting job, I'll need you to be pretty easy-going in all sorts of practical ways—it's that I want you behind me, morally speaking, interested in what I do. Can't you see that?" And she looked at him pleadingly.

Thanet was torn. Half of him acknowledged that what she said was true, that she had been a good wife, put his well-being and comfort first, always. But the other half was rebellious. Couldn't she see that what she was asking was unreasonable? He'd told her last night to go ahead. What more could she ask? He couldn't be expected to change his feelings, could he?

"Of course I see all that," he said, and was relieved that the irritation wasn't showing in his voice. "And I told you last night, go ahead. Investigate the possibilities. Find something you'll really enjoy and I'll back you all the way." But the words lacked conviction and he knew it.

So did Joan. She looked at him dubiously. "You really mean that?"

"Darling, how many times d'you want me to tell you?"

A million times would not be enough, he realised, so long as he felt this way. Joan knew him well enough to sense that he was lying, however convincing he tried to be. He told himself that it couldn't be helped, that he couldn't change the way he felt, that she would just have to be satisfied with what she'd got. He felt aggrieved. Surely he had done all that could be expected of him, and more? Not many men would have done as much, he was sure.

Perhaps she had acknowledged this, for she smiled at him now, gave him a thank-you kiss. And, reluctant as he had been to enter into the discusson, he realised that it was after all better to have talked; now at least they could relax.

Thanet meditated, not for the first time, on the way people function on two different levels simultaneously. On the public one they speak, gesture, apparently react; but it is on the other, the private one, that they are truly themselves. Here lie their secret thoughts, fears, hopes, fantasies; shared but occasionally, and only with those they really trust, those with whom they can allow themselves to be vulnerable.

He had always thought that he and Joan were lucky. They were able to be themselves with each other—or so he had always imagined. Now he was learning that he had been wrong; all this time, Joan had been hiding away from him the side of herself that dreamed, aspired. As he, now, was hiding from her his true feelings on this subject. Perhaps their relationship was going to go the way of so many he had seen; perhaps their best and closest years together were over. It was a depressing thought and something that he was determied to prevent, if it was in his power to do so. But it seemed that if he was to succeed, somehow he was going to have to change his attitude towards this job business. And how could he do that?

How could one change the way one felt?

In bed later he lay listening to Joan's even breathing and thought back over his day. In the darkness and the silence he gradually became aware of something hovering on the edge of his consciousness. He had no idea of its nature, but there it was, on the very periphery of his awareness. What could it be? The significance of some fact, so far dismissed as unimportant? Or some insight, vital to his understanding of the case? But it wouldn't come. Perhaps, while he was asleep, his subconscious would give it a shove and in the morning there it would be, waiting for him when he awoke. It had often happened that way in the past. It was as if that submerged level of the mind was able to operate better when the surface ones were not functioning. From which level, he wondered, did the impulse to murder come?

This meaty question occupied him until he fell asleep.

15

"Inspector Thanet?"

"Speaking."

"Paul Ennerby here, vicar of Nettleton. Do you think you might be coming out to Nettleton this morning?"

"Yes, I'll be along shortly, as a matter of fact."

"Only, I've got something to tell you. Do you think you could call in at the vicarage?"

Words to gladden any policeman's heart, thought Thanet. Perhaps they would compensate for the fact that his subconscious had let him down; no dazzling revelation had awaited him this morning. "By all means," he said. "What time would suit you?"

"Fairly early? I've got a Mothers' Union coffee morning at ten thirty. I'll be working at home till then."

"Nine thirty, then?"

"Fine. Thank you. Goodbye."

Lineham had just come in.

"The vicar of Nettleton is about to Reveal All, by the sound of it," Thanet said. Then, "You're looking remarkably cheerful this morning, Mike."

"I told her," said Lineham, beaming.

Evidently he had plucked up the courage to tackle his mother.

"You said you'd go ahead regardless?"

Lineham nodded. "Not quite as bluntly as that, though. I . . . er . . . wrapped it up a bit."

"Naturally," Thanet said. "And there's no need to ask how she took it, by the look of you."

Lineham was going to tell him anyway. He was positively bubbling over with it. "To be honest, sir, I was scared stiff. Well, I thought, perhaps she'll have a heart attack here and now, and she wouldn't have if I hadn't told her, if you see what I mean, and then I'd wish I'd kept quiet." He stopped, looked hopefully at Thanet, as if wondering whether Thanet was following him.

"Quite," said Thanet encouragingly, pleased at the success of Lineham's stand (and relieved, too, for if Mrs Lineham *had* had another heart attack it was he, Thanet, who would truly have been responsible, no doubt about that) but impatient to get out to Nettleton to see the vicar. It must surely be important, or Mr Ennerby would not have bothered to phone. Perhaps someone had confessed to him? No, it couldn't be that. The secrets of the confessional were sacrosanct.

"So she said . . ." Lineham was saying. He was obviously determined to give a blow-by-blow account of the conversation and Thanet didn't have the heart to discourage him. Thanet couldn't help rejoicing for his sergeant. He looked as though the troubles of the world had suddenly been lifted from his shoulders. Mrs Lineham had apparently been a little tearful to begin with, but when she realised that her son really meant what he was saying, she had given in gracefully. "D'you think I could just give Louise a ring, sir?" Lineham finished up. "I can't wait to tell her and I didn't like to ring from home . . ."

"Go ahead," said Thanet resignedly, thinking for the umpteenth time that he would be glad when all these traumas were over and Lineham was comfortably settled into married bliss. "You can follow me out to Nettleton. I'm going to see the vicar first, but then I want you with me when I see first

Mrs Selby, then her husband. We really must find out whether or not Carrie went to the Selbys' after leaving the Pitmans'. Susan says she must have, because Major Selby was not expected home until Tuesday, but it's only an assumption on her part. I'll see you in the church car park around ten."

The uncertain weather of the last few days had vanished overnight and it was a sparkling March morning. A frisky wind propelled fluffy white clouds briskly across the sky and tree branches dipped and swayed in the gardens as Thanet sped past.

When he got out of the car in Nettleton he stood quite still for a moment or two, taking deep breaths of country air. There was a builder's lorry parked opposite the end of the footpath which ran along the back of Church Cottages and two men were unloading sacks on to the narrow pavement. One of them set off along the footpath as Thanet passed on his way to the vicarage gate. He was trundling two of the sacks in a wheelbarrow.

The other man was Arnold, the builder. He was systematically marking each thick paper sack with a wide-tipped black felt pen. Thanet stopped, intrigued.

"Morning," he said.

Arnold glanced up, returned the greeting. "Bloody waste of time," he muttered. "If you lot did your job properly, I wouldn't have to be doing this."

Thanet came closer, peered down at the marks Arnold was making: a circle approximately six inches in diameter, with a capital A inside it. "What do you mean?" he said.

"Some perisher's been nicking my stuff, hasn't he? Bag after bag of cement, sand, ballast . . . You name it, he's had it."

"All in one go?"

"Naw. Bit at a time. But it all adds up. Lost nearly fifty quid's worth of stuff, I have, in the last month. And your lot have done damn all about it."

"You've reported it, then?"

Arnold stood up, glanced impatiently along the footpath. "You bet. And a fat lot of good it's done me. Where the devil's Bill got to? Bill!" he yelled.

"So you decided to mark it. Good idea."

"Only if we spot any of the stuff after. But believe me, if I do, I'll knock the bleeder into the middle of next week."

"Much more sensible to let us know, first," Thanet said

mildly. "You wouldn't want to end up on a charge of assault, would you?"

"Justice!" muttered Arnold. He took one or two steps away from Thanet and peered along the footpath. "*Bill!*" he bellowed.

The sound of the wheelbarrow heralded Bill's appearance.

"Where the hell've you been?" said Arnold. "We haven't got all day, you know."

"I . . ."

"Don't give me any of your guff," Arnold said. "Been chatting up that bird from next door again, haven't you?"

Bill did not deny the accusation, merely bent to lift another sack into the wheelbarrow.

"Mr Arnold . . ." Thanet said, when Bill had set off once more.

"Yeah?" Arnold was reaching across to ease a large sheet of plasterboard off the lorry. It, too, had been marked, Thanet noticed.

"The night of the murder," Thanet said. "Was anything taken?"

Arnold slid the plasterboard into a vertical position and leaned it against the side of the lorry. Then he shook his head. "Nothing's been nicked since the weekend. Saturday night it was, the last time. A yard of ballast! Makes you think, don't it? I mean, it must be someone local. The bleeder must have carted it off in a wheelbarrow. Well he ain't building Buckingham Palace at my expense, I can tell you. If anything else goes missing I'll camp out in the house at night until I get him. I'm hoping this murder might've scared him off. It's an ill wind, they say. . . . Now, if you'll excuse me." He lifted the sheet of plasterboard and set off down the footpath, crabwise.

Pity, thought Thanet, watching him go. If the thief had been at work on the night of the murder he might possibly have seen or heard something and it would have been worth making an all-out effort to catch him.

All the same, he thought as he pushed open the vicarage gate and walked up the path, the fact that nothing had been stolen on the night of the murder did not necessarily mean that the thief had not been in the garden of number two that evening. He might have gone along to steal something and been disturbed. Say that he had heard someone coming. . . . He would have hidden—there was plenty of cover. He might even have seen or heard the murderer as he dumped Carrie's body in the privy.

The vicarage door stood ajar and Thanet knocked absently, his mind far away. It could even be, he realised, that the thief himself was the killer. Say that on her way home Carrie had seen or heard something suspicious—someone carting something away in a wheelbarrow, for instance. Arnold might well have complained to her about the pilfering, told her that he suspected a local. He might even have asked her to keep her eyes open. Suppose, then, that she had recognised the thief. . . . This might be the reason why, after the initial blow on the head, the murderer had decided to finish her off: he could not afford her to recover consciousness and reveal his identity.

Surely, though, this would have been rather a thin motive for murder? But people had been killed for far less, he reminded himself. In any case, if the thief had killed her, or even if he had simply seen the murderer, he would surely have gone away empty-handed, if he had any common sense at all. He would not have risked drawing attention to himself.

At this point Thanet had a strong feeling that there was something he should be remembering. Not that elusive fact or insight which had been floating around last night, no, but something which had been triggered off by this most recent train of thought. What *was* it? He shook his head, scowled. He was losing his grip.

And where was the vicar?

Lurid thoughts flashed through his mind, born of detective novels in which those with interesting information to impart invariably met a sticky end before they could disclose it. He pushed the door wider, stepped into the hall.

"Mr Ennerby?" he called.

No reply.

He went to the foot of the stairs, called again.

A door banged at the back of the house, making him start.

"Is that you, Inspector?" The vicar appeared in the kitchen doorway. "Sorry, have you been here long? I just popped out to the greenhouse while I was waiting." He extended grubby hands. "I'll just wash these. Come on in, won't you?"

The kitchen was just as hospitable by day as by night. Sunshine streamed in through the window and a kettle was hissing on the Raeburn.

"Cup of coffee, Inspector? Do sit down."

Thanet shook his head and took one of the chairs at the formica table. The room was neat and tidy, breakfast dishes cleared away, work surfaces uncluttered. The Reverend Paul Ennerby obviously coped very well without a wife.

"I hope you didn't mind my asking you to call," the vicar began, seating himself opposite Thanet.

"Not at all."

"It's just that... oh, dear, I really do find it extraordinarily difficult to...." He was gazing fixedly at his hands, which were clasped on the table in front of him, and now he glanced up at Thanet. The grey eyes were—what were they? thought Thanet. Embarrassed? Shamefaced? Pleading? He began to wonder what was coming.

"You might think," said the vicar, having apparently decided on an approach to the subject, "that I am a bachelor, or a widower, perhaps." And he glanced around the kitchen, as if to underline the absence of a wife in this most feminine of provinces.

"Well I had..." began Thanet.

"Well you'd be wrong. I am married, but my wife isn't here. She's... she's in a mental hospital. I won't go into the details, but she's been there now for ten years or more, and they say there's no hope of a recovery."

Ennerby paused, but he wasn't asking for sympathy. He was simply sketching in the background of what he had to say. Thanet simply sat and waited. It was evident that the difficult part was coming next. The vicar's knuckles were now white with tension, and he moistened his lips before managing to summon up the resolution to continue.

"Forgive me, Inspector," he said, with a nervous little laugh, "but as you will see.... The fact of the matter is," he went on, his voice suddenly much stronger, "that after you came to me the night before last with that absurd rumour about Miss Pitman and Mr Ingram, I... Well, I know that in a murder investigation all sorts of things turn up, are uncovered, so to speak, that have no relevance to it. And I am well aware that those who have something to hide can quite easily fall under suspicion even though what they are hiding might have no connection whatever with the case.... In short, for Miss Pitman's sake, I felt I had to explain to you that if you feel she is holding anything back she is, in fact, trying to protect... me." His voice tailed away and he bowed his head.

Thanet still wasn't sure what the vicar was trying to tell him, but the man's embarrassment seemed to point to only one explanation. He remembered the note of relief in old Mr Pitman's laughter at the suggestion of a liaison between Marion and Ingram. "You mean," he said slowly, hoping that he hadn't got it wrong, "that you and Miss Pitman . . ."

"Yes," said Mr Ennerby. And then, quickly, "Oh, not in the conventional sense, Inspector. I mean, we haven't . . . it hasn't been an *affair*, so to speak. But we are in love, yes, although we know that the situation is hopeless. My wife . . . although her mind has gone, she is physically healthy and is expected to live for very many years.

What a miserable, miserable situation, Thanet thought. No doubt, for a vicar, divorce and remarriage would be out of the question. He would probably have to leave the church. All very well if his religion was hollow, but if it was not. . . . He looked at the Reverend Paul Ennerby's fine, strong face and knew that his was not.

"The point is, you see, that no one knows about this. Even though we have nothing to hide in the conventional sense, if it came out there would be a great deal of talk and inevitably Miss Pitman would suffer. She has a difficult enough life as it is, though she never complains. And I know that out of a sense of loyalty to me, she would say nothing to you about our . . . relationship. Vicars, as you no doubt realise, are especially vulnerable to gossip. I felt I must explain all this to you myself so that you wouldn't misinterpret any evasiveness on Miss Pitman's part. I hope you don't feel that I am insulting you when I add that all this really is in the strictest confidence."

"It won't leak out in the parish through me, I can assure you," Thanet said. "Unless, of course, it has some bearing on the case."

"It hasn't," said the vicar eagerly. "The very fact of my having been frank with you shows how confident I am that it hasn't."

Thanet hoped that he was right. "Did Miss Birch have any inkling of this?"

"No, certainly not. I told you, I'm one-hundred-per-cent certain that nobody has. Except Miss Pitman's father, of course, and he is absolutely to be trusted. If they had, there would have been whispers, glances, innuendoes—you know the sort of thing—and I would have been bound to be aware of it. I just felt that it would be better to get in first with the truth than have you suspicious of Miss Pitman for the wrong reasons."

"I can see that," Thanet said, rising and holding out his hand, "and I appreciate your confidence."

"There was one other thing," Ennerby said quickly.

Thanet sat down again.

"I should have remembered before, I suppose, but it wasn't until last night that it came back to me. My study is at the front of the house and when I have phone calls at night I tend not to bother to switch the light on. I know the study like the back of my hand and in any case I usually leave the study door open so that the light from the hall shines in. I never draw the curtains. It wasn't until last night, when I answered the phone about nine thirty, that I remembered having had a phone call towards the end of the PCC meeting on Monday night. I think it was because the circumstances were exactly reproduced—I was standing there, gazing absentmindedly out of the window into the darkness and it suddenly came back to me. Just before that call ended, the one on Monday night I mean, I saw Miss Birch coming along the pavement on the other side of the road."

Thanet's stomach clenched with excitement. It was almost as though he had caught a glimpse of her himself.

"Where was she, exactly?"

"On the far side of the Pitmans' bungalow, walking this way. I assumed she'd been to the Selbys', but I may be quite wrong."

But he probably wasn't, thought Thanet. The old vicarage was the last house in the village. Where else would Carrie have been coming from, at that time of night? Here was confirmation that Mrs Selby had lied. "You're sure it was she?"

"Absolutely. I know it's some distance along the road, but when I saw her she was just coming into the light of that street lamp which is outside the Pitmans' gate. I saw her pretty clearly, and besides, she was a very individual figure, you know."

"And you're sure she was on the far side of the Pitmans' house?"

"Certain."

"She couldn't simply have been letting herself out of the Pitmans' drive?"

"No. Absolutely not."

"And this was just before the end of the PCC meeting, you say?"

"Yes, at about, let me see, say ten to ten?"

"Did you see where she went?"

"I'm sorry. I just caught this glimpse of her at the very moment when I was putting the phone down. And of course, I didn't think anything of it at the time. The next second I'd turned away. I was anxious to get back to the meeting."

A pity, but it couldn't be helped. Ennerby could be lying, of course, but Thanet didn't think so.

"Thank you for suggesting Mrs Gamble as a substitute for Miss Birch, by the way," the vicar said as he preceded Thanet to the front door. "Miss Pitman spoke to her about it and she's agreed. Miss Pitman's over the moon about it."

Thanet made self-deprecatory noises but couldn't help feeling distinctly smug.

Lineham was sitting on the churchyard wall. When he saw Thanet emerge from the vicarage he jumped down and crossed the road to meet him.

"Anything interesting?" he said.

"Could be." Thanet gave him a brief summary of the interview.

"So Mrs Selby was lying," said Lineham.

"If we believe Mr Ennerby's story, yes."

"Don't you believe him?"

"I don't think he's lying," Thanet said, "but he could be mistaken. There's only a few yards in it, and it was some distance away, and in the dark. I've been here at night, and that lamp outside the Pitmans' isn't all that bright."

They had walked rather aimlessly a few paces along the road while they were talking and were now at the entrance to Church Lane. As they waited to cross to the old vicarage a blue van with BARRET'S on it in bold white lettering turned into the lane and pulled up in front of old Miss Cox's cottage.

"Just a minute," Thanet said, putting a hand on Lineham's arm to restrain him from setting off across the road, and the two men watched as the driver jumped out of the van, went up to the door of number five and knocked.

Barret's, Thanet remembered, was the store for which Miss Cox made loose covers, a skill presumably learned years ago before she became a recluse. Aware that he was wasting time, but driven by sheer curiosity to see how she handled this sole contact with the outside world, Thanet began to stroll along the lane. With a puzzled glance Lineham fell into step beside him.

"I forgot to tell you," Thanet said, as they passed number two, where sounds of vigorous hammering could be heard. And he recounted Arnold's information about the sneak thief. "After we've seen the Selbys, scrape together as many men as you can and put them all on to going through the village with a fine-toothed comb. We'll see if we can find any of Arnold's marked materials, flush this character out."

Miss Cox's door had opened and she and the driver exchanged a few words. Then Miss Cox went back into the house, leaving the man standing on the doorstep. As Thanet and Lineham approached the cottage Miss Cox reappeared, slowly backing towards the front door in a half-stooped position. The van driver said something, bent to touch her on the shoulder and she stood aside for him. He leant forward, swung the large, plastic-wrapped bundle she had been dragging on to his shoulder and set off briskly down the path to the van. Thanet caught a glimpse of swathes of floral material through the plastic covering before the driver closed the double doors of the van. Miss Cox, he was aware, had seen himself and Lineham approaching.

"Morning, Miss Cox," he said, raising a hand in salute. "Lovely day, isn't it?"

She croaked something, presumably a greeting, then began to hobble down towards the front gate. She was using her stick again today. The crutches, yesterday, had presumably steadied her for sweeping the path.

Thanet and Lineham pressed themselves back against the picket fence as the van reversed down the lane. They then turned to the old woman. There was something infinitely pathetic about that combination of masculine garb and vulnerability, Thanet thought.

"Have you made any progress?" she said in that rusty voice of hers.

"Oh yes, we're coming on, aren't we?" said Thanet looking to Lineham for confirmation. "Definitely."

"Definitely," echoed Lineham, nodding like a mechanical toy.

"How much longer?" she asked. Her face was screwed up with anxiety.

"Oh, it'll be soon now, I hope," Thanet said, with what he hoped was hearty reassurance. "Very soon."

She peered into his face and then, apparently satisfied, gave a tight little nod, turned and lurched awkwardly back towards the house.

"Extraordinary, the unspoken pressure that woman puts on one, have you noticed?" Thanet remarked as they returned to the main road.

Lineham nodded. "You really think it will be soon?"

Thanet shrugged. "I repeat: I *hope*. But strangely, in a way, yes. I feel that the pattern's beginning to emerge, that any minute now I'll see it. All last night I felt that it was there, waiting to be understood...." He shook his head. "D'you know what I mean?"

"Not really. It all seems a mess to me, a jumble of people and motives, little mysteries that don't seem to have any relevance..."

"Yes, but don't you see?" said Thanet. "The fact of the matter is, that there *is* a pattern, there *is* an explanation, it's simply a matter of uncovering it. And we're getting closer all the time, if only we could see it. It's like a view that's just around the bend in the lane. You know it's there, it's just a question of waiting until you've turned the corner."

Lineham said nothing. It was obvious that he did not share Thanet's optimism.

16

It was again necessary to knock several times before Irene Selby opened the door. When she saw who it was she stood back without speaking, then led the way once more to the conservatory.

Now that he was aware of the nature of her sickness
Thanet wondered how he could have failed to recognise its
symptoms, so obvious were they to the enlightened observer
His attitude towards her had, he found, changed considerably
since his conversation with Susan yesterday afternoon. Mrs
Selby was no longer a middle-class housewife with a drink
problem but a frustrated concert pianist denied the natural
expression of her gift by a repressive husband.

Nevertheless this was a murder enquiry and Irene Selby
had lied. The effort which Thanet had to make to suppress his
newly-awakened feelings of compassion for her made him
sound unusually brusque and he was aware that when he
spoke Lineham glanced at him in some surprise.

"Mrs Selby, when I came to see you yesterday I asked you
if Miss Birch had called here after leaving Mr Pitman on
Monday evening. You told me that she hadn't, because your
husband was expected back that evening and a visit was
therefore unnecessary."

"That's right, yes."

"I have since learned that he was not due back until
Tuesday."

Silence for a moment, while Irene Selby stared down at
her tightly clasped hands. Thanet could almost feel her
willing herself not to look at the bottle, which she had hidden
in the same place as yesterday; he could just see the tip of it
projecting above its screen of leaves.

Mrs Selby put up her hand to brush away that tic again.
"Originally that was so. But he got through his business
much more quickly than he expected, so he rang me early on
Monday evening to say that he would be arriving home
around ten o'clock that night, instead of next day. He asked
me to let Carrie know that it wouldn't be necessary for her to
call in."

"So you went across to see her?"

"No. I knew that there was a PCC meeting that evening
and that she would be looking in on Mr Pitman during Miss
Pitman's absence, so I went out to the front gate at a few
minutes before nine and caught her as she went in. She was
always as regular as clockwork. It was easy enough to time it
exactly."

What a pity it wasn't summer time, Thanet thought. Old
Mr Pitman's mirror would no doubt have reflected this en-

counter, if it had taken place. "Why didn't you tell me this before?"

She shrugged. "You didn't ask. And it didn't seem important."

"What time did your husband ring?"

"I'm not sure. Between six and seven, I think."

And if this story had not already been agreed between them, there was no doubt that Irene Selby would be ringing her husband the moment Thanet and Lineham left, to make sure that Major Selby knew of this phone call he was supposed to have made.

Had made?

Could Susan's assumption that Carrie had called to see Mrs Selby that evening be wrong? Could the vicar have been mistaken? Or lying?

No, Thanet thought, as he and Lineham returned to the car and set off for Major Selby's place of work, he was convinced that it was Irene Selby who had been lying. He said so, to Lineham. "What do you think, Mike?"

Lineham didn't hesitate. "I agree, sir."

"So, why?"

Lineham considered. "Protecting her husband, I should think. He could have got back earlier than he says he did. Like you said, when Susan heard him he could have been coming back into the house for the second time. Say he got home first between nine thirty and nine fifty, when Carrie was still there—and found his wife dead drunk. He could have lost his temper with Carrie, lashed out at her . . . he looks just the type to have a nasty temper, don't you think?"

"He does, I agree."

"Or," said Lineham eagerly, getting into his stride, "Mrs Selby herself could have killed her. Say Carrie tried to take her last bottle of drink away and Mrs Selby tried to get it back, struggled with her. They could have toppled over and Carrie could have hit her head as they fell."

"But why finish her off? I can see Mrs Selby trying to get her bottle back, but even if she was drunk I honestly can't see her smothering an unconscious woman, can you?"

"I suppose not," said Lineham reluctantly. "And then, of course, she'd have had to get the body across the road and into the garden of number two, somehow. I shouldn't think she'd be strong enough."

"And she'd still have had to drink herself into a stupor

before Susan got home. There just wouldn't have been time. Unless Susan is lying too, which I don't think she is."

"She could have disposed of the body later?"

"Then where was it in the meantime? No, it just doesn't feel right."

"But none of this applies to Major Selby, does it, sir? I mean, I shouldn't think he'd have any scruples about finishing Carrie off, would he, not from what you say of him? If she'd been blackmailing him, he might have thought it the ideal opportunity to get rid of her."

"He could have hidden the body in the stables," Thanet said. "Then he could have waited until everyone was asleep, carried her across the road . . ."

". . . and dumped her in the privy at his own convenience," Lineham finished eagerly. "Do you think that's how it could have happened?"

"Let's not get carried away," Thanet said. "Or committed to any one idea yet. There are too many other possibilities. Carrie *could* have got knocked out in a struggle with Mrs Selby, but my guess is that Mrs Selby would then have departed in triumph with her bottle and proceeded to drink herself into oblivion. Then when Major Selby arrived home he could have found Carrie unconscious and seized the chance to put an end to what must have been a pretty intolerable situation for a man like him. Anyway, let's see what he has to say for himself."

They had arrived at Stavely's and were quickly ushered into Major Selby's office. The Major was standing behind his desk. He gave his secretary a terse nod and the second she had left the room exploded into outraged speech.

"This is intolerable!" he said. "Absolutely intolerable!"

"What is, Major Selby?" said Thanet innocently.

"This . . . this invasion of my office," spluttered Selby. He strode fiercely across to the window and back again. "I have a position to maintain here, you know, and I really cannot see, in any case, why you should be . . . harassing me at all. My connection with Miss Birch was of the most tenuous nature."

"Perhaps you wouldn't mind telling us, Major, exactly what that connection was?" Thanet said.

Selby stopped his pacing and lowered his head, glowering at Thanet from beneath those luxuriant eyebrows. "What, exactly, are you insinuating, Inspector?"

"Not insinuating, Major, merely enquiring. May we sit down?"

Selby waved a hand in impatient permission, then went to sit behind his desk.

Perhaps, Thanet thought, he hoped by this move to establish his control of the interview, underline his authority as managing director of a thriving business. Certainly the office lent weight to the image. It was luxuriously appointed, with a thick, fitted carpet, antique furniture and an impressive array of up-to-date telecommunications equipment on the highly polished desk. A moment later it became apparent that Major Selby, Captain of Industry, had decided to change his tactics.

"I'm sorry, Inspector," he said, with an attempt at a smile. "You've caught me at a bad moment, I'm afraid. A minor crisis . . . Would you and your sergeant take some coffee? Or a pre-lunch drink, perhaps?"

Thanet preferred the man when he was fighting. What was more, the sudden switch was patently out of character. If I hadn't been suspicious before, he thought, I would be now.

"Thank you, no," he said. "I simply wanted to ask you one or two more questions about Monday night. Now," he went on smoothly, as Selby opened his mouth, no doubt to protest that he had already told him all there was to tell, "I understand that you were not due back from your business trip until Tuesday?"

"That's right, but . . ."

"And that when you were away, Miss Birch used to call at your house morning and evening?"

"Certainly, but what on earth . . ."

"So that, in the normal way of things, not expecting you home until Tuesday, she would have called in on Monday evening. Yet, she apparently did not do so. Could you tell us why that was, Major?"

"Because," said Major Selby, leaning forward across the desk and more or less spitting out his words, "I rang my wife on Monday evening, told her that I would be home at about ten and asked her to let Miss Birch know that it wouldn't be necessary to call. And now, Inspector," he said, rising, "I really am a very busy man, so if you'd excuse me . . ."

Thanet did not move. "I haven't quite finished yet, I'm afraid," he said.

Selby's face flamed. It was obvious that he was quite unused to having his authority challenged. "Very well," he said, controlling himself with a visible effort. "But I wish to make it clear that I consider this intrusion into my private life absolutely inexcusable."

"You don't consider murder sufficient excuse?" Thanet said quietly. "Look, Major," he went on, "I think it only fair to tell you that we know why you employed Miss Birch to keep an eye on your wife."

Silence. Thanet could almost have felt sorry for the man. The high colour seeped slowly out of Selby's face and in ten seconds he seemed to age as many years.

"I don't know what you mean, Inspector," he said, but his eyes avoided Thanet's and there was no conviction in his voice.

"I think you do, Major. So could we please cut out the skirmishing and stick to plain facts?"

Selby said nothing.

"You didn't really ring your wife on Monday evening, did you?"

Selby looked up. "Certainly I did." There was a note of—what?—defiance in his voice now. Clearly he had decided to stick to his story. A predictable reaction, Thanet thought. Selby was the sort of man who, more than most, would find it difficult to admit to having lied. A pity. For a moment there Thanet had thought the man's defences sufficiently breached to make him acknowledge defeat. "At what time do you claim to have made this phone call?"

Selby did not react to the implication. "About six thirty."

"From where?"

"A call box at a motorway service station."

Untraceable, of course. "And you arrived home at what time?"

"Just after ten, as I told you."

It was obvious that Selby was not going to budge.

"Thank you, Major," Thanet said briskly, and stood up.

Selby looked up at him with a slightly dazed expression, as if he could not quite believe that the interview was at an end.

"We'll see ourselves out."

He and Lineham were almost at the door before Selby reacted. "Wait!" he said urgently, and came hurrying after them. "Just a minute. Er... look, Inspector," and he swallowed, as if the words he was about to say were stuck in his gullet, "I apologise for over-reacting just now. As I said, we're in the middle of a minor crisis here and of course my wife is very

upset about this business.... The County Council Elections
are coming up next month.... A man in my position has to
be seen to be above reproach.... What I'm trying to say is,
what you said just now, about knowing the reason why Miss
Birch used to... er... keep an eye on things for me while
I'm away..."

Thanet couldn't stand it any longer. Selby trying to be
ingratiating was a nauseating sight. "Don't worry, Major," he
said, "we're not in the habit of broadcasting people's secrets
unless it's absolutely necessary."

"Yuk!" said Lineham, when they were safely out of earshot.

"My sentiment exactly," Thanet said.

Despite his earlier conviction that they were drawing close
to a solution to the case, Thanet suddenly felt depressed,
partly because of the abortive interview with Major Selby,
which he felt he had perhaps mishandled, partly because he
knew that they had now reached the stage in the case that he
always loathed: it was time to sit down at his desk and work
systematically through every single report that had been
made since the beginning of it. It was astonishing just how
fruitful this task could be. It gave one an overall picture,
enabled one to see the wood instead of just the trees, and at
the same time refreshed the memory. Facts, remarks, com-
ments, observations which earlier, in isolation, had appeared
to have little or no significance, took on new meaning when
they were linked with others which had surfaced or been
made subsequently.

"Desk time, I think," he said to Lineham, with a rueful
grin.

Back at the office, Lineham organised a thorough search of
Nettleton for any trace of Arnold's pilfered building materials
while Thanet made sure that all the reports were up to date
and at hand. Lineham ordered coffee and sandwiches for a
working lunch, then they settled down to it.

For the next three hours the atmosphere of concentration
in the room was almost palpable. The telephone rang from
time to time and occasionally one of the two men would
query some point or comment upon something of significance. Otherwise the silence was unbroken save by the
scrape of a match and the little popping noises made by
Thanet as he puffed at his pipe.

At five o'clock Mallard poked his head around the door.

"Good grief," he said disgustedly, fanning away the coils of tobacco smoke which by now were as dense as one of the celebrated old London smogs. "Look at you!" he said as Thanet and Lineham raised dazed faces from the heaped papers on their desks. Then, striding across the room, he flung up both sash windows. Sweet, fresh air poured into the room. "It's a miracle your brains are functioning at all," he said. "Next time I'll bring an oxygen mask with me."

"Nonsense," said Thanet with a grin, laying down the report he had been studying. "Ideal working conditions, aren't they, Mike?"

"Well..." said Lineham, who didn't smoke.

"There you are," Mallard said. "If you're not careful, Luke, you'll be up on a charge of poisoning off your subordinates." He propped himself against the window ledge. "How's it going, anyway? Still with the delectable Miss Birch, are you?"

"So so," said Thanet. "Nothing definite yet, I'm afraid. Though there've been one or two surprises." And he told Mallard about the money and the clothes.

"Not really so surprising, I suppose," said Mallard. "Fairly typical pattern. Domineering mother, repressed spinster daughter. It's got to come out somehow."

"Ah yes," said Thanet. "But that's just the point. How, exactly, did it come out? I agree, the clothes are understandable enough, but where did she get the money? Did she earn it, win it, steal it, or did she get it by blackmail? I forgot to tell you that she was a snooper. There's a very interesting old man, used to be her headmaster years ago. He knows her pretty well, she used to clean house for him. Anyway, he thinks that her real passion was the sense of power it gave her to know other people's secrets. He thinks that just to know was enough for her—but of course, there's always the possibility that it didn't remain enough, that sooner or later she was tempted to use what she'd learned."

"And was there anything—anything she could have used for blackmail, I mean?"

"Nothing earth-shattering. But then, the things which matter most to ordinary people are not usually sensational, are they? Just grubby little secrets which they'd rather nobody else knew about. And we've turned up a number of those, haven't we, Mike?"

Mallard wrinkled his nose in disgust, heaved himself off the window ledge. "Rather you than me. Give me a nice healthy corpse any time. Well, let me know when you come up with something definite." He looked at his watch. "Got to be off. I'll leave you to your dirty washing."

"And that's the trouble, isn't it, Mike," Thanet said when Mallard had gone. "That's all it appears to be, dirty washing." He waved his hands at the mounds of papers. "All this, and no real evidence of any kind."

"Oh I don't know. If Miss Birch had known about Ingram's affair with the hairdresser . . ."

"If. That's the point. If. There's not a shred of proof anywhere that his relationship with Carrie—if such it can be called—was anything but what he claims it was, absolutely superficial. In all the stuff the men have dug up there's not one reference to any significant connection between them."

"She would have been pretty careful not to be seen talking to him though, surely."

"Why? Who would have suspected that the innocuous Miss Birch was indulging in a spot of blackmail? And in any case, if there's no evidence, Ingram's in the clear as far as we're concerned, isn't he?"

"What about Major Selby?" said Lineham. "He's much more promising."

"True. But again, there's no evidence. I admit he's got a lot to lose, especially with the elections next week . . ."

"Don't you think it's pretty peculiar that he should employ someone like Miss Birch as a sort of watchdog for his wife, sir?"

"I do. But then, it was Hobson's choice, wasn't it? His daughter is at school all day and you know what alcoholics are like about hiding their supplies. Carrie would have been bound to be aware that Mrs Selby drank, cleaning the house as she did, and I suppose Selby thought he might as well cash in on the fact that she knew and pay her well enough to make sure she kept her mouth shut."

"Perhaps that's where all the money came from."

"I very much doubt it. There was just too much of it, for that."

"Perhaps she got greedy, sir?"

"Possibly. Who can tell? And that's the trouble with this case. There's too much speculation, and speculation just isn't enough. Sooner or later we've got to have something more concrete."

The two men sat in silence for a while, thinking.

"Mike," said Thanet eventually. "Major Selby..."

"Yes?"

"How did he strike you?"

"Not my cup of tea."

"I know that, but what did you think of him?"

"Typical army type."

"Too typical?"

Lineham frowned. "What do you mean?"

"Well, just think about him for a minute. I mean, he's almost a caricature, isn't he? Clothes, appearance, manner, the lot. You don't think it's just a bit too much?"

"You mean, he's an imposter? But he's managing director of Stavely's!"

"I'm not talking about that," said Thanet with an impatient wave of the hand. "I'm talking about the army bit. These titles, Major and so on, they carry social weight, don't they? And that's something Selby is rather fond of, I should think."

"You'd like me to check? Where should I begin?"

"You'd need to know his regiment first. I'll ring Mr Pitman now. He'll be sure to know. Then you'll have to check in the Army lists. They're in the Public Record Office at Kew. They'll be shut now. Get on to it first thing in the morning."

Thanet had been dialling the Pitmans' number as he spoke and now a brief conversation with Marion Pitman produced the information he needed. "He was in the North Kents," he said, replacing the receiver. "If he was a fraud and Carrie found out, while she was poking through his desk, perhaps, then that really would have given him good reason to want to get rid of her."

Thanet surveyed his untidy desk, groaned and began to shuffle papers together, stopping now and again to glance once more through a report. He felt discouraged. The afternoon's work had been a waste of time after all.

"What about the vicar?" said Lineham, who was doing the same thing. "Or Miss Pitman?"

"Shouldn't think so," said Thanet. "I really cannot see him killing someone to preserve his secret. Oh, I know it would be unpleasant for both of them if it came out, but they'd weather it all right. It's surprising how people rally to the support of their vicar when things go wrong."

"Chris Gamble, then?" suggested Lineham.

"Another dead duck," said Thanet. "Theoretically, Susan doesn't want her father to know, but I have a feeling she wouldn't be exactly heartbroken if he did. Young Jenny Gamble said something of the sort, and I think she was pretty near the mark."

"Chris Gamble might not know that, though."

"Even so," said Thanet with an air of finality. He thumped the last report down on the pile. "Let's face it, practically everyone connected with the woman has some sort of motive. I bet we could even find one for poor old Miss Cox, if we tried hard enough."

"What, for example?"

"Well, let me see. What does Miss Cox value most? Her privacy. Carrie could have threatened that, in some way."

"How?" said Lineham. "Miss Cox wouldn't let her over the doorstep, we know that."

"She could have sneaked in somehow," retorted Thanet. "Let me see. Yes. If you remember, the cat got shut in the shed that night. Perhaps Carrie heard Miss Cox down the garden, calling it, and realised that this was her chance to have a quick snoop around. After all, just think what a frustration it must have been to someone like her to live next door to a hermit. She must have been dying to take a peek. So she grabs her chance and then Miss Cox comes back and finds her."

"Surely she would have made sure she was out of the house by the time Miss Cox got back?" objected Lineham.

"Perhaps she got carried away, didn't realise how quickly the time had gone. Miss Cox was only away about ten minutes."

"So Miss Cox finds her snooping, takes a swipe at her..."

"... with her walking stick!" said Thanet. "The ideal weapon, literally to hand."

"And then puts a cushion over her head and finishes her off?"

The two men grinned at each other. "All right," said Thanet, lifting his hands in a mock gesture of defeat. "It was a nice little exercise in fantasy, I agree. The rest I can see: Carrie grabbing her chance, Miss Cox being angry, hitting out at her—though even that is straining the imagination a bit. But then deliberately to finish her off..."

"And manage to drag her all the way to the privy in the garden of number two with that broken leg..."

"Well, it was a nice idea," said Thanet. "And it proves my point. Look hard enough and there's a motive under every

bush. What we need are some nice hard facts. Perhaps the
men will have turned up something about that pilferer. . . . Oh,
to hell with it. I'm going home to sleep on it and you can do
the same." He grinned. "Only one more day before Saturday,
now. Then you'll be a staid old married man."

Lineham blushed.

"All being well," he said.

17

The streets of Sturrenden were quiet, almost deserted, as
Thanet drove home. Darkness was coming swiftly now and
light from illuminated shop windows spilled softly on to the
empty pavements. Only outside the old Embassy Cinema
was there any sign of activity; this had been converted to a
bingo hall some years ago and a steady trickle of women was
flowing towards its brightly illuminated facade.

The pace of Thanet's driving reflected his state of mind. He
felt sluggish, as if every last ounce of mental energy had been
sucked out of him by the sustained effort of the afternoon.
And all for nothing, he thought dully as he left the shops
behind and turned into the Ashford Road. So lethargic did he
feel, however, that even this dispiriting reflection aroused no
more than the faintest flicker of disappointment in him.

He was not allowed to remain in this state for long. The
second he opened the door two small bodies supercharged
with energy came flying towards him.

"Hey", he said, reeling under the impact and squatting to
gather both of them into his arms at once, "what're you two
doing up at this time of night?"

"It was Peter's party, Daddy. We *told* you." Bridget's eyes were shining, her face flushed.

Ben had already wriggled out of Thanet's grasp and disappeared into the kitchen. Now he came running back with a red balloon bobbing at the end of a piece of string, a paper bag in his hand. "Look what Mrs Darwin gave me, Daddy," he said, opening the bag and peering inside as if to reassure himself that his treasures had not disappeared, before thrusting it under Thanet's nose.

Thanet duly inspected the contents (an apple, an orange and a bar of half-melted chocolate) before making impressed noises and handing it back to Ben.

"They're terribly over-excited," said Joan, as Thanet and the children entered the kitchen. She was obviously trying to get supper going before putting the children to bed.

How was she going to cope with this sort of situation if she started a full-time job, Thanet wondered, as he said, "It's all right. I'll get them bathed. And there's no hurry for supper. I shouldn't have to go out again this evening."

"I'm afraid it'll be a job getting them calmed down," she said, stopping what she was doing to come and give him a grateful kiss. "We might well have tears before long, I should think."

"Don't worry, I'll cope," said Thanet. "Right, you two! Off we go."

It was a rare treat for their father to be home in time to bathe them and put them to bed and Thanet managed to tone down their almost frenzied state of excitement by the simple expedient of telling them that if they didn't quieten down he would go downstairs again and they could put themselves to bed bathless and storyless. He couldn't help feeling pleased with himself when, half an hour later, he was able to say to Joan, "No problems. They'll be asleep in two minutes, I shouldn't wonder. Looking as though butter wouldn't melt in their mouths, of course, as usual."

Joan had been busy in the meantime. There was an appetising smell in the kitchen and a welcoming fire in the living room. Thanet sank down in front of it with a sigh and picked up the newspaper. Strangely, he felt much less tired than when he had arrived home. The interlude with the children had refreshed him; for a whole half an hour he had been able to put his work out of his mind entirely.

Now, however, he found himself unable to concentrate on

the lines of newsprint. Snippets of information and conversation relating to the Birch case kept floating into his mind and distracting him.

"What's the matter?" Joan said as she came in to lay the table.

"Nothing. Why?"

"You were frowning."

"Was I?"

"Positively scowling, in fact." She was briskly unloading table mats, cutlery and glasses from the tray she was carrying. "Supper's just about ready now," she said.

Abstracted as he was it was not until they were eating dessert (lemon meringue pie, one of his favourites) that Thanet became aware that Joan was secretly excited about something. He had seen that look before. It was in the lightness of her movements, in the lift at the corners of her mouth, the extra sparkle in her eyes when she smiled.

For the first time in their marriage his immediate reaction to it was a sudden sinking of the spirits. *She's found a job*, he thought, and was tempted to pretend he hadn't noticed. But this would have been quite out of character for him. He would have to pretend that nothing was amiss.

"Well," he said, laying down his spoon and looking at her expectantly. "When are you going to tell me?"

"Tell you what?"

"Come on, darling," he said. "No point in pretending with me. I can read you like an open book."

"What it's like," she said, gathering up the dishes and marching off towards the kitchen, "being married to a policeman!"

He couldn't help grinning and his spirits rose a notch. Perhaps he was wrong, perhaps Joan's news would be perfectly innocuous after all.

She waited until they had settled down with their coffee and then she said, "You were asking just now..."

"Mmm?" he said, pretending abstraction.

"What I had to tell you."

"Ah, yes. I thought you said there wasn't anything."

"One of these days, my darling, you'll get a cup of coffee poured over your head, if you're not careful! Now, do you want to hear it or not?"

He shrugged. "If you insist," he said, then put up his arm

in mock self-defence as she raised her cup in the air. "Just as you like, dear," he said, with exaggerated meekness.

But she couldn't waste time playing games any longer. "Well," she said, wriggling herself into a more comfortable position. "I went along to the probation service this morning."

"Oh?"

His wariness must have shown in his voice, for she glanced at him doubtfully before continuing.

"I thought, well, I've always been interested in probation work and although I didn't think that there was the slightest chance that they would be interested in me, as I have no qualifications whatsoever, I thought it might just be worth enquiring. . . . Well, anyway, it seems I was wrong. Apparently there's more than one way of becoming a probation officer, and the fact that I've done regular voluntary work with the mentally handicapped over the last couple of years while Ben's been at playgroup means that they might be prepared to take me on either as an unpaid volunteer or, what's even more exciting, as an assistant probation officer, with a view to seeing whether I suit the work. Then, if all went well and they were satisfied with me, they might sponsor me through a proper training. That means they'd actually pay me, while I was doing the training! Isn't it exciting!"

"I don't quite see what working with mentally handicapped children has to do with the probation service," Thanet said carefully.

"The fact that it happens in my case to be handicapped children has nothing to do with it, really," Joan said. "What matters, apparently, is that I've worked for the community in what they called a caring capacity."

"A caring capacity indeed! You're picking up the jargon already."

"It was their expression, not mine. And what else would you call it?" Joan said rebelliously. "You know perfectly well what I mean and you're deliberately ignoring the point."

"Which is what?"

"That they may be prepared to take me on despite my lack of formal qualifications."

"I must say that piece of information does not exactly inspire confidence in the probation service."

"Now you're being ridiculous! I've just explained that of course I'd have to do a proper training, but not until they were satisfied that I'm suited to the work."

She was right, of course. He was being petty and mean-spirited and his attitude could lead only to disaster. He took a deep calming breath.

"Sorry, love. Look, I accept that you need to find something interesting to do. But does it have to be this?"

"It doesn't *have* to be, I suppose, but why not? It's a fascinating job, and the running-in period would give me a chance to see if it would really suit me, before I start the proper training course. Oh darling, why not? It would be ideal, don't you see?"

"Ideal for whom?"

She stared at him. "Well for me, of course. What do you mean?"

"Have you thought how it could affect us?"

"Us? In what way?"

"You haven't thought that there could be a certain, well, clash of interests?"

"No. Why should there be?" She had drawn away from him and was sitting rigidly upright against the arm of the settee. She looked wary, hostile.

He sighed. "Look, the probation service and the police, they're often poles apart in their attitudes to criminals."

"But they're both on the same side really, surely? They're both concerned to maintain peace and order in society?"

He shook his head. "Maybe. But that doesn't stop them frequently being in conflict. I don't suppose you've had much to do with probation officers, but I have. And I grant you they do very fine work, many of them. But that's not the point. The point is, as I say, that their attitudes to criminals are different. Don't you see that it's impossible to shed one's working attitudes in one's private life? They become an integral part of one, as basic as breathing. I can see all sorts of situations in which this thing could become a barrier between us."

"How, for example?"

He shrugged. "Well, for one thing, I've always shared my work with you, haven't I? Told you everything, without reserve, knowing that I could trust you not to talk about it."

"But I still wouldn't," she cried. "You know that, surely?"

"Maybe you wouldn't talk about it, but your attitude to what I tell you would be bound to be different, don't you see? It's inevitable that you'd be looking at the whole question of crime from a different point of view, from the side of the criminal, his guilt, his rehabilitation, whatever. . . . Darling, don't you see that? You must, surely."

"Not necessarily. Probation officers have to be detached, they can't afford to identify with their clients or they couldn't work properly."

"And what if it turned out that we were both working on the same case? That I had arrested someone for a crime and you had to do a social enquiry on him? And suppose then that it was your evidence in court that got him off even though I strongly felt that he should have had a sharp sentence to bring him to his senses?"

"I would think that the chances of that happening would be very slight. And if it did happen, couldn't one or the other of us request that we should be taken off the case?"

"And that would create a barrier between us, too. Joan, you must see it. It would limit us, put restrictions on our work. We'd be bound to resent it. And there would be other barriers—just in ordinary life, in casual conversation, we'd have to be guarding our tongues, watching what we say to each other . . ."

"I think the truth of the matter," she said tightly, "is that you don't want me to work at all."

"It's not that . . ."

"Isn't it?" she cut in. "Are you sure? Oh," she went on miserably, "I was so excited about it. To think that I could have a really interesting, challenging job despite my hideous lack of qualifications . . ."

She was near to tears and she stood up abruptly, pulling away from his restraining hand. "It's all right for you," she said. "You really love your work, don't you? Well, why shouldn't I be able to do something I enjoy, too?"

"Darling," he said, in what he hoped was an eminently reasonable tone, "I'm not saying you shouldn't. I'm just saying, does it have to be this?"

"Well, I'm still not convinced that that is all you're saying. Oh, what's the point in talking about it any longer. I'm going to have a bath." And she swung away and walked quickly out of the room before he could stop her.

Thanet looked gloomily after her. The situation seemed to be deteriorating by the day. And this idea of hers . . . It was crazy, absolutely crazy. Not that he couldn't see that she would enjoy the work, probably be very good at it . . . Oh, to hell with the whole business, he thought. He glanced at his watch. Nine o'clock. He would watch the news.

He switched on the television then sat back on the settee, tried to relax. At first it was impossible, but when the news ended there was an interesting documentary on behavioural patterns in the criminal and he gradually became absorbed in the programme.

When it ended he switched off the television, unplugged it and listened to the silence of the house. Joan must have gone to bed long ago. He fixed a spark guard firmly in position in front of the fire, checked that both front and back doors were securely locked and went upstairs.

In the bedroom the little lamp on his bedside table was still burning and Joan was merely a humped shape, turned on to her side away from the light. Presumably she was asleep, or pretending to be. She did not stir as he entered the room, came and went to the bathroom, undressed and got into bed.

Thanet switched out the light and composed himself for sleep. But the darkness, the silence (broken only by Joan's soft, even breathing) and the absence of any form of distraction combined to create the perfect conditions for his mind immediately to start working again in top gear. Unable to prevent it functioning, and unwilling to discipline it to logical thought, he let it go free. Like a dog newly released from the lead it ran about with abandon, briefly following one train of thought then switching abruptly, for no apparent reason, to another.

At first he brooded over his recent argument with Joan and then he meandered off into disjointed thoughts about the case: fleeting images of the people involved, snatches of conversation, fragments of the reports he had read that afternoon. Lineham appeared briefly from time to time, commenting on the case or expressing anxiety about the wedding. And in and out of it all, a pathetic, elusive and really rather unpleasant little wraith, floated Carrie Birch.

Despite what he had learned about her, Thanet found to his surprise that he still felt sorry for her. Who knows what she would have been like, if the circumstances of her life had been different? Shaped and moulded by that monstrously self-centred and domineering mother, Carrie had been forced to find her secret satisfactions or perish as a person. Who could really blame her if those satisfactions had taken a form distasteful to those fortunate enough not to have been warped by their upbringing? God forbid that he and Joan should ever cripple Bridget and Ben in that way, he thought.

In a philosophical mood by now, Thanet reflected on the damage caused by possessiveness. Convinced as he was that it was in ferreting out some secret that Carrie had brought about her own death, he thought now that in all justice the true murderer was Carrie's mother, Mrs Birch. Although it was a fate that he would not wish upon any one, perhaps in a way it was only poetic justice that she should have ended up alone, unwanted and abandoned—for can love not flourish only and above all where it is freely given?

Look at Marion Pitman and her father, he thought, warming to his theme. The old man asked nothing and in response was loved without reserve, to the point of self-sacrifice on Marion's part; whereas so many of the other poeple in the case seemed to have been crippled in one way or another by possessiveness.

Take the Ingrams, for example. Thanet was willing to bet that if Joy Ingram had not been so fiercely and unremittingly jealous of her husband he would never have been driven to find consolation elsewhere.

And then there were the Selbys. Susan, panting to get away, seething with bitter resentment against her father; and poor, pathetic Irene Selby, her fine talent gone to waste, driven to the bottle for the comfort which her life with that pompous, posing little monster of a husband could never give her.

And there was poor old Miss Cox, self-condemned to a life of loneliness, shying away from any kind of personal contact simply because many years ago she had invested all her loving in a boy who died.

Nearer home there was Lineham's mother, in danger of losing her son altogether because she had sought to bind him too closely to her.

How strange it was that these people, the ones who demanded the service, allegiance and obedience of their nearest and dearest as a right, could never see that in the long run it was they themselves who were the losers.

At this point in the catalogue Thanet stopped. For the last few minutes he had been aware of a feeling of pressure inside his head, a sensation of—what?—restlessness in his limbs. The atmosphere of the room seemed suddenly to have become oppressive and he felt stifled, found that he was sweating slightly.

Could he be ill? Perhaps he was going to have a heart attack. He had heard that these frequently occurred in the small hours, though he had never understood why. It really was suffocating in here. He had to have some air.

The absence of pain in his chest decided him that it was quite safe to get up. Taking care not to wake Joan he slid out of bed and crossed to the window. It was slightly ajar, but easing up the catch he opened it wide and leaned out to breathe in great gulps of the chill night air.

After a moment or two he felt calmer but still uneasy and very wide awake. He decided that he would go down and make himself a pot of tea.

Downstairs it was chilly. The central heating was always switched off at night and the kitchen had no other form of heat. He unearthed an electric fire from the cupboard under the stairs and plugged it in while the kettle boiled. Soon, with the tea made and a comforting glow emanating from the bars of the fire he was sitting at the kitchen table.

With nothing to do but think.

And this, he discovered, he was reluctant to do.

Why?

Cautiously, like someone gently testing an aching tooth with the tip of his tongue, he groped his way back into his previous train of thought.

He had been thinking about Mrs Birch.

And about Joy Ingram.

And Henry Selby.

And old Miss Cox.

And Lineham's mother.

And there it was again, the same sense of pressure within his brain, the same need to get up and move about, as if his body were telling him, run, run like hell.

He stayed where he was, putting his head down between his hands and pressing his fingers to his temples.

What was the matter with him?

And then, suddenly, he knew. The moment of revelation was sudden, blinding and exquisitely painful. He closed his eyes as if to blot it out, but of course the knowledge remained, once perceived never again to be denied, ignored or hidden away from his consciousness.

Just as all these people had in one way or another crippled their relationship with those they would claim to love the most, *so was he crippling his relationship with Joan.* By seeking to hold her he would most surely lose her.

He found that he was staring fixedly at the wall, sitting rigidly upright with hands clenched into tight fists. He stayed that way for a minute or so longer, braced against further pain. Then, slowly, he began to relax, to hold this revolutionary new idea up for scrutiny.

He was exaggerating, he told himself. How could his relationship with Joan possibly be compared with these others? Had he not always been a faithful, appreciative husband? But, he admitted with painful honesty, that wasn't the point. Relationships do not remain static and what might have been satisfying to them both in the past sufficed no longer. From what Joan said it was clear that her dissatisfaction had been growing for some time.

What a fool he had been, he thought, remembering the arguments of the last few days, the widening rift between them—what a blind, selfish fool! After all, what right had he to expect that Joan should sacrifice herself to his needs, deny herself a fuller life simply because it would bring inconvenience, discomfort to his? What was the point of forcing her to remain in a role which was preventing her from developing her abilities to the full, if by so doing he would be stultifying, perhaps destroying the relationship which he had always counted one of the most precious things in his life?

He stood up abruptly. He couldn't wait to tell her, to apologise, to ask her forgiveness and explain the reasons for his change of heart. Upstairs in the bedroom, however, his newly-awakened guilt and contrition made him hesitate. Why wake her up, just to satisfy his own need for expiation? Quietly, stealthily, he slid into bed and, contemplating pleasurably the prospect of her delight in the morning when she heard what he had to say, composed himself at last for sleep.

But it still wouldn't come.

Stimulated by his new insight he felt as alert as ever and returned to thinking about the case. Once again the principal characters marched across the stage, parading themselves for his inspection. One by one he contemplated them, thinking back over facts, conversations, snippets of information picked up disjointedly here and there, trying to penetrate the secret places of their hearts.

And then there came to him an idea so monstrous, so bizarre that his eyes snapped open and he sat bolt upright in bed.

Was it possible?

Joan stirred, mumbled and he froze, scarcely daring to breathe. His desire to talk to her had evaporated, ousted by his need to think. She settled back into sleep and, careful not to disturb her again, he lay down. Was it possible? he thought again. Could it be true?

It was a fact that the person he had in mind had once behaved in a totally uncharacteristic manner, but surely this was not sufficient ground upon which to base a theory so outlandish, so truly extraordinary?

He began to think back over the case in the light of this new idea and found that it had radically changed his thinking. Behaviour which at the time he had interpreted in one way he now saw could equally well be interpreted in another. It began to seem that his theory could hold water. Above all it provided him with a motive, a motive so powerful that he now understood at last why it had been essential for Carrie to be silenced.

Yes, it all made sense at last.

18

"But where are we going, sir?" Lineham sounded positively plaintive, as well he might. No sooner had he arrived at the office than he had been scooped up by an impatient Thanet and whisked downstairs to the car.

"To see an old friend of mine."

Thanet had awoken with a name in his mind: Harry Pack.

"You see," he explained to Lineham, "yesterday, after Arnold had been talking about his sneak thief, there was something nagging away at the back of my mind. You know how it is, when you just can't put your finger on it. Anyway, this morning I realised what it was. The first time I arrived in Nettleton, with Doc Mallard, there was a crowd of onlookers at the entrance to the footpath behind Church Cottages. I had them sent packing, of course, but just as they were all drifting off I realised that I'd recognised somebody in the crowd. You know what I mean. I'd seen him, without it registering properly, and I just had this vague feeling that I'd glimpsed a familiar face. I didn't bother to follow it up at the time. I didn't think it could be important and anyway I wanted to get on with the job."

"You mean, it was someone with a record?"

"Yes. A man called Harry Pack. He's a petty thief, a pathetic specimen—you know the type, in and out of job after job, spends most of his time living on social security, has swarms of kids and a wife who can't cope and is so useless he can't help getting himself caught every time he puts a toe outside the law. I happened to be in court on another case the last time he came up. He was put on probation for what they assured him was the very last time. If he was caught again he'd be inside quicker than he could pick a lock."

"You think he might have been in the garden of number two, the night of the murder?"

Thanet shrugged. "It's a bit much to hope for, but you never know. The point is, if he was, he'd never have dared to come forward because if he did he'd have to say what he was doing there and he'd be virtually sending himself to prison."

"In that case, he'll never admit it anyway, surely?"

"I don't know. We might just be lucky. Harry's so dim that if he's the pilferer he's bound to have left some evidence lying around. Even if I hadn't remembered seeing him that first morning, the men would have turned him up in the end, I'm sure. I checked their reports this morning and they haven't got as far as Harry's council estate yet. I could be wrong, of course. He might be in the clear. But I don't think so. It all fits, somehow. It's just typical of Harry to set out to pinch a bag of cement and find himself involved in a murder."

"But . . ." said Lineham, and stopped.

"But what?"

Lineham shook his head. "Nothing."

"Oh come on, man. It's obvious there's something. How's your mother, by the way?"

"Fine, so far."

"Excellent. Well?"

Lineham still hesitated. "Well, sir, I don't quite see why all the rush. OK, Harry Pack may be the thief and he may have been there that night, but, well, it's very much a routine enquiry, isn't it? And you're not usually so . . . keyed up as this."

Thanet grinned. "On the ball, aren't you, Mike? You're quite right, of course. Certainly I'm interested in what Harry'll have to say, but there's something else I'm far more interested in checking. But just in case Harry *was* there and did see something, well, I want to see him first. So I'm in a rush to get him over with, so to speak, because I want to get on with the other thing."

"I gather I don't get to hear what that is, yet?"

"No need to huff," Thanet said. "No, I'm not telling you at the moment, but not because I don't trust you. It's just that I'm afraid of looking a fool."

"You mean you think you know who the murderer is?"

"I might. Now look, Mike, stop fishing. I'm not telling yet, and that's that."

"But you're pretty sure, aren't you?"

"What makes you say that?"

"Well, because you're looking so . . ."

"Smug?" Thanet laughed out loud. "Well, I may be, but that's nothing to do with the case." He remembered with satisfaction Joan's reaction this morning when he had told her of his change of heart.

"I really mean it, darling," he'd said, smiling at her. "Go ahead. With whatever you want to do. And I'll back you all the way."

She had naturally been reluctant to believe him, had thought at first that once again he was only seeking to placate her, but he had managed to convince her at last and their reconciliation had been sweet.

What a relief it was, Thanet thought now, to know that everything was all right between them once more.

Nevertheless his euphoria was tinged with sadness. Examining his theory about the murder in the cold light of morning, he still thought that it might well hold water; but his initial elation at having solved the mystery had faded as its implications sank in.

It was at times like this that he felt that he was perhaps not cut out to be a policeman after all. There was a softness at the core of his nature, a lack of single-mindedness, perhaps, which so often prevented him from experiencing undiluted pleasure in the apprehension of a criminal such as this one.

Many of his colleagues, he knew, had no such qualms. For them, right and wrong were white and black; whereas for Thanet there were many shades of grey between. It was ironic that the very qualities which made him so successful in the solving of such cases as the present one—his intuitive understanding of people, his ability to grasp the subtleties of their motivation and their relationships—were the very qualities which in the end robbed him of unqualified satisfaction in his success. Having entered into the mind of the criminal, he found it all too easy to understand the crime—and even (and he found it very difficult to admit this, even to himself) to excuse it. It was only because murder was truly abhorrent to him, because he passionately believed that no one had the right to take the life of another human being, that he was able at times like this to go on functioning as an instrument of justice.

And so it was that this morning he found himself divided. Part of him was anxious, as he had told Lineham, to forge ahead, prove his theory correct; while the other part held back, shrank from inflicting the pain which would be inevitable. There was never any doubt in his mind which part would win. He just wished that it could be a more comfortable process.

He shifted uneasily in his seat as Lineham made the now-familiar left turn into Nettleton.

"Pack lives in the little group of council houses on the right, half way through the village," he said. "Number nine."

Number nine stood out from its neighbours by virtue of its squalor. Most of the other gardens were trim and neat, bright with daffodils and forsythia, but Harry's was a square of balding grass and weeds, strewn from end to end with broken plastic toys, rusting tricycles, bits of rope, empty Coca-Cola cans and crisp and sweet packets.

Two toddlers were scratching in the dirt with bits of stick and broken china, both of them dressed in grubby clothes much too big for them. Neither of them looked as though he had seen soap and water for some time. As Thanet and Lineham pushed open the gate they glanced up with slack faces and eyes devoid of interest or curiosity. Poor little devils, thought Thanet, smiling at them. He couldn't help contrasting their appearance and behaviour with that of his own alert and lively children. What chance did they have, with a home like this? They reminded him unnervingly of the old people he had seen in the geriatric ward when he had visited Mrs Birch.

Lineham had to knock several times before the door was finally opened. The woman who answered it was carrying a baby's feeding bottle and the child's thin, protesting wail rose from somewhere at the back of the house.

The woman herself, though probably in her early thirties, looked a good fifteen years older, Thanet thought. Her sagging breasts, protruding stomach, blue-veined legs and lank, greasy hair proclaimed that continuous child-bearing and the inability to meet the demands of a large family had long ago destroyed her will to do anything more than survive with the minimum of effort. Families such as these were the eternal despair of the social workers.

"'E's still in bed," she said, in response to Thanet's request.

"Could you tell him we'd like a word with him? We'll wait outside, in the garden," Thanet added.

If such it could be called, he thought, as he and Lineham strolled around to the back of the house. Here, too, was the same neglect, the same detritus of living. There was, however, one interesting feature. He and Lineham exchanged significant glances at the sight of the straggling, uneven concrete path which stretched two thirds of the way beneath the washing line. It was clearly still under construction; broken planks shored up its sides.

"Got him, I think," said Thanet with satisfaction, making for a pile of rubbish against the fence. He stooped to pick up an empty cement sack. On its side, clearly visible, was the sign with which Arnold had been marking his property. He folded the sack up and whipped it behind his back as the rear door of the house opened and Harry appeared, bleary-eyed and unshaven. He was a small man with a whippet-like face and cringing manner.

"Sorry to interrupt your beauty sleep, Harry," Thanet said. "Just one or two little questions we wanted to ask you."

Pack stood aside as Thanet and Lineham approached, and led the way through a urine-smelling kitchen to a grubby living room.

"You know why we're here, of course," Thanet said, declining the invitation to sit down. He smiled benignly at Harry, who darted a nervous glance at the notebook and pencil which Lineham had ostentatiously taken from his pocket.

"Don't know what you mean, guv'," Harry mumbled.

"This, Harry," said Thanet. And, careful to keep the marked side away from Harry he produced the sack, unfolded it and displayed it like a magician who has just conjured a white rabbit out of thin air. "This."

Harry licked his lips, said nothing.

"You know what it is, of course."

Harry glowered.

"Precisely. It's a sack. And we both know what was in it, don't we? *Don't we*, Harry?" he said more fiercely, when there was still no response.

"How should I know what was bleedin' in it?" said the little man sullenly.

"Oh, come on," Thanet said wearily. He gave the sack a little shake and a fine powdering of cement dust drifted down to coat the accumulated layers of dirt upon the floor. "That's a very fine path you've been laying out there, isn't it, Harry?"

"It was the wife," said Harry defensively. "On and on about it, she was, the mess what got carried in after she'd been hanging out the washing..."

"Never mind the excuses, Harry. Just give us the facts. No, don't bother, or we'll be here all day. I'll give them to you instead. This sack contained cement and you stole it from the garden of number two, Church Cottages, didn't you, Harry?"

"That's a bleedin' lie," Harry burst out.

"Is it?" Thanet shook his head, clicked his tongue. "Poor old Harry, you do have bad luck, don't you? Trust you to nick something that's marked." And indeed, he couldn't help feeling sorry for the man. He was one of life's natural victims. It showed, now, in the look of resigned despair in Pack's eyes, as if he had been half expecting something like this to happen.

"Marked?" Harry's voice was little more than a croak.

"I'm afraid so, yes." Thanet turned the sack about, to display the circle with the A in it. "A for Arnold. Mr Arnold—that's the builder who's renovating number two, Church Cottages—got a bit tired of someone walking off with his building materials and decided to lay a little trap."

"I've never seen that sack before," Pack said desperately.

"Blew over the fence, did it? What a shame. Let's hope the magistrates believe you. What was the suspended sentence? A year? But, let's face it, you'll be inside a lot longer than that. Murder's a very different matter from pinching a few tea spoons, isn't it?"

The unhealthy pallor of Pack's skin became suffused with a pink which faded as quickly as it had come, leaving him ashen. He opened his mouth, but no sound emerged.

"Did you say something, Harry?" Thanet said.

Pack tried again. "Murder?" he croaked. "What d'yer mean?"

"Oh come on, Pack," Thanet snapped. "Stop playing games. You bumped into her that night, didn't you? Miss Birch? She caught you in the act, didn't she? So you had to shut her up, make sure she didn't talk because if she did, as we both know, don't we, Harry, you'd have been inside before you could have said, 'probation'. So you bashed her on the head with a handy bit of wood and then..."

"*No! No, I never*," said Harry desperately. He had been watching Thanet like a rabbit mesmerised by a stoat, but now he could contain himself no longer. "It wasn't like that, I swear it wasn't..."

"Then what was it like, Harry?" Thanet said softly. "You tell us."

Pack looked at Thanet's face, then at the marked sack in his hand. His thought processes were almost audible. What's the point in not coming clean? he was asking himself. They've got me anyway. Then his eyes narrowed as a new idea occurred to him and he stiffened, gave Thanet a calculating look. "What if I did see something... something that could be useful to you, like...?"

Thanet said nothing.

"Well, I mean to say, if I help you..."

"You scratch my back and I'll scratch yours, eh, Harry?" said Thanet. He folded his arms across his chest and gazed at Pack sternly. "Come on, now. You know I can't make bargains like that. All the same..."

"Yes?" said Pack, pathetically eager.

"Well, it's nothing to do with me, mind, but the authorities do tend to look more favorably upon those who've given us a helping hand..."

"You'd put in a word for me?"

"Let's hear what you've got to say, first. And, mind you, I

want the strict truth. No frills. My sergeant here'll be taking it all down, word for word."

"Well it was like this," said Pack.

"Just a moment. I think we'd all better sit down," said Thanet.

Pack took the sagging armchair by the empty fireplace and Thanet and Lineham chose two upright wooden chairs which appeared to be reasonably clean.

"Right," said Thanet when they were settled. "Let's hear it."

Thanet listened to Pack's story without surprise. It had all happened exactly as he had envisaged it. Lineham, however, had difficulty in concealing his amazement and kept glancing at Thanet as if expecting him to challenge the truth of Pack's tale.

Thanet, however, was convinced. Pack had been there. Every detail of his story tallied with what they already knew. When he had finished Thanet took him back over it, querying, probing, questioning, but he could not shake the man. His evidence would convince any jury. Carrie's murderer was in the bag and Thanet only wished that the thought gave him more satisfaction.

But there was something else worrying him now and a growing sense of urgency was making him restless. For the last ten or fifteen minutes his mind had been working on two different levels simultaneously: the surface part had been applying itself to an examination of Harry's evidence, but the subterranean part had been questing back yet again over his last encounter with the murderer. What was it that was causing this pricking unease, this itching impatience to be gone?

Suddenly, he had it: it was not so much what had been said that was worrying him, but how it might have been interpreted—or rather, misinterpreted, in the light of what he now knew or could guess of the murderer's character and motive. And if he was right. . . . He stood up abruptly, cutting Pack off in mid-sentence.

Both Pack and Lineham glanced up at him, surprised.

"Let's go," he said, terse in his anxiety.

The other two came to their feet, still looking puzzled.

"We'll have to hurry," he said. "Get your coat, Harry, quickly." By the time Pack and Lineham joined him at the front door he was practically dancing with impatience.

"What's the hurry all of a sudden?" asked Lineham as they bundled Harry into the back seat.

"Later," said Thanet. "I'll drive."

They took off in a cloud of dust, paused to scoop up Bentley who was coming out of one of the council houses as they went by, and turned the corner into the main street of Nettleton with a squeal of tyres. The sense of urgency was overwhelming now and Thanet cursed himself for not having been more percipient before. Perhaps it was already too late.

They skidded to a halt in front of number five, Church Cottages. With a hurried word to Bentley to stay with Pack, Thanet and Lineham flung themselves out of the car and ran up the path to the peeling front door. The curtains were still drawn and the house had a forlorn, abandoned look. There was no response to their repeated knocking.

"Gone?" said Lineham.

Thanet shook his head tightly, compressed his lips. "We'll break in," he said. They had no warrant, but his degree of certainty was such that he brushed the thought aside.

The Yale lock on the door presented no problem and in a matter of seconds they were inside. The darkened sitting room within was deserted. But not completely. Lineham cannoned into Thanet from behind as he came to a dead stop.

"Look at this, Mike."

It was Tiger, stretched out stiff and cold in their path. The sight convinced Thanet, as nothing else could have done, that he had been right to be afraid. No doubt, now, of what they would find upstairs. Nevertheless it was just possible that they were not too late and they pounded up the narrow staircase one behind the other. The doors to all the bedrooms stood open and a quick glance inside showed that they were empty.

"The attic," said Thanet, remembering the window he had noticed in the gable end of this house, the last in the terrace.

A cupboard-like door in the corner of the landing revealed the even steeper flight of stairs leading to the roof space. There was no door at the top and the room itself was in pitch darkness. Thanet fumbled for a light switch on the wall nearby and as Lineham came up behind him, found it. The room sprang to life in the sickly yellow glow of artificial light in daytime.

Both men froze.

It was as if they were seeing double: twin beds, twin

bodies, each with cropped grey hair, faces overlaid with the unnatural pallor of death, both dressed in identical garb of corduroy trousers, men's shirts.

It was only on closer inspection that the mirror-image impression splintered and resolved itself into male and female.

"Her brother Joseph," said Thanet heavily, gazing down upon the weak, unshaven face of the slighter of the two bodies. "The only person she ever cared about in her whole life."

"But how did you know?" Lineham's face was a study in amazement.

"Something old Mr Pitman told me. He said. . . ."

"*Sir?*" The voice reverberated through the empty house, reaching them only faintly. Its note of urgency, however, was even at this distance clearly audible.

Both men made for the head of the stairs. "Up here," Thanet called. "In the attic."

Bentley appeared at the bottom of the staircase, puffing slightly. "Sir, message on the car radio . . ."

"Well? Get on with it, man," Thanet snapped.

"It's Mike's . . . DS Lineham's mother, sir. She . . . she's had a heart attack, been taken to Sturrenden General." Bentley peered miserably up the stairs at Lineham's frozen face.

"Sorry, Mike," he said.

19

"Now then," said Joan, settling herself into the passenger seat with a sigh of relief, "tell me all."

It was half past one the following afternoon. Ben and Bridget were safely parked with friends and Joan and Thanet were setting off for the little country church where Louise and Lineham were to be married. It was wedding weather— bright sunshine, cloudless blue sky and a little breeze which set the daffodils nodding in the gardens as Joan and Thanet went by.

This was their first opportunity to talk. When the news of Mrs Lineham's heart attack had come through, Thanet had insisted that Lineham leave at once for the hospital. Fortunately the attack had once again proved to be mild and although the hospital insisted on keeping her in bed and under observation for a few days Lineham had been able, after some qualms of conscience, to stick to his ultimatum and go ahead with plans for the wedding. On Louise's suggestion, the newly married couple would visit Mrs Lineham in hospital in their wedding finery and present her with the bridal bouquet before changing to leave on their honeymoon.

Meanwhile, of course, Thanet had found his workload doubled. In the aftermath of the deaths of Matty and Joseph Cox there had been much to do. Joan had been in bed and asleep by the time Thanet had finally crawled home last night, and this morning he had had to return to the office to try to clear away the accumulation of paperwork which was the inevitable accompaniment to the end of a case. Until now there had been no time to give Joan anything but the bare details.

"It's difficult to know where to begin," he said.

"Start with how you guessed. However did you? What made you suspect Miss Cox in the first place?"

Thanet frowned, thinking back. "It's difficult to tell, really. It wasn't so much that at one particular point I said, ah, there's something fishy about that. It was more an accumulation of things which in themselves didn't seem to have any special significance but when added together pointed to only one conclusion."

"What sort of things?"

"Well, in a case like this you have to try to get inside the skins of those involved. The sort of people who lived in Carrie Birch's world don't go around killing each other for nothing. The trouble was that, as so often happens, once we began investigating all sorts of unpleasant secrets began to surface."

"Like poor Mrs Selby's drinking, you mean?"

"Yes. That's a typical example. And there's no doubt about it, they do confuse the issue for us. Mrs Selby had no idea we knew about her drink problem and her main concern was to prevent us finding out. Looking back, I think that the real reason why she lied to us about Carrie having been there that evening was because she was so drunk that she didn't remember anything about the visit and thought it would be simpler to lie than to risk being questioned about it."

"You think Carrie did go to the Selbys' that night, then?"

"I think she must have, because of the timing of what happened later, in Miss Cox's house."

"And Major Selby lied because his wife had asked him to?"

"Yes. All of which, of course, made us highly suspicious."

"I suppose that if you look hard enough, most people would have something in their lives that they're ashamed of, either in the past or in the present."

"That certainly applied to the people in this case," Thanet said. "Which gave us plenty of grounds for suspicion when we discovered that Carrie was a snooper."

Joan wrinkled her nose. "Nasty."

"Yes. But, be fair, in her case it was understandable. If you'd met that mother of hers. . . . Poor Carrie. Her secret indulgences just weren't enough to satisfy her. I would guess they were too inward-turning, too . . . sterile. She wanted something real, involving other people. But she was incapable of making good relationships with them so she settled for finding out about them instead."

"And you think that was enough for her?"

"I do, yes. I don't think it ever entered her head to use that knowledge in blackmail. Certainly there's no shred of evidence that she did. Prying is a nasty, shabby business and perhaps she deserved some kind of punishment. But to pay with her life . . . it does seem altogether out of proportion to her crime, if crime it can be called."

"But if she didn't get the money from blackmail, where did she get it from?"

Thanet grinned sheepishly. "Would you believe it? From bingo."

"Bingo? Oh darling, no! I just don't believe it!" Joan began to laugh. "What a let-down, after all those dramatic explanations you thought up—blackmail, theft, gambling. . . ."

"Well bingo is a form of gambling, of course . . . But it just

shows that it doesn't pay to let your imagination run away
with you. It's a sad and rather dreary fact of life that the
obvious explanation is often the true one. And in this case
well, it really should have been obvious to me that she was a
bingo sort of person. I must admit I felt a bit of a fool when
we found out."

"How did you find out?"

"As so often happens, when we were following quite an
other line of enquiry. The men were on house-to-house
trying to track down the sneak thief, and Bentley came across
this woman who was also a bingo addict and regularly used to
see Carrie on bingo night at the Embassy. Carrie had quite a
reputation for being lucky, I gather.... Where was I?"

"Talking about Carrie's snooping."

"Ah yes. Well anyway, when I began to understand just
how nosey Carrie was, I started to think about Miss Cox. Just
imagine how frustrating it must have been for a woman like
Carrie to live next door to someone who is a complete
enigma. For years she must have longed to get her foot inside
Miss Cox's front door. I expect that when Miss Cox broke her
leg and accepted Carrie's offer to help with the shopping
Carrie thought that she was going to make it inside number
five at last—but no, she never got over the threshold. And I
could imagine her planning all sorts of stratagems to worm
her way in. It might well have become an obsession with her
Burning curiosity and the determination to satisfy it... in
certain circumstances they can be a pretty fatal combination
as Carrie found out."

"I see!" said Joan. "So you think that's what happened. She
managed somehow to get inside Miss Cox's house and either
saw brother Joseph or something which betrayed his
presence..."

"And Miss Cox came back and found her. Yes, that's how it
was, I'm certain of it. I'd guess Miss Cox lashed out in anger
at first, with the walking stick she was using—forensic have
confirmed that that was the weapon used to knock Carrie
out—and then, realising that if Carrie were allowed to live
the secret would be out, decided that there was only one safe
place for her from now on and that was in a wooden box, six
feet under."

"Poor Carrie. I suppose that the second she put her foot
over the threshold of number five she had, in effect, signed
her own death warrant. But I still don't really understand

why. Why was it so important to keep Joseph's presence a secret?"

"He was a deserter," Thanet said. "After being shot down in the Berlin raids he must somehow have made his way back to England and headed for home instead of reporting to the authorities. He was a quiet, timid lad and I should think he would have found his war experience more shattering than most. And then, well, once she had him safely home again I bet his sister persuaded him to stay. Even at that stage I expect they would both have been afraid that if the truth came out he would be arrested."

"What was the penalty for desertion?"

"Well, that's the point. I expect they thought he would be shot. Deserters were, during the first world war, and during the second the myth persisted that they still would be. In fact, it would probably simply have meant a term of imprisonment."

"I suppose one could understand them feeling like that while the war was still on, then, but afterwards . . . Surely there was an amnesty for war-time deserters?"

"That's the tragedy of it, there was. I checked. In February 1953. After that he could safely have come out of hiding at any time. If only they'd known. But they were very simple people, living such circumscribed lives. If they hadn't actually come across the information by chance, either on the radio or in the newspapers, I'm sure they'd never have thought of enquiring. For that matter, I'm not sure they would have known what an amnesty was if they had heard about one."

"So how d'you think Carrie did manage to get in, in the end?"

"On the night of the murder, Tiger—Miss Cox's cat—went missing. She was very attached to it and when it didn't come to her call she went out to look for it. It had got shut in the shed at the bottom of the garden, she said, and she blamed the wind for banging the door closed. It may have done, of course, but I've wondered since if Carrie might not have shut the cat in the shed on purpose, knowing that Miss Cox would go out to look for it. Miss Cox, like Carrie herself, was very much a creature of habit and Carrie would have been able to anticipate her movements exactly. Miss Cox still had a leg in plaster and Carrie would know that it would take her some time to get down the garden path, locate the cat and get back again, long enough for Carrie to slip into the house and have a quick snoop around."

"But if Miss Cox had a leg in plaster how on earth would she have been able to move the body from her house to where it was found? It was some distance away, wasn't it?"

"A hundred yards or so, I'd guess. Yes, that leg was one of the things which threw us off the scent and made us tend to discount her. But it is extraordinary what one can achieve with sufficient incentive and determination. I think she must have rolled the body—and Carrie was a small woman, remember—on to one of the big plastic sheets which she used for wrapping up those loose covers she made for a living. Then, when all the lights were out in Church Cottages and everything was quiet, she dragged the body down the garden path, along the footpath and into the back garden of number two—where, unluckily for her, Harry Pack had gone to pinch another sack of cement for his wife's concrete path. He told us he'd left home at midnight, so it must have been about twenty past when he had the fright of his life and almost bumped into her as he was coming back out on to the footpath. Although he couldn't see exactly what she was doing, he didn't wait to find out. He was terrified of being caught red-handed, knowing that it would mean prison this time, so he dodged back into the garden and hid behind the privy."

"Where she hid the body!"

"Exactly. When she'd gone, curiosity made him peep inside. You can imagine how he felt when he saw what was there."

"And he's quite sure it was Miss Cox?"

"Certain. He knows her well by sight. There was a fitful moon that night and enough light for him to identify her beyond any shadow of doubt. There was that leg in plaster, too. He must have had a very nasty half an hour or so while she laboured to cram Carrie's body into the privy only feet away from him."

"But surely, the fact that Miss Cox hid the body doesn't necessarily mean that she was the murderer?"

"You mean, Joseph might have done it?"

"Why not? It would have been natural for her to cover up for him, wouldn't it? And everything you've said about the murder could equally apply to him. Carrie could have come upon him, startled him, and he could have killed her in the shock of discovery."

But Thanet was shaking his head. "No, I can't agree. It's all wrong. Just think about that relationship, Joan. When Matty Cox lost her mother she invested all her loving in that baby. It wasn't so much that he needed her—I'm sure that if she hadn't looked after him, somebody else would have—but that she needed him, emotionally speaking. He was her lifeline and the intensity of her love for him increased rather than diminished with the years. He became, if you like, her raison d'être. Think how she must have felt when he was called up, how she would have grabbed with both hands at the chance of keeping him at home, when he eventually turned up after making his way back from Germany. I'd guess she would have done anything, anything at all, to prevent his being snatched away from her again—well, she did, didn't she? She killed for just that reason."

"But did she? I agree with all you're saying, and yes, I can see she might well have done the killing, but I still think it could equally well have been Joseph."

"Well, look at it this way. Think of the effect that that kind of obsessive love would have had upon him. She cocooned him in it so thoroughly that, over the years, I should think his will-power would have been completely destroyed. I'd guess that by now he would have been incapable of any sudden act of aggression, let alone one as violent, as extreme as murder. Faced unexpectedly by Carrie, I should think that his instinctive reaction would have been to turn to his sister for rescue, just as hers was to strike out in his defence. No, I'm as certain as I can be that he couldn't have done it."

"Yes," Joan said slowly, turning it over in her mind. "I see what you mean. Yes, I suppose you're right." She shivered. "It's frightening, isn't it, to think what one person can do to another, in the name of love?"

"Yes," said Thanet, remembering grimly how he himself had so narrowly escaped that particular trap. "It certainly is."

Joan was silent for a while, thinking.

"But I still don't understand how you cottoned on to the idea that Joseph was still alive and living with his sister," she said at last.

"It was something old Mr Pitman said. You see, peculiar as people can be, they are usually consistent in the things which really matter to them.

"We're both too young to remember it, but I understand that many, many women whose men were reported 'missing, believed killed' in the last war refused to accept that they were dead, preferring to think that they were really stuck behind barbed-wire fences in some prisoner-of-war camp. And, of course, a lot of them were. Usually news filtered back from camps before the war ended, but there were plenty of cases when men turned up unexpectedly some considerable time later. After hearing about young Matty Cox and her singleminded devotion to her brother Joseph, I was surprised that she hadn't gone on hoping that this was what had happened to him long, long after most women would have given up. But she didn't. Mr Pitman told me that she stopped expecting him to come home about a year after he went missing, towards the end of 1944—*long before the end of the war*.

"The Pitmans apparently thought that this was because it was too painful for Matty to go on living in perpetual disappointment, that the only way she could cope was to accept that he was dead—but I bet that was the moment when he finally arrived back home. It was also at that point that she abruptly became a recluse. People accepted this, of course, thought that the shock of losing her brother had unhinged her. And I don't know, but I would guess that it was then that she gradually began to adopt a mannish appearance."

"You mean, so that if by chance anyone should catch a glimpse of Joseph, they would think it was her?"

"That's right. And they did indeed look very similar, dressed alike and with the same hairstyles—cut by Miss Cox herself, I imagine."

"But just think," said Joan with awe, "to live like that for more than thirty years, shut up in one room . . ."

"Not necessarily in one room. At night, with the curtains drawn, I should think he would have been able to have the run of the house." Thanet remembered his recurring feeling of being watched by someone in number five, and for the first time he wondered: could that have been Joseph, not his sister? It was possible.

"What was it like, the attic?"

"It take up the entire roof space. The partition wall between number five and number four had been heavily insulated, presumably so that he wouldn't have to worry too much about keeping quiet all the time—and the room itself... you should have seen it. He had everything he wanted up there, I imagine, and yet it was so pathetic, somehow, a substitute for life. There was a vast model railway layout on a properly constructed base, books on bird-watching and on almost every aspect of country and wild-life, and some very fine binoculars. There was a carpenter's bench with a splendid set of tools—most of the furniture in the house had been made by him, by the look of it. Games, records, you name it, he had it. I should think Miss Cox spent every penny she could spare on keeping him happy.

"And yet, it was almost as if Joseph had never become a man at all, as if he was a small boy whose hobbies had to be indulged.... I suppose he'd grown used to it. I expect he'd lost the will to live in any other way and would have found the modern world a bewildering and perhaps frightening place. No, I think that the most astounding aspect of the whole affair is that he could have lived in a terraced house in an English village for that length of time without anyone once suspecting that he was there. I suppose if he'd ever been seriously ill the game would have been up."

"It's no good. I *still* don't see how you guessed. I wouldn't have, in a million years."

Thanet laughed. "Flattery will get you everywhere," he said. "Did I tell you how gorgeous you're looking today, by the way?"

Joan was wearing a new spring suit in a deep hyacinth blue which suited her fair colouring to perfection. On her head was perched a minute straw hat decorated with tiny blue and white flowers.

"That," he went on, "is the most ridiculous and adorable hat I have ever seen in my life."

Joan looked pleased and a faint flush of pleasure bloomed in her cheeks. "I'm glad you like it," she said demurely, "but you're not wriggling out of it like that. You still haven't explained to me..."

"My word, you certainly deserve full marks for persistence," Thanet said with a grin. "Well, I admit there was something else... something apparently quite irrelevant. By itself it would have had no significance, but linked to Carrie's love of snooping and Miss Cox's inconsistent behaviour over her brother's reported death... You see, at one point I began to suspect that Major Selby was a fraud."

Joan looked blank. "I'm not with you at all," she said. "What's the connection?"

"It just seemed to me that he was too much of a good thing. As I said to Lineham, he was almost a caricature of what an ex-regular Major should be."

"I still don't see the point. Was he?"

"Was he what?"

"Genuine?"

"No idea. We never got around to checking. Patience, darling," he said, as Joan made an exasperated sound. "Patience, and all will be revealed. I know it's a bit tortuous, but you did ask. . . . You see, the point is that once I'd started thinking along those lines—about the army and the war in general—I side-slipped on to Joseph Cox. I remembered thinking how strange it was that Miss Cox had suddenly given up hope of his return, when there was really still quite a strong possibility that he hadn't been killed at all, but picked up and put into a POW camp. And then I thought, what if he hadn't been killed *and he hadn't been picked up, either.* What if he'd lain low for a time and then managed to find his own way back to England, as many men did. . . . You see? Once I'd reached that point, my whole thinking about the case altered. I saw that I could have been misinterpreting Miss Cox's behaviour all along."

"What do you mean?"

"Well, I had thought she was afraid. And I was right, of course, she was—but *not,* as I had imagined, because the murderer was still at large. What she was really frightened of was that I should learn the truth. The tragedy was that in trying to reassure her, by telling her that the end of the case was in sight, I achieved precisely the opposite effect and pushed her into action. If I hadn't done so she wouldn't have panicked and both she and her brother would still be alive. I can't help feeling guilty about that."

"You mustn't blame yourself. How could you have known?"

"That's beside the point."

"No, it isn't!" Joan cried passionately. "You were simply trying to be kind. And anyway, how much better off do you think they would have been if they were still alive? You said yourself that Joseph would have been lost if he'd had to cope with present-day living. What do you think it would have been like if he had had to do so without his sister to help him? And how absolutely miserable she would have been, if she'd had to go to prison and not only have to live without him but know that he was hopelessly ill-equipped to fend for himself?"

Thanet was silent for a few moments and then he gave Joan a shamefaced grin. "I hadn't thought of it quite like that," he said.

"That's because you're always too ready to blame yourself for everything that goes wrong. But when it comes to taking the credit..."

"Here's the church," interrupted Thanet with a smile. "Just at the psychological moment, before you get well and truly launched on that one."

Joan released an exaggerated sigh of mock exasperation. "Sometimes, my darling, you are well and truly impossible!" she said. But her curiosity had been satisfied now and she was leaning forward to look eagerly out of the window, eyes shining in anticipation. "I am glad they've got such a lovely day," she said. "Oh look, the bridesmaids are arriving."

And there they were, one girl in her early twenties and two tiny ones, all of them looking like spring flowers themselves in their pretty pastel dresses.

"It's a shame Mrs Lineham couldn't have been here," said Joan, as she and Thanet walked along the ancient flagstones to the church porch.

"I don't want to sound hard," Thanet said, "but in a way she has brought this on herself, you know. All the same, I do agree. It is a pity. But I think Mike made the right decision in going ahead regardless. If he hadn't . . ."

"True. He'd never have got away, then. I don't think Louise could have borne a third postponement."

Thanet and Joan took their places on the bridegroom's side of the church. Half the police force of Sturrenden seemed to be present, unfamiliar in their Sunday best. Thanet thought how glad he was that with the Birch case solved Lineham would be able to go off on his honeymoon with a clear conscience.

Briefly, his mind skimmed back over the case, pausing to rest for a moment on each of the main characters. For a very little while he had impinged upon their lives and they upon his. Some of them would stick in his memory, he knew: old Robert Pitman, for example, with his unquenchable fortitude and zest for life—and, yes, Carrie Birch herself with her pathetic daydreams, her thirst for vicarious living. She would never know it, but he would remember her with gratitude. For did he not, after all, in some strange way, owe her Joan? He shivered involuntarily to think how close he had been to losing his wife.

"Cold?" she whispered.

He shook his head, smiled at her.

Lineham and his best man were rising now, moving to take their places for the ceremony. The bride must have arrived. Heads turned, seeking a first glimpse of her, as the congregation came to its feet.

Then the organ burst forth into the gloriously triumphant opening chords of the Wedding March and Louise began to move serenely down the aisle on her father's arm.

Thanet felt for Joan's hand and pressed it, savouring the quick response. They exchanged affectionate glances.

Yes, he was whole-heartedly in favour of marriage, himself.

ABOUT THE AUTHOR

DOROTHY SIMPSON is a former French teacher now living with her husband and three children in Kent, England. She has written eight Thanet novels. Her fifth, *Last Seen Alive*, won the 1985 British Crime Writer's Association Silver Dagger award. Her other books are: *Suspicious Death, Element of Doubt, Dead on Arrival, Last Seen Alive, Close Her Eyes, Puppet for a Corpse, Six Feet Under,* and *The Night She Died.*

The following is a preview from

SUSPICIOUS DEATH
by Dorothy Simpson

to be published by Bantam in
February, 1990

The heavy frost had thawed, but the wind had not yet dried out the residual moisture and their boots made a swishing, squelching sound as they moved through ankle-high grass across ground still sodden from the winter rains. Nearer the water the ground fell away, sloping down to the footpath along the river bank which in summer was rarely without its complement of dog-walkers and strolling couples. This morning it was deserted save for the flurry of activity near the trees. A small, nattily dressed figure was approaching, bald head gleaming and half-moons twinkling in the sunshine.

"Ah, reinforcements have arrived. Morning, everyone."

"Morning, Doc," they said, Thanet smiling with genuine pleasure. He was very fond of the little police surgeon, whom he had known since boyhood, and it always delighted him to see Mallard in the ebullient mood which had enveloped him since his second marriage. For many years before that Mallard had been a lonely embittered figure after the lingering death of his first wife.

"You beat us to it, I see," said Thanet. "What's the story?"

"Well, she's dead, all right." Mallard peered mischievously at Thanet over his glasses. "That what you wanted to know?"

Thanet tutted. "Come on, Doc, stop playing games."

"The young are always so impatient," murmured Mallard, putting down his bag and pulling out a notebook. He flipped it open. "Female, white, mid-forties, height 5' 6", weight about 9 stone, cause of death . . ." he paused.

"Well?" demanded Thanet.

Mallard shut his notebook with a snap. "I'm not too sure I want to commit myself, as yet."

"She didn't drown, then?"

"She might have. On the other hand, she . . ."

". . . might not have!" finished Thanet.

"Precisely. Look, I'm sorry, but I can't pronounce yet on this one. You know how tricky drownings can be. She might have had a cardiac arrest or a laryngeal spasm as a result of the shock of falling into the water, or . . ."

"Or?"

Mallard shrugged. "There's a nasty gash on the right temple. It's difficult to tell, at the moment, whether or not she got it before or after she went into the river."

"You'll do a diatom test?"

"Definitely, yes."

Thanet knew that this test would settle whether or not the woman had died before or after entering the water. Diatoms are microscopic algae, found in both sea and fresh water. Water is sucked into the lungs during drowning, and diatoms enter the bloodstream and are pumped to the heart, entering the body tissues. The presence of diatoms in these is therefore proof that the victim was alive on entering the water.

"How long had she been in the river?"

Mallard shrugged. "Difficult to tell. But by the condition of her hands and feet . . . she went in some time last night, I'd guess." The doctor picked up his bag. "Well, must go now. See you later."

As they made for the trees. Thanet was interested to note that he was feeling none of his usual qualms at viewing the body. The first sight of a corpse normally filled him with a complex and uncomfortable mixture of emotions, soon past but hard to endure while they lasted. This morning, however, his stomach was steady, his mind clear of the customary clogging apprehension. Why was that? he wondered. Because all signs of violence would have been washed away by long immersion? Or was it possible that at last he had outgrown his weakness?

Trace, the Scenes-of-Crime Officer, came to meet them. "Morning, sir. It looks as though she went into the water somewhere further up river. The undergrowth along the bank just here is pretty dense and there's no way anyone could have dragged her through and dumped her without leaving traces of her passage. I understand they had problems enough getting her out . . ."

Thanet nodded a greeting at the two ambulancemen waiting near by before moving towards the body which was stretched out at the foot of a tree. Mallard's description had told him what to expect, but the bald facts had conveyed no image of the reality. The woman, even in death, had an interesting face: high cheek-boned, with jutting nose and powerful jaw. Deep vertical creases between her eyebrows hinted at bad temper, short sight or periods of intense concentration. A strong character, he guessed, and perhaps a difficult one. He noted the gash on the right temple, mentioned by Doc Mallard, and stooped to look more closely. Yes, it had been quite a nasty blow. Her long hair, he saw, had been dyed; it darkened perceptibly at the roots.

Closer proximity made him notice her jewellery too: large, tear-drop pearl earrings with gold mounts and a triple choker of pearls. If genuine, they would cost a packet. He glanced at her left hand. Yes, there was a wedding ring, plain gold, and a modest engagement ring with three small diamonds. On the same hand she wore two other rings, both apparently gold, one of a twisted rope design, the other elaborately chased. And on her right hand she wore a large diamond cluster which, again if genuine, would probably pay the deposit on a modest house.

Her shoes were missing but her clothes, too, were interesting: a quilted anorak over a peacock blue cocktail dress with a heavily beaded and sequinned top. A strange combination, surely? He pointed it out to Lineham.

"Hardly the sort of coat to wear over a dress like that."

Lineham frowned. "Perhaps she was entertaining at home and just slug the anorak on to go outside for some reason"

"Possibly." Thanet glanced up at Trace, who was watching him. "Anything in the pockets?"

"Just a handkerchief and a set of car keys, sir."

"Car keys . . . Did you notice any cars belonging to members of the public back there, Mike?"

Lineham invariably noticed cars.

The sergeant shook his head. "No, sir."

"We'll check on the way back. So," mused Thanet, "no means of identification, so far."

"Sir?" It was Swift, looking uncomfortable.

"Yes?"

"I don't know whether I ought to say anything, as it's so vague, but . . . I'm sure I've seen this woman before, somewhere."

"But you can't remember where?"

"No sir. It's so frustrating. I've been racking my brains." Swift stared down at the dead face, as if willing it to provide him with the information. He shook his head. "It's no good."

Thanet clapped him on the shoulder. "Don't worry, it'll come. Just put it out of your mind, that's the best way." He walked across to the river bank. To his right, a couple of hundred yards upstream, was the weir; eight or ten feet below him the swollen waters of the Sture, obscured by a dense tangle of undergrowth. Broken branches and trampled twigs confirmed Trace's words about the difficulties of retrieving the body. "This where you got her out?"

"Yes, sir." One of the uniformed PCs pointed. "If it hadn't been for that tree, she'd be miles down river by now, we reckon. Her hair had caught on that tangle of branches. Apart from that she was floating free."

The tree in question must have come down during the winter storms; it projected some fifteen feet into the river, its upper branches submerged and well out into the main current. Thanet could visualise the scene clearly, the body carried along by the swollen waters, accelerating as it approached the rush of water over the weir, the twisting tumble as it was carried over the lip into the churn of waters below, the sudden check as the woman's abundant hair caught in the web of branches lying in wait beneath the surface . . .

"Have you checked the bank upstream?"

"We had a quick look, sir, but there's no sign of a struggle, or of anything out of the ordinary."

"Good." But they would take another look all the same, thought Thanet. In any case, there was little point in cordoning off the area or setting up screens. He told the ambulancemen they could take the body away, then turned back to the uniformed men. "Who was first on the scene?"

"We were, sir."

Thanet addressed the older of the two patrolmen. "I assume it was a member of the public who discovered the body?"

"Yes, a woman out walking her dog, sir. She lives in the cottage on the corner just up there, where you turn off the Sturrenden road to come down to the car park. We thought it would be OK for her to wait at home to give her statement. She was pretty shaken."

"Fine. Right. So this is what we do."

Thanet despatched young Swift to take a statement from the witness, then ordered a further search of the river bank upstream, both above and below the weir.

"Any news, report back to me. DS Lineham and I are going back to headquarters."

Trudging back across the field Lineham said, "Looks as though we might have a problem with identification, sir."

"Mmm. I don't know. It wouldn't surprise me if it's not too long before someone reports her missing. She looks pretty well-heeled, don't you think? I should say she's come up in the world."

"What makes you say that?"

"Those rings. Modest engagement ring, the rest of her jewellery—if it's genuine—pretty expensive. Either her husband has had a successful career, or she has."

"She could have come downriver for miles," said Lineham.

Something in the Sergeant's tone made Thanet glance at him sharply. Now that he came to think about it, Lineham had been unusually subdued all morning. Normally the prospect of a possible murder investigation aroused all the Sergeant's enthusiasm.

"Anything the matter, Mike?"

"No. Why?"

Now Thanet was certain. He knew Lineham too well. But if the Sergeant didn't want to talk about it . . . "Just wondered . . . Anyway, I think we'd better take a good look at a map. Come on."

Back in the CID room they were still studying a large-scale map of the area when Pater, the Station Officer, came on the line. "I've got someone on the phone, sir, says his wife is missing. Sounds as though she could be the woman we pulled out of the river this morning."

"What's his name?"

"Salden, sir. Lives at Telford Green."

Which was in the right direction, upriver from Sturrenden on the river Teale, a main tributary of the Sture. "Put him on."

"Mr. Salden? Detective Inspector Thanet here. I understand your wife is missing?"

"Yes. I didn't find out till this morning, but her bed hasn't been slept in."

"I wonder, could you describe her for me?"

"She's five six, slim, long blonde hair, brown eyes . . ."

"How old is she?"

"Forty-five."

"I see. And do you happen to know what she was wearing last night?"

There was a pause. Then, "A deep blue cocktail dress, with those shiny things on the top . . . What d'you call them. . . ?"

"Sequins?"

"Yes, that's right, sequins." The man's voice suddenly sharpened. "Why?"

Thanet sighed. This was one of the worst parts of his job, and he especially hated having to communicate news like this over the telephone. But it would be unfair and rather pointless to keep Salden in suspense while they drove out to Telford Green.

"I'm sorry, Mr. Salden, but I'm afraid I might have some bad news for you."

*   *   *

"Here we are, sir."

For the last few minutes the two police cars had been running alongside the tall red brick wall of Telford Green Manor, where Salden lived, and now the gates had come into view. Lineham turned in past the little octagonal gatehouse and as arranged the other car continued on into the village.

Salden was due back shortly from a visit to the mortuary where, Thanet knew, he had confirmed that the dead woman was his wife. Thanet wasn't looking forward to the interview. Above all things he hated questioning the newly bereaved, having to probe at a raw wound when the witness was least able to bear the pain. It had to be done, however, and if this turned out to be a murder case . . . well, Thanet was as aware as the next man that in cases of domestic murder it is the husband who is the most likely suspect.

Meanwhile, he and Lineham had been doing their homework and studying a large-scale map of the Telford Green area. The main road to Sturrenden, which lay five miles to the east, ran at this point more or less parallel to the river Teale, which flowed into the Sture two miles downriver. The road to Telford Green, a small community with a population of around 500, cut away diagonally, crossing the Teale in the center of the village. The Manor grounds were sandwiched between the two roads and ran right down to the Teale on the far side of the bridge in the village.

The rest of Thanet's team had been detailed to go into the centre of the village and work their way along the river bank, looking for signs of anything out of the ordinary.

The driveway to the Manor was about half a mile long, curving to the left between impressive mature oaks and copper beeches before straightening out in an avenue which afforded a fine view of the house, which was black and white, long, low and timbered.

Lineham whistled as it came into sight.

"They can't be short of a penny."

As this was the Sergeant's standard reaction to every dwelling bigger than a four-bedroomed detached, Thanet ignored it. What interested him much more was what was going on in front of it. A bulldozer was parked between a car and a police motorcycle, and a group consisting of a uniformed policeman, three men and two women seemed to be having a heated discussion. All six turned to look as Thanet's car approached.

"Wonder what's up?" said Lineham, parking neatly alongside the bulldozer.

They both got out.

"Detective Inspector Thanet, Sturrenden CID," said Thanet, addressing the company at large. "What's going on?"

They all started to speak at once, And Thanet raised a hand. "One at a time, please."

One of the women stepped forward. "Is it true?" she said. "About Mrs. Salden?"

She was around fifty, short and dumpy, with untidy fluffy brown hair, a round ingenuous face and unfashionably uptilted spectacles. Her clothes were drab—brown tweed skirt, cream blouse with Peter Pan collar and a shapeless brown speckled cardigan.

"Sorry," said Thanet, "you're. . . ?"

The woman flushed, an ugly brick red. "Edith Phipps," she said. "I'm Mrs. Salden's secretary. And this is Mrs. Pantry, the housekeeper. And will you please tell these men that in the circumstances nothing can be done, for the moment, now that . . . Is it true?" she repeated. "Is Mrs. Salden really. . . ?"

Thanet dragged his attention back from the fact that, without a single word being exchanged, he had taken an instinctive dislike to Mrs. Pantry the housekeeper. "Er . . . yes, Miss Phipps, I'm afraid it has been confirmed. Mrs. Salden is dead."

"Then I should think that settles it," said the uniformed PC to the other three men. "Sorry, sir, PC Kimberley. This is my patch, and Miss Phipps called me in to try and settle a dispute. These men are bailiffs. Mrs. Salden has an order for possession against a chap called Greenleaf who's been living in her woods and they've come to enforce it, as he's been refusing to move after the notice expired."

"And the bulldozer?" said Thanet.

"Greenleaf lives in a ramshackle sort of hut, sir, that he built himself. The bulldozer was to demolish it."

"And I'm simply saying," broke in Edith Phipps, "that they can't go on with this, now that the circumstances have changed." She was holding herself under a tight control, her hands, tightly clasped and white-knuckled, betrayed her agitation. "We don't know if Mr. Salden will still want to go ahead, and anyway he certainly won't feel like being bothered with all this, when he gets back, he'll be too upset. Please," she said to Thanet, "send them away. Otherwise there'll be so much trouble . . ."

"Trouble?" Thanet looked at PC Kimberley.

"The village people are opposed to the eviction, sir. A number of them are waiting down in the woods, near Harry's—Greenleaf's hut. I've sent to headquarters for reinforcements."

"Then I agree," said Thanet. "The eviction should be postponed. Mr. Salden will have too much on his mind to be bothered with this sort of problem."

The taller of the two bailiffs shrugged. "So long as you're willing to take the responsibility, Inspector."

"I am."

"OK." He glanced around, as if reassuring himself that there were plenty of witnesses, then said, "Come on then, Ted, we'll be off." And to the bulldozer driver, who had been standing by smoking a cigarette and looking bored, "You too, mate."

The bailiffs got into their car and drove off. The other man shrugged, took his cigarette out of his mouth, spat, replaced the cigarette and then climbed into the seat of his cab.

"Right," said Thanet. "If you'd just wait here, Kimberley, I'd appreciate a word with you later." He turned to the two women. "Shall we go indoors?"

His words were drowned by the full-throated roar of the bulldozer starting up, and he had to repeat them. Mrs. Pantry led the way through the heavy oak front door into a huge entrance hall open right up to the roof rafters. A wide, highly polished oak staircase led up to a galleried landing. The stoneflagged floor was incongruously adorned with a modern bordered carpet square in strident tones of orange and green.

"May I enquire which of you two ladies saw Mrs. Salden last?"

The women looked at each other.

"I did," said the housekeeper, reluctantly.

"What time would that have been?"

"About twenty to ten last night, when she left to visit her mother, in the village."

"I haven't seen her since yesterday afternoon," said the secretary.

"Right, well perhaps I could have a word with you later, Miss Phipps." He looked at the housekeeper. "Is there somewhere private, where we could talk?"

"We could go into the kitchen."

"Fine."

Thanet's sitting-room and dining-room would both have fitted comfortably into the kitchen, which had evidently been built on to the house in the days when there was no servant problem and there would probably have been eight or ten people sitting down for meals at the long pine table. A row of bells, each labelled with the name of a room, hung near the door. Apart from its size it would be a pleasant room to work in, with a chestnut brown Aga exuding a comforting warmth, a more than adequate supply of oak-faced units, and yellow and white checked curtains at the windows, which looked out on to the back garden. A smell of baking hung in the air.

They all sat down at one end of the table.

"Now then," said Thanet, "perhaps you could tell us about last night?"

While she talked he studied the housekeeper, seeking a reason for that apparently irrational recoil he had experienced upon being introduced to her. She was a big, raw-boned woman in her sixties, heavily built and . . . no, not clumsy, exactly . . He sought the word. Graceless, yes, that was it, graceless in all her movements. Although she was wearing a flowered dress beneath a blue nylon overall she looked as though she would have been much more at home in trousers, her feet planted firmly apart on the quarry-tiled floor. Her hair was cropped, the ends chunky and uneven as though she had cut it herself, standing in front of a mirror. It was an unbecoming style, emphasising the strong masculine planes of her face, the heavily unplucked brows and beginnings of a moustache. Thanet wondered about the circumstances that had brought her here. Was she a live-in housekeeper or a daily, imported from the village? He asked her.

"Oh, I'm full-time, live-in."

"And how long have you been with the Saldens?"

"Eighteen months, now."

Thanet was intrigued by the note of bitterness in her voice and he glanced at Lineham. *Take over*. He and Mike had worked together for so long they were like an old married couple, Thanet reflected as Lineham went smoothly into action. In this sort of situation there was rarely a need for them to communciate in words and Lineham was used to having to take over without warning. Thanet knew that one can often learn more about a witness by watching and listening than by conducting the interview oneself.

Mrs. Salden's disappearance had apparently been discovered at 7:30 a.m. when Mrs. Pantry took up a tray of early morning tea. Her bed had not been slept in and although the housekeeper was surprised she was not really alarmed. She simply thought that Mrs. Salden must have spent the night at her mother's cottage in the village. It had happened before, from time to time.

"Where was Mr. Salden?"

"They have separate rooms." The housekeeper's mouth tightened in disapproval.

"So what did he say, when you told him that his wife's bed hadn't been slept in?"

"He seemed, well, confused, like. Put his hand to his forehead, as if he was trying to pull his thoughts together. He had just woken up, you know," she added defensively.

So Mrs. Pantry's loyalty lay with Salden rather than his wife, thought Thanet. Interesting, but scarcely surprising.

Remembering the dead woman's strong, determined face, he couldn't really imagine her getting on well with this woman. What had soured the housekeeper so? he wondered. He tried to imagine her face transfigured by a smile or softened by tenderness, and failed. What a joyless life she must lead.

"In fact, he told me he hadn't got home till four this morning," she added.

"Where had he been?"

"At his mother-in-law's place. She died about half-past three."

"And his wife was there, too?"

"No. But I didn't know that then, did I?"

"Look," said the sergeant, "I'm getting a bit confused. Let's go back, start at the beginning. Were Mr. and Mrs. Salden both here last evening?"

"Early on, yes. They was having a dinner party, see."

Hence the beaded dress, thought Thanet.

"Many guests?" said Lineham.

"No, only two. Mr. Lomax and . . . *Miss* Trimble."

An interestingly scornful inflection, there, Thanet thought.

Lineham frowned. "Lomax . . . An unusual name . . . That wouldn't be Mr. Douglas Lomax, the borough councillor, by any chance?"

"Yes, that's right."

Well done, Mike.

"And Miss Trimble?"

"Lives in the village. She's always round here. Mrs. Salden encouraged her." Mrs. Pantry gave a disapproving sniff and brushed an imaginary piece of fluff off her nylon overall as if dismissing the undesirable Miss Trimble as of no importance.

"She works here?"

A derisive snort. "She's a hairdresser in Sturrenden. That unisex place at the bottom of the High Street."

It certainly sounded an ill-assorted dinner party, thought Thanet. With an unusually small number of guests. A married couple might invite another couple for an informal supper, but to give a dinner party for a borough councillor and a hairdresser . . . He scented intrigue. What had been going on?

"I see," said Lineham. "So what time did these guests arrive?"

"Josie—Miss Trimble—came first. Bang on 7:30." *Unfashionably punctual*, her expression said. "Mr. Lomax got here about a quarter of an hour later."

Mrs. Salden, it seemed, had come downstairs shortly after Josie's arrival and had come into the kitchen to tell Mrs. Pantry that dinner might have to be delayed, as the nurse had rung from old Mrs. Carter's cottage to say that the old lady was asking for Mr. Salden. He had left at once, having arranged to ring at about eight to tell his wife what time he was likely to be back.

"Odd, wasn't it?" said Lineham. "Asking for him, rather than for her daughter?"

A reproving look. "Mrs. Carter was very fond of Mr. Salden. Like a son, he was, to her."

"I see. So it wasn't unusual for the nurse to ring up and ask him to go and see the old lady?"

"Well . . ." For the first time, Mrs. Pantry seemed unsure of her ground. "I dunno. I can't say, I'm sure. I don't know what half their phone calls is about. It's just that last night I had to know, see, because of dinner getting spoiled."

"Quite . . . so what happened then?"

At eight o'clock Mr. Salden had rung to say that he would be staying on at the cottage for a while, and that dinner should proceed without him.

"Mrs. Salden didn't think of cancelling the dinner party?" said Lineham.

"Oh no. Why should she? She wasn't to know it'd be any different this time. Mrs. Carter has been ill for over a year, very ill . . . Cancer . . . There's been many, many times when they thought she wouldn't last the night, but she did. And when that keeps on happening, you get to expect just another false alarm, don't you?"

Lineham nodded. "True."

Mrs. Pantry had then served dinner, and as soon as they had finished the last course, at about half-past nine, Mrs.

Salden had apparently rung the cottage, because a few minutes later she had come into the kitchen to say that she was just going to pop down to see her mother and to ask Mrs. Pantry to serve coffee in the drawing-room. She didn't expect to be long.

"The guests didn't leave at that point?"

A disapproving sniff. "Not they. Anyway," she added grudgingly, "As I was carrying the tray of coffee through I did hear Mrs. Salden ask that Josie wait till she got back, as she especially wanted to speak to her."

"But she didn't come back?"

"Not to my knowledge. Mr. Lomax left about a quarter or twenty past ten, and I went to bed soon after."

"So you didn't hear either Mr. or Mrs. Salden come in, or Miss Trimble leave?"

"No. But she stayed till eleven, I believe."

"What makes you say that?"

"There's a note for Mr. Salden, on the table in the hall. I was dusting," she added defensively, "and couldn't help seeing it."

Lineham was looking at Thanet. *Anything else you want to ask?*

Thanet gave an imperceptible shake of his head and stood up. "This note, Mrs. Pantry. Is it still on the table in the hall?"

"I think so, yes."

"Let's go and see, shall we?"

He waited while she reluctantly dragged herself to her feet.

Kinsey Millhone is...

"The best new private eye." —*The Detroit News*

"A tough-cookie with a soft center." —*Newsweek*

"A stand-out specimen of the new female operatives."
—*Philadelphia Inquirer*

Sue Grafton is...

The Shamus and Anthony Award winning creator of
Kinsey Millhone and quite simply one of the hottest
new mystery writers around.

Bantam is...

The proud publisher of Sue Grafton's Kinsey Millhone
mysteries: